IMMORTALISED
TO
DEATH

The Dunston Burnett Trilogy
Book One

LYN SQUIRE

LEVEL
BEST BOOKS

Historia

IMMORTALISED

TO

DEATH

Older brothers play an important role in the lives of their younger siblings. Mine did. I dedicate Immortalised to Death to his memory.

Old Time heaved a mouldy sigh from tomb and arch and vault; and gloomy shadows began to deepen in corners; and damps began to rise from green patches of stone; and jewels, cast upon the pavement of the nave from stained glass by the declining sun, began to perish.

—CHARLES DICKENS, THE MYSTERY OF
EDWIN DROOD, 1871

Contents

Characters

MAIN CHARACTERS

- Dunston Burnett, Retired bookkeeper
- Nick Sharpe, Dunston's manservant
- Georgina Hogarth, Charles Dickens's sister-in-law
- Dulcet, Georgina's parlour maid
- Isaac, Georgina's stableboy
- Frank Beard, Charles Dickens's physician
- Mr Clatterbuck, Charles Dickens's lawyer
- John Forster, Charles Dickens's literary advisor
- Archibald Line, Scotland Yard's Chief of Detectives
- Dinky Dryker, Leader of a gang of robbers
- Snatcher, Nobbler, Stingo Pete, Members of Dinky's gang
- Ellen (Nelly) Ternan, Former stage actress
- Earl of Toxington, Member of The Athenaeum Club
- Lord Magnus Lavelle, Man about town
- Luke Mallick, Owner of a painting shop
- Snodrick Wurmsey, Acquaintance of Georgina Hogarth

CHARACTERS IN *THE MYSTERY OF EDWIN DROOD*

- John Jasper, Choirmaster at Cloisterham Cathedral
- Rosa Bud, Young lady orphaned in childhood
- Hiram Grewgious, Rosa Bud's guardian
- Edwin Drood, Young man betrothed to Rosa Bud
- Datchery, Former policeman

Chapter One: In the Study

Kent; Thursday, June 9, 1870

A slight tingle in his right arm, enough to pause his quill mid-word, but nothing to worry about. The writer ran his left hand over his scraggly, almost-white beard, straightened the sleeve of his velvet-collared jacket, and returned to his task.

The sharp spasm that jolted him only three sentences later could not be so easily ignored. Shaken, he set the quill down and sat up, seeking relief, reassurance, finding neither. Nor any respite. Powerful convulsions shuddered through his body before he could take a single calming breath.

A moment later, the onslaught was over, the damage done. With an ebbing-tide sigh, his head dropped to his chest; his torso, poised for a split-second, followed suit, thudding onto the desk with the doomful finality of a cell door slamming shut on a condemned man.

The sun, as if in sympathy, withdrew behind the clouds. With it went the light that had so gloriously brightened the book-lined study throughout the early June morning, leaving in its stead, a leaden gloom intended, or so it seemed, to hide from view the items scattered across the parquet floor by flailing arms: blood-red geraniums, his favourite, bleeding from a small decorated vase; a bronze statuette of duelling toads locked forever in mortal combat; white oblongs of writing paper, trailing towards the door like a fleeing murderer's footprints.

The minute hand on the study's eight-day chiming clock dawdled through a quarter-turn before the sun, energy restored, burst from its retreat, its brilliance revitalising the study… and the sorry shape draped across the desk. Like a mummy rising from its sarcophagus, the stricken man struggled to raise head and shoulders, a trivial task for most, but monumental for this wreck of a human being. He pushed himself upright and sat there unmoving, gasping for breath, head bowed, eyes unfocused.

Several minutes passed before his right arm reached out, combing the desktop, circling blindly like an eyeless tentacle, not resting until his trembling hand grasped its prize. He leaned forward, dipped the quill into the inset inkpot, and with the spirit of a life-long writer burning in his breast, sought to record his final words.

But it was not to be, his dying effort to document his passing cut cruelly short by another more destructive wave of pain, striking him before he'd completed even a single word. The gutted effigy stared for a woeful moment at the four letters he'd scribbled and then slumped forward like a weathered gravestone toppling to its final resting place.

Struck down well before his three score and ten, Charles Dickens, his latest tale only half told, lay dead at his desk, a barely legible scrawl his final message to the world.

Chapter Two: An Awkward Reunion

When her brother-in-law didn't appear for lunch at the usual hour of one o'clock, Georgina Hogarth rose from the sofa, crossed the drawing room, and glanced across the hallway to the study door. It was closed, his signal that he was not to be disturbed. He usually emerged well before lunchtime, but if the literary juices were flowing or he had a pressing deadline, he'd stay locked away until mid or even late afternoon and then surface, announcing proudly that his pen had 'flown across the page' for four, five, even six hours. Georgina returned to her sewing.

Another hour passed still without any sign of Charles. She set her needlework aside, smoothed her sensible light grey day dress, restored a stray lock to its proper place in her equally sensible bun, and rose from the sofa for the second time. This time, she stepped across the hallway and tapped on the study door. No answer. She tapped again and peeked in… and there he was… slumped over his desk, arms spread as though preparing to take off on a flight of fancy the like of which only the author himself could imagine.

She didn't faint – Georgina was not the fainting type. She entered the room and saw at once that the mighty literary force she'd supported, protected and defended all her adult life was dead. She called to the servants to fetch Dr Steele. Only then did she give free rein to her feelings.

Her breath coming in short gasps, she approached the still form, gently lifted the novelist's right hand, removed the quill, his sixth finger as he called it, and carefully eased his gold signet ring from his lifeless finger. She raised it to her lips, let it rest there briefly, then slipped it in her skirt pocket. Tears flowed down her cheeks as she laid a farewell hand on his shoulder, turned and left the study. It was all over in a matter of minutes, but she knew those soul-shafting moments would stay with her as long as she lived.

Three hours later, a carriage topped the rise and turned into the semi-circular drive leading to Gad's Hill Place, Charles Dickens's home in Higham, Kent, thirty miles east of London. The crunch of iron-rimmed wheels on gravel snapped the softly weeping woman out of her quiet grieving. She pressed her lips to the gold ring she'd been fondling, returned it to her skirt pocket and stepped to the drawing room window. 'A visitor?… At *this* time?… Whoever can it be?' She frowned, clearly dismayed her private moment was being interrupted by some untimely intruder. 'Goodness gracious! Is that… it can't be. Oh, no, it is – Dunston… Dunston Burnett.'

The solitary passenger glanced out of the carriage window and saw for the first time the author's modest, red-brick Georgian house with its large, bevelled windows, one in each quadrant of the two-storey structure, above them, a narrow strip of attic tight under the roof, between them, a pillared portico. As he descended from the carriage, the heavens, playing England's time-honoured game of solar hide-and-seek, darkened the sky again. The Union Jack, waving so proudly from the cupola on first approach, collapsed, gently enfolding the flagstaff, much as the regimental colours sheath the coffin of a fallen comrade. On any other day, weather and omen would have sent the new arrival scurrying away. Not today. Today, he walked straight towards the short flight of steps leading to the front door.

Forty-year-old Dunston Burnett had not seen Miss Georgina for twenty years. During his school years, he'd read everything then written by Dickens, his 'uncle', as he persisted in calling him even though they were only distantly related. He was so entranced by the wondrous story-telling, it wasn't surprising that the young man, his education complete, took every possible opportunity to visit Number One Devonshire Terrace, his uncle's home then in London. It was there that he first met Georgina.

He'd been a bit fond of her at that time, but his uncle was all that really mattered to him, his every waking hour spent trailing his hero like an insignificant speck caught in the gravitational pull of the brightest star in the literary universe. Dunston, naturally, had writing ambitions of his own but his uncle, increasingly infuriated by the young man's constant pestering, had brutally squashed that dream. 'Dunston,' he'd said, 'the transit of a camel through the eye of a needle is simplicity itself compared with wringing even a *single* literary phrase out of you, let alone a novel.'

A week later, Dunston's humiliation was complete. The deadline for the next monthly instalment of *David Copperfield* was looming and Charles had had enough of the annoying nuisance. With the tacit agreement of Dunston's great aunt, the young man's guardian, Charles heartlessly packed him off to earn a living as bookkeeper for a Southampton-based shipping company. There Dunston had remained, out of sight and mind, too insecure to venture ever again into his uncle's presence... or Miss Georgina's.

Dunston's knock at the door was answered by Dulcet, Georgina's parlour maid, a local girl, slender, quick of movement, no more than sixteen or seventeen. New to the household and eager to please, she smartly showed the visitor into the drawing room.

'Miss Georgina, I'm... I'm so sorry,' Dunston began. 'Came as soon as I heard. I'm retired now – small inheritance from my great aunt – and living barely two miles away in Strood. My neighbour, Dr Steele, told me he'd just come from Gad's Hill Place and that Uncle Charles was... that is, he told me... the sad news. A stroke, he said. So, *so* sorry.'

Georgina stared speechlessly at the speaker. He was considerably stouter... and shorter, if that was possible, than the Dunston of two decades ago. Unlike that Dunston, he wasn't wearing one of those gaudy waistcoats in imitation of his idol, but missing that touch of colour, his attire was drab as a penitent's sackcloth. That bemused expression, though, that vagueness typically associated with absent-minded professors, or, in his case, a middle-aged bookkeeper with more liabilities than assets, was still plain as the bulbous nose on his chubby-cheeked face.

'Dunston... yes... thank you... thank you for coming,' she finally managed. 'Yes, a stroke. Your uncle... his body... in the study... if you'd like a few minutes with him ...'

With those few awkward words, the only ones passing between them, they parted, he to the study, she remaining in the drawing room.

A quarter hour lapsed before Dunston returned to find Georgina seated at a round, Spanish mahogany table in the salon. 'Miss Georgina, I-I... well, I don't know what to say. Words... words fail me. Perhaps... perhaps, it's best if I show you what I found.' He took the chair opposite her and passed her an ink-bespattered sheet of foolscap paper. 'It was on the desk under Uncle's left hand.'

Georgina took the single page and squinted at the lettering scribbled towards the bottom.

'Those four letters are the last Uncle ever wrote,' Dunston said. 'Not much, but it's clear what he was trying to tell us. Death must've taken him before he could finish the word.'

Georgina, still, silent, stared at the scrawl, clearly struggling to come to grips with the meaning of those four hateful letters.

'*Poison*, Miss Georgina. He was trying to write *poison*.'

Chapter Three: A Second Opinion

The next morning, Dunston was standing outside Woods View House, his home in Strood, folding a single sheet of paper before placing it carefully in the inside pocket of his charcoal grey jacket. He hoisted his trousers, a full inch too long for his stubby legs, undid the bottom button of his waistcoat, a full inch too tight for his prominent belly, and clambered into the waiting carriage, shouting to the driver as he did so, 'Gad's Hill Place.'

Ten minutes later, his knock on the front door was answered by Dulcet, and he was ushered into the drawing room.

'Good morning.' Georgina, sombrely attired in a black crepe mourning dress, smiled in greeting. Dunston, however, could sense the worry behind the forced warmth of her welcome. Yesterday's events were obviously weighing heavily on her.

'Good morning.' Dunston reached into his breast pocket. 'Miss Georgina, I have—'

Before he had a chance to say more, the drawing room door opened and Dulcet ushered in the morning's second caller.

The newcomer's dapper, assured bearing proclaimed that nothing, not even his early departure from London, could disturb the orderliness and crispness of his appearance, an observation applying as much to his well-tailored, dark suit and starched, white shirt as his neatly groomed moustache and perfectly-in-place, grey-tinged, black hair. He'd taken the day's first train to Higham, a journey he'd made many times before, the gentleman in question being Dr Frank Beard, Dickens's personal physician and close friend.

'Frank. I'm *so* glad you're here.' Georgina's smile for him was full of genuine affection, noted a slightly miffed Dunston. 'Dr Steele said he would contact you.'

'He did. His telegram arrived late last night with the terrible news.' Frank took her hands. 'Charles's passing is such a loss I can't begin to tell you how sorry I am. And I thought he was doing so well. You must be devastated. Are you alright?' His calm, brown eyes searched her face for signs of stress. They were easily spotted, but so was her characteristic, steely determination.

'It's difficult but I'm coping as best I can,' she replied. 'Dr Steele is the local doctor, just opened his practice in Strood. He came yesterday and confirmed that Charles died of a stroke as we'd long feared, but then after he'd left, Dunston—Oh, forgive my manners, not quite myself today. I'm sure you remember Dunston Burnett, Charles's nephew.' Frank nodded amiably to Dunston. 'Dunston found… found… this on Charles's desk.' She handed him the ink-splashed sheet of paper with its four horrid letters. 'Dunston thought Charles was trying to write *poison,* but that can't be right, can it?'

Frank glanced at the half-finished word, sucked in his breath and returned the paper to her. 'Steele completed his studies at Barts only recently,' he said, referring to St Bartholomew's Hospital, London's premier teaching hospital. 'Attended some of my lectures.Not the sharpest scalpel in the operating theatre, if you take my drift. Perhaps, I should take a look?'

'Yes, of course. Come, he's been laid out in the billiard room.'

As soon as Georgina returned, Dunston tried again to catch her attention. 'Miss Georgina, I brought—

'Not now,' she said sharply. And then, moderating her tone, 'Dunston, I'm so sorry. Please excuse my shortness. If you don't mind, perhaps you could allow me a minute to myself.' She paced the length of the drawing room twice, and then sat at the salon's round table, her face set. Dunston joined her and there they waited in silence for Frank's return.

He was soon back. He sat next to Georgina, took her hand and said quietly but firmly, 'My dear, I'm afraid I have shocking news.' He paused, allowing her time to compose herself. 'Charles died from strychnine poisoning.'

'*Strychnine poisoning?*' Georgina stiffened, her free hand flying to her throat. 'Are... are you sure? Dr Steele seemed so certain it was a stroke.'

'Quite sure,' he answered with authority. 'I'm so sorry, Georgina. A novice like Steele might easily have mis-diagnosed the cause of death, especially given Charles's medical history, but I've seen cases like this before. Charles died from asphyxiation resulting from paralysis of the respiratory muscles. That, plus the wide open eyes and the *risus sardonicas* – the fixed grin – are clear signs of strychnine poisoning.'

'Forgive me, Frank, I didn't mean to doubt you, but this... this is the worst possible news. If it was poison, then... then... Charles must have—'

'No, no,' Frank cut in quickly. 'Don't think that for even a moment. Charles would *never* do that. He *burned* with a will to live, *especially* when he was in the throes of one of his novels.'

A small nod from Georgina.

'He was *so* excited about his current book, and with good reason,' he continued. '*The Mystery of Edwin Drood* was to be his *first* mystery, a tale surely destined to become a classic. But it was far from finished, and he would never... *never* do away with himself in the midst of creating one of his masterpieces, especially one that would hold a *unique* place among all his great works.'

Another small nod.

He waited to see if she'd grasped the implication of his words – if not suicide, then...? – but she remained silent, face blank. 'Georgina,' he finally said, 'I fear Charles was murdered.'

Unshakeable Georgina was clearly shaken. 'Wh-what? H-how can that be?'

'His tonic... it was laced with poison,' he explained.

'His tonic? The one you prescribed for the pain in his foot?'

'Yes.' He gave her the small brown bottle of Battley's Sedative Solution he'd found in the study. 'It contains strychnine. The mixture is heavily sweetened to mask the laudanum's unpleasant taste, but the contents of this bottle – I sampled a few drops on my tongue – have the bitter tang of strychnine. Once Charles reached for this bottle, he was doomed. The poison would've struck fifteen to twenty minutes later. He'd have been dead within an hour.'

'How terrible.' Georgina shuddered, still visibly unsettled but doing her utmost to regain her composure.

'I know, my dear,' Frank sympathised. 'Regrettably, strychnine's not difficult to obtain. Eight pence will buy an ounce in any apothecary in England.'

'So, *anyone* could have... well, you know,' she said.

'Anyone who could get into the study,' Frank clarified.

Georgina bolted upright. 'Frank! The robbery! How could I forget? Somebody broke in through the study window... a week ago.'

'Really? What happened?' Frank asked.

'The desk drawer where Charles kept some letters and his notes for the Drood novel had been forced open and the contents removed, but nothing else was taken.'

'Georgina,' Frank exclaimed, 'You see what this means, don't you? The intruder didn't break in just to take a few papers. His real purpose was to *poison* Charles. This intruder murdered Charles.'

'Oh, Frank, whatever do we do?'

'Well, we'll have to notify the police,' he replied. 'But I should warn you, Georgina, once we do that the newshounds will descend like sharks scenting blood, splashing ugly headlines across all the front pages. Charles is so famous, his death in this manner will be fodder for the scandalmongers for weeks to come.'

Georgina sat up, grabbing Frank's arm. 'Charles's reputation! It will be torn to shreds. His legacy! Destroyed.'

Hearing the despair in Georgina's voice, the third and so far silent member of the party finally spoke. 'Um... pardon me. Perhaps it won't be... er... necessary to involve the police.'

'Whatever do you mean, Burnett?' Frank asked. 'Of course, it will. They investigate every suspicious death, and the death certificate in this case can hardly say death by natural causes, can it?'

'Actually... it can. You see, Dr Steele has already signed Uncle's death certificate... and submitted it to the General Register Office. This,' Dunston was nervously holding up a sheet of paper like a surrender-minded foot soldier waving a white flag, 'This is Miss Georgina's copy. He asked me to bring it since I was on my way here. It clearly states that Uncle Charles died from a—'

'Stroke!'

'Exactly, Miss Georgina,' Dunston said proudly, suddenly the conquering hero returning home with the spoils of war. 'This certificate means the police won't have to know he was poisoned, nor the newspapers.'

Dunston knew from their previous acquaintance that Miss Georgina – Miss Truthful-To-The-Core Georgina – would rather cut her tongue out than tell a lie... *except* when it came to anything that threatened the reputation of the man she'd devoted her life to, and then she could be surprisingly artful, a Scottish Machiavelli. So it was today. He could see she was willing to go along with his idea. But what about Frank? A much tougher nut to crack. Dunston glanced at him.

'My goodness, a remarkable suggestion, Burnett,' Frank began. 'Medically speaking, it might work, I suppose. The corpse's facial muscles will gradually relax so the cause of death won't be noticeable externally.' He frowned. 'Of course, your proposal, as you must realise, goes against everything I stand for as a doctor, but that's *not* what bothers me most. Let's not forget, Charles was *murdered*, and I for one am not willing to let the villain get away with killing my friend, my patient and the most celebrated novelist of the age. The police *must* be brought in,' he said, his tone brooking no argument.

Had Dunston's idea been squashed? Perhaps, perhaps not. He watched closely as Frank's expression shifted from resolute to more second-thoughtish. It looked as though he was debating whether to say more or leave matters where they were.'Say more' was the decision.

'I don't know where this takes us,' he said, 'but I feel *very* strongly about one other aspect of this sad business, and that is that Charles's funeral not be diminished by any... distractions. He deserves to be put to rest with all the ceremony, all the respect and all the accolades that he's earned throughout a lifetime of bringing smiles and tears to countless readers.'

'There might be a middle way,' volunteered an emboldened Dunston. 'Just thinking aloud, but perhaps we could wait until Uncle's been properly buried with all the attendant tributes he so richly deserves *before* informing the authorities of the... the true nature of his passing. Once Uncle has been appropriately memorialised, we could tell the police about the poison in the bottle of Battley's, saying we'd only just discovered it, and ask them to investigate.'

Georgina looked hopeful, Frank dubious. 'But what of the murderer in the meantime?' the latter asked. 'We can't sit back and—'

'If I may,' interrupted Dunston. 'We are, I'm sure, all agreed that Uncle's killer *must* be brought to justice, but instead of a full-blown police investigation, it might be better if we conduct our *own* more *discrete* inquiry, at least initially. After all, we three know more about my uncle than the police ever will, so we are best placed to determine who wanted him dead. Then, once Uncle is at rest, we can hand over to the police any evidence or suspects we might have uncovered, making their job that much easier.'

Frank nodded, but his look made clear he was only half convinced.

'I might add,' Dunston said, 'that if the official record says Uncle's death was due to a stroke, the villain will believe his crime has gone undetected, and may drop his guard to our advantage.'

More nodding, but it still took much discussion before they were fully agreed. In the end, they settled on a grace period of one month after the novelist's death before involving the authorities. Time enough for the family, the nation and indeed the entire world to mourn and honour Charles John Huffam Dickens, in a manner worthy of the beloved storyteller, and, thought Dunston, time enough for me to track down the intruder who murdered Uncle.

Chapter Four: Market Day

The Saturday morning market in Rochester, Strood's sister-city sitting on the opposite bank of the River Medway, was in full swing under the forbidding shadow of the massive stone walls of the town's ancient castle. Nothing, not even the royal revelries of yesteryear or the jousting tournaments of bygone days, could compare with the joyful confusion that was market day.

Stalls of early summer vegetables and fruit; pens of pigs, sheep, goats; a juggler barely keeping five skittles in the air; a roving salesman with a tray of winkles, whelks, jellied eels and the like; a hot pie man attracting a steady stream of customers despite stiff competition from a girl selling toffee-apples; the sight was colourful enough, but the clamour of the crowd took the breath away. Raucous shouts, boisterous haggling, spirited bantering, the cheap jacks' constant touting of their glassware and earthenware from Birmingham and Sheffield, all mingled and intensified, overwhelming the senses.

'What d'yer think of that?' The speaker nudged his mate and pointed.

The two gentlemen of the road were standing off to one side. From there, they had an uninterrupted view of the jostling hotchpotch of tradesmen, performers and customers, all grist to the mill in the eyes of these two fellows, scavenging hyenas, ever ready to feed on the flesh of others and, if one or two throats were slit in the course of business, well, that was too bad.

'Looks like a tidy pair of bubbies to me,' was the second footpad's assessment of the day's latest diversion. 'All I've had of late is them whores in town an' they're so long in the tooth they got tits like mashed 'taters.'

'Not what's in her bodice, yer stupid baboon,' the other snarled. 'Look how she's clutching her purse to her body.Now, why d'yer think that is?'

'Don't rightly know. Wouldn't mind if she clutched my Nelson's Column like that, I can tell yer,' the bosom-watcher remarked.

'For God's sake, get yer hand out of yer pants and listen. She's clutching her purse 'cos there's something in it, and since she's just come out of the bleeding jeweller's, chances are its SOMETHING VALUABLE! And what did I say our business was?'

'Don't rightly remember.'

'Thieving! And for thieving, you needs brawn and you needs brains,' his fellow traveller explained for the umpteenth time. 'That's why we teamed up. You've got more beef than you knows what to do with, and I got the wits, and that's just as well 'cos your head's empty as me bladder after me first-of-the-mornin' piss, yer dumb ape.'

'Ape' was right. Brawn was indeed simian to the point where he'd be greeted with open gorilla arms if he ever found himself in the forests of Borneo. Were it not for his few articles of clothing – battered cap, patched jacket, open-necked shirt, ragged trousers tied at the knee with yarn, mud-spattered boots – he'd be carted off to the nearest zoo to become the most admired specimen in the apery.

Not so Brains. His clothes were in no better repair but they hung on his slender frame with more distinction, hat drawn over one eye, jacket fitting across the shoulders, trousers hitched to leg-length. His carriage too was more, well, more *human*, more upright and jaunty, arms of mankind proportion rather than apelike span, and his features markedly less Neanderthal, the hint of softness in mouth and chin offset by a steady, forthright look in his pale blue eyes. Even though no more than twenty, several years younger than his muscular mate, he was clearly the undisputed leader.

The young woman being eyed by the pair was Dulcet, Georgina's parlour maid. Earlier that morning, Georgina had handed her Charles's signet ring, the one she'd taken from his finger the day he died. 'Dulcet,' she'd said, 'I want you to take this ring to the jeweller's in Rochester and ask him to clean it thoroughly. Once he's done, bring it straight back. Do *not* let it out of your sight at any time. It's the master's signet ring and I must replace it on his finger, there to go with him to the grave exactly as he requested.'

Dulcet, face aglow at being entrusted with such an important task, had looked with interest at the gold ring. She saw a string of letters engraved on the inside. She counted them – eleven, ten almost worn away, the eleventh, still clearly defined. She glanced up inquiringly, only to find her mistress's face closed. She was not to be privileged with their history.

Brains watched her make her way back through the market at a steady pace until a milling throng in front of The Bull's Head Inn caught her attention and she slowed down. The tavern, a mismatched collection of buildings surrounding an old-fashioned coachyard, was temptingly close to her route. She paused, the child in her obviously debating whether or not to take a quick look at whatever was causing all the excitement. Brains smiled when the maid, apparently persuaded by a loud cheer, eased her way into the crowd.

What a fantastic sight greeted her marvelling eyes. She saw a girl, no more than ten, in a patterned pinafore standing on a bucket, singing with great purpose but little melody; a burly man, red in the face, holding a drum in one hand and beating it energetically with the other; and in front of them, the star attraction – a dancing bear. Her obvious delight in the magic of the moment was in no way diminished by the animal's sorry state – fur more grey than brown, with running sores and patches of exposed skin – or its feeble understanding of choreography as the beast, chained to a stake, shuffled round its fixed circuit, as though marking time on a faceless clock.

No matter how piteous the bear, such attractions were made for the likes of Brains.He glided silently towards his prey like a silhouette sliding across a screen, and stole through the outer ring of onlookers, untouched, untouching. He noted the purse strings, loose around the girl's wrist. Slash, slash, he thought, grab the purse, shove her into the bear, and scarper. He edged his knife out of his pocket, and slipped into position behind his quarry.

At a signal from the drummer, the youngster stopped in mid-song, jumped down, picked up the bucket and made ready to collect whatever the spectators were willing to share with the threesome. Dulcet moved on before she was obliged to contribute to the bear's well-being, although from what she now saw the hobbled creature's being was less than well, the profits from today's performance surely destined for The Bull's Head, not the bear's stomach. She tightened her grip on the purse and set off through the thinning crowd.

The knife was slowly returned to its hiding place and the silhouette glided away.

'Where'd the little lady go?' Brains growled.

Brawn pointed with his huge paw towards the iron bridge over the River Medway.

'Thought so. She's heading for Strood, then she'll take the road to Higham.'

'How d'yer know that, then?'

'She's one of the maids in that house top of the rise, that's how I know. And all you needs to know is we'll be waiting for the little luv'ly at Dillywood Lane, just before she reaches Gad's Hill Place.'

Chapter Five: A Wild Goose Chase

Two days after Dickens's death, Georgina was sitting in front of her dressing table, running through in her mind all the arrangements for the funeral.

Still as trim as when she first joined her brother-in-law's household as a mere fifteen-year old, her sparkling blue eyes and trace of a Scottish burr were her most endearing features. Presentable, but hardly eye-catching; well-read, though not overly intellectual; a firm disciplinarian with a caring centre; the sum of these parts had made her the ideal nanny for the children. Never Miss Hogarth, not even Miss Georgina, but always Aunt Georgy, she was the most important person – nurse, teacher, friend – in each child's early life.

The duties of hostess fell to her eight years later when husband and wife separated less than amicably, a pivotal moment in her young life. Her duty as younger sister to Catherine, a wife of fourteen years and ten live births, was clear, yet she sided with the husband, effectively ostracising herself from the Hogarth family. She confronted that challenge, as she did all others, with Christian resolve and common sense. Now in her forty-third year and firmly entrenched in spinsterhood, regret for what might have been occasionally nagged at the soft under-belly of her self-belief, only to be rooted out in short order.

The opening and shutting of the front door interrupted her planning. A visitor. She rose, smoothed her black mourning dress, and went downstairs to find Dunston waiting for her in the drawing room.

'Good morning, Dunston.' She'd been hoping her Saturday would be free of callers – so many details to attend to – but she was more than willing to make an exception for the deceased's nephew. 'Come to have a farewell moment with your uncle before the funeral, have you? How thoughtful. His dear body's still laid out in the billiard room. Let me take you there and give you some time with him by yourself.'

'No, no. That won't be necessary,' Dunston said quickly, clearly having no desire to be alone with a two-day old corpse. 'Actually, I'm here to lay out my... my *sleuthing* strategy.'

'Sleuthing strategy?'

'Yes, you see, I feel it my duty to Uncle Charles and, of course, to you, to spare no effort in personally hunting down the blackguard who took his life, and now that I'm retired, I have ample free time to devote to the task.' He smiled in anticipation of glowing words of praise.

Oh, Heavens! Georgina groaned to herself. Dunston as Charles's avenging angel? What a fiasco that could be. She'd half suspected this might happen and, being Georgina, had prepared just in case. 'Perhaps we should sit.' She gestured to the small round table. 'Then you can tell me what you have in mind.'

'Yes, of course,' he said. He held her chair for her before taking his own seat. 'Miss Georgina, I've come up with the perfect method of investigation, one worthy of the redoubtable Inspector Bucket in *Bleak House*,' he announced. 'I've compiled a two-part list of suspects – first, family members all of whom might be hoping for something in Uncle's will; second, fellow authors, competitors who'd be pleased to see him removed from the literary scene.

'The clever part, though, is this: I will question all of them without arousing *any* suspicion.' He paused, then blushing with pride, he laid the crowning glory of his strategy before her, 'I'll tell them I'm writing Uncle's *biography*.'

Georgina remained motionless and, fortunately for Dunston, speechless, her mind racing in a dozen different directions but whatever the direction, the final destination inevitably had disaster written all over it. This was even worse than she'd feared. She was horrified at the thought of socially-awkward Dunston intruding on the grief of Charles's family or grilling England's literary luminaries. Time for her plan.

'I see you've given this much thought,' she began. 'A very… clever strategy indeed, but questioning the *obvious* suspects is a *routine* task that anyone can handle. Whereas, there's a more challenging line of inquiry, one that can *only* be undertaken by someone who understands Charles's approach to writing, knows his compositional tendencies, and has read *everything* he's ever written, and you, Dunston, are the *only* person I can trust with this assignment.' A large helping of flattery, that should do the trick. 'Can I count on you?' She looked straight into his eyes.

'Certainly, I'm at your service,' replied the innocent, totally unaware he was being led by the nose.

'Excellent.' So far so good. 'You see, what bothers me is the timing of Charles's death. Think of it. He was working on the only mystery he ever wrote, and suddenly before the story's complete, he's struck down. It crossed my mind that someone may have wanted to prevent him from finishing the tale.'

'Why for Heaven's sake?' Dunston asked.

'Because Charles loved to draw on *real* people and *real* incidents for his novels.' A good lead-in since it was true. 'Of course, by the time he'd finished, reality had become larger than life, but often enough, you could see the original behind his embellishment.'

Dunston nodded. A good sign, but still a long way to go.

'Now *The Mystery of Edwin Drood*,' she resumed, 'is set in a cathedral town called Cloisterham which is obviously a fictional version of Rochester, so it's possible Charles was building his story around some foul deed that *actually happened* in Rochester. If so, the guilty party would do anything to make sure the story was never finished.'

'Seems rather farfetched to imagine that one of the good citizens of Rochester would go to such lengths to prevent Uncle completing a novel,' Dunston said dubiously.

'Ah, but don't forget the break-in I told you about yesterday.'

'The break-in?' He couldn't see any connection. 'What does that have to do with it?'

'Remember I told you the drawer in your uncle's desk was robbed? He found it half open when he entered the study in the morning. I was in the drawing room and heard him call "Georgina! Georgina!" Not Georgy as usual, a sure sign something was amiss. When I got there, he turned to me, and cried, "They're gone!" The intruder had taken some letters *and* his notes for the rest of the Drood story.' She paused to let her words sink in. No reaction.

'Don't you see? The burglar was *desperate* to know what was to be revealed in the novel.'

She waited for him to grasp the link between the missing notes and the murder. Silence. She willed the penny to drop. More silence. The penny, far from dropping, was stuck firmly in the silly man's peat-bog cranium.

'Hmm… well… if the intruder found something in the notes,' Dunston finally began, 'something that seriously threatened his reputation, what was he to do? He had to take the notes… hence the theft. But he also had to silence Uncle Charles… hence the murder. By Jove, the burglar stole the notes *and* poisoned Uncle!'

'Exactly. Now are you persuaded that Charles was murdered to prevent him finishing the book?' Georgina asked.

'Ye-es,' he said, sounding decidedly uncertain. And then more positively, 'Yes, I believe I am.'

'Good. And you'll help me?'

'Willingly,' Dunston said, 'but where would I start? Did the burglar leave any traces in the study that might help?'

'No. Charles didn't report the break-in to the local constabulary for fear of gossip, but he did ask his friend, Inspector Line of Scotland Yard, to have a look around the study unofficially. The inspector, for whom Charles had the highest regard, as do I, was only too happy to oblige, but despite a thorough examination of the study window and the desk drawer, he found nothing of use.'

'Well, there you are.If a Scotland Yard inspector couldn't make any progress, what hope have I?' Dunston asked reasonably.

'Ahhh, here's the difference. *He* investigated the *burglary*. I want *you* to investigate the *novel*.'

'The novel?' Dunston was unsure he'd heard correctly.

'Yes. If there is something truly damaging planned for the denouement, I want you to find out what it is. I want you, Dunston, to scrutinize *every* word, dissect *every* sentence, tear apart *every* paragraph that Charles has written so far and learn everything you can about how he intended the story to conclude *and*, God willing, uncover who stood to gain most by his death.'

Dunston looked at her doubtfully. 'I'll do whatever I can,' he said, 'but I'm not sure I'll find much. After all, Uncle's written only three monthly instalments, barely a quarter of the novel.'

'*Published* only three instalments, Dunston,' Georgina said coyly. 'But I have three *unpublished* ones!'

'Three *unpublished* instalments!' Dunston exclaimed.

'Three,' Georgina confirmed. 'John Forster, Charles's literary advisor, has seen the fourth and fifth in draft as have I, but nobody's eyes, *nobody's*, Dunston, not Forster's, not mine, have gazed on the words in the sixth except those of the author himself.' A lie, just a minor remoulding of the truth really, akin in her mind to a re-arrangement of the drawing room furniture, but a lie all the same, Georgina having read every single word in the supposedly unseen sixth instalment.

'Charles was writing the final words of that instalment when the poison took him from us.' She was confident now that Dunston was thoroughly hooked, a gullible river trout flapping ecstatically on the end of her line. 'I want you, Dunston, to be the *first* to read these pages.' The spellbound fish leaped from hook to frying pan. 'I want you to analyse all *six* instalments right up to the last page he ever wrote and, when you do, I'm sure you'll be able to shed light on the story's ending *and* discover who took Charles's life. Wait, I'll get them.'

A few minutes later, Georgina returned and handed Dunston the Fourth, the Fifth and the as yet, according to her, unseen, unread Sixth Instalment. She smiled at the sight of the speechless, breathless man in front of her, his hands shaking so much he could barely take the manuscript. Observing his delight, she felt, much to her surprise, a pleasant tingling like the spreading warmth of hot porridge in her childhood tummy on a raw, Scottish morning.

Her pleasure at his pleasure, though, was a distant second to her satisfaction at the success of her ploy. From what she'd read, the poor man would never be able to figure out how the story concluded. He'd be tied up for weeks banging his head against a brick wall, and Charles's grieving family and fellow novelists would be spared Dunston's investigatory intrusions.

Georgina had played her cards well, but she'd rest less easily if she knew Dunston had not entertained the slightest thought of giving up his sleuthing strategy. There was more weft to his weave than that. He might not have lion-hearted courage or Samson-like strength, but he had a quiet determination, a powerful sense of purpose and… the perseverance of King Bruce's spider. The three additional instalments would certainly occupy his immediate attention, but questioning each of his suspects was still high on his agenda.

Chapter Six: Dillywood Lane

An oversized, brawny man coming in the opposite direction and occupying more than his fair share of the highway, obliged Dulcet to shift to the right side of Gravesend Road. She was approaching Dillywood Lane, weary from her long walk and glad to be within sight of Gad's Hill Place after her long walk from Rochester. Drat! The stupid man was veering into her path.

She pulled her skirt tight about her and tacked to the other side. The lumbering lump performed a mirror-image manoeuvre, rapidly closing the distance between them. She glanced up, the first flicker of fear lighting her eyes, all her attention fixed on the hulk directly in front of her, blocking her way.

'AAAHH—'

Her cry was cut off by the arm snaking around her neck, snapping her head back, and squeezing shut her windpipe. The two-person ambush! One in front as decoy, one behind to do the business. THE RING! Warning bells clanged in her head as a knife sliced through her purse strings. The business was done. Or almost, the ribbons severed, but the purse still clutched to her breast.

'Give us the purse, me luv'ly, or it'll be worse for you,' the burly ruffian snarled.

He lifted her as easily as a gunnysack of hay and hurled her onto the summer-hard ground. She landed heavily on her left side, pain racking her body from shoulder to hip.

'All we wants is the purse… least ways, for now. Ha! Ha!'

23

He was reaching down to grab the small linen bag, when his eyes fell on the exposed flesh above the girl's bodice. Blinded by the lust suddenly inflaming his loins, he failed to spot the flash of work-toughened nails, but he definitely felt them raking his face with desperate fury. He rocked back on his heels, grasping his bleeding cheek, the purse forgotten. Glaring death, he reached for the maid's throat.

'WHOA! Let her go!'

A whip slashed across the brute's back, once, twice, thrice before he had a chance to turn and assess the unexpected threat. His eyes fell upon a slender lad, lashing out with all his might but little effect. He snatched the whip from him, snapped it in two across an anvil-solid knee and threw it aside. Totally defenceless, Isaac, Georgina's stable-boy, took a step back, then another only to find himself gripped from behind by two hands as hard and unyielding as iron shackles. The lout's knife-wielding accomplice had joined the action.

'You can have this one. I'll deal with her.' Brains pushed the stable-boy towards Brawn, and turned back to the maid. She was curled up on the ground, looking more like a pummelled punch-bag than a young woman. He reached down, and with one short, sharp tug, wrenched the purse from her grasp.

Brawn smiled at Isaac, his intent only too clear. Someone was going to be hurt like he'd been hurt, only much, MUCH worse, an eye for an eye a totally inadequate judicial code for the likes of him. And there stood the girl's would-be champion. Brawn stepped forward and swung his massive fist. The lad ducked, and stumbled backwards, his courage crumbling as surely as a child's sandcastle succumbed to the incoming tide. Brawn laughed. Isaac shuddered.

'Let him go, you lout!' a new voice barked.

Brawn half-turned to see who'd caused this latest interruption. A mistake. The stable-boy's kick aimed at the oaf's groin, landed with a solid thud.

'Scarper! I've got the purse,' Brains yelled and took to his heels.

No so Brawn, his thirst for blood far from quenched. He stepped towards the lad, murder in his eyes, poised to deliver one last, crippling blow. Like hammer to nail, his clenched fist sped towards his quarry's cowering head.

'RUN, you fool!' The new arrival's desperate yell immobilised the villain in mid-swing. Glimpsing the latest entrant to the fray heading his way, Brawn hesitated for a second, then turned and lumbered off after Brains.

'I'll get yer, yer slimy piece of shit,' he bellowed at the stable-boy. 'Larrup you all to pieces when I gets hold of you.'

Isaac, shaking violently, turned to greet the newcomer with gratitude in his heart and thanks on his lips.

'No need to thank me,' said Nick, Dunston's manservant. 'You was the one what saved the young lady. Take my hand, sir. You're a brave man.'

Dulcet was already sitting up with the assistance of Dunston who'd watched the rout of the footpads from the safety of his carriage. The next few minutes were devoted entirely to her welfare. While her three rescuers scurried to and fro aimlessly, she discreetly checked her injuries. Her shoulder and hip were sore and stiff, the bruised flesh no doubt already turning various shades of black and blue. No broken bones though as far as she could tell. Feeling a little more self-possessed, she regarded her three heroes.

Isaac, it turned out, was returning in the one-pony trap from Mrs Hulkes's nursery on the outskirts of Strood where he'd collected roses for the funeral wreaths. The lad, only nineteen or so, was almost girlish in appearance with high cheek bones, full lips and long curling brown locks, but to the young maid he was the most handsome fellow she'd ever seen. Slim and smallish in stature, his carriage – body held erect, head tilted back – conveyed the impression of a taller man, a bantam strutting like a rooster. His dress was neat with just a touch of the dandy evident in his coxcomb-like, scarlet neckerchief, a flourish apparently endowed with some powerful magnetic property judging by its effect on Dulcet.

She beamed a special smile at the first of her saviours. 'You was so brave, Isaac. Never seen nothin' like it.' She blushed and smiled again as he acknowledged her thanks with a shy nod.

'And you Nick, thank you so much.'

With his wiry, twenty-year old frame, cropped, russet-toned hair, and crystal-clear, hazel eyes, Nick was no less handsome than Isaac but there were no blushes for him. And no lingering looks.

'Oh! Begging yer pardon, Mr Burnett, should've thanked you first for yer kindness, sir.' Definitely no blushes for him. Nor any below-the-lashes peeks.

'My dear, least we could do,' Dunston said gallantly. 'Very fortunate I was returning home after visiting Miss Georgina. Now, young lady, we must get you back to Gad's Hill Place where your injuries can be properly attended to.'

And so, with her three good Samaritans in close attendance, she was assisted towards the two waiting carriages. Without a word being spoken, all four pairs of feet made towards Isaac's trap and not Dunston's more spacious phaeton. Who was guiding the four? Dulcet? Or one of her entourage sensing the lay of the land? Or perhaps all four recognising the moment belonged to Isaac and Dulcet. Whatever the truth, she was gently placed in the trap amidst a chorus of well-intentioned but largely useless instructions shouted from all sides.

THE RING! For the second time, the object of her errand screamed its presence in her mind, and, in short order, the same was shrieked aloud. 'The ring! The master's signet ring! It's gone! Miss will never forgive me. What'll I do? It was inside the purse the pikeys took. They've got the ring.'

'You're probably right, my dear,' Dunston said, 'but perhaps we should search the area just in case it was discarded during the tramps' hasty retreat. Um... Isaac, if I have your name right, could you and Nick take a look around?'

Isaac nodded, and immediately set to. Nick, as was his wont, rolled his eyes. Having grown up in the every-one-for-himself harshness of a London slum, life had taught him to protest any and all demands on him. A complainer by schooling, then, not by nature. Indeed, Nick greeted life in the main with wry humour and good spirit, and more often than not, a friendly smile.

Dunston had 'acquired' him when he moved into Woods View House, the property left to him by his great aunt. Having made his way out of London as a sixteen-year old, Nick had been taken on as the household's jack-of-all-trades. The only servant on hand when Dunston arrived, Nick informed him that he'd be 'happy to stay on and continue serving as… ahem… valet, sir.' The new master, unused to servants, had accepted this statement without question, and over the next few months had come to rely more and more heavily on his self-appointed manservant, a stalwart Sam Weller to Dunston's Mr Pickwick.

The maid waited in an agony of suspense while the two young men scoured the area. Seconds passed like hours. Then she saw Nick stoop and pick something up and her heart leapt. Had he found the purse? No, not the purse, because whatever it was, glinted in the sunshine. The ring! It could easily have fallen out during the fracas. He was examining it intently, her spirits rising the longer he studied it. Evidently sensing her eyes on him, he glanced in her direction, and with a slight shake of his head dashed her hopes.

'Got it!' Isaac yelled. He held up a small purse, four severed ribbons clearly visible. Dulcet was so excited she could barely wait as he ran to her, a big grin on his face. 'Found it,' he announced proudly as he handed the prize to her. She looked inside. No ring. She hunted with her hand. No ring. She turned it inside out. No ring.She groaned and thrust the purse at Isaac. He searched it thoroughly. No ring.

The robbers! They threw away the purse but took the ring. Dulcet was inconsolable, the three men at a loss as to how to help her. At length, the maid recovered her composure sufficiently to ask Isaac to take her to Gad's Hill Place. She must tell her mistress.

Isaac climbed into the driver's seat and with what was left of his whip set the pony on its way. Dulcet, still upset, felt a small glow warming her as she sat watching his back.

'Isaac,' she said to the back. The back concentrated hard on its driving. 'You risked your life for me. Don't know what would've happened if you hadn't saved me.' The back remained motionless but definitely listening. 'I wants you to know that if there's ever anything I can do to repay your kindness and your bravery, I will, cross my heart and hope to die if I don't.'

This was said to the back with such feeling that immobility was no longer a permissible response. The back straightened, the head nodded.

Dulcet smiled to herself, satisfied.

Chapter Seven: The Separation

llow me to introduce myself. Well, not my name. That's not in the least bit important. No, what's important is my avocation, my mission in life as I think of it. I consider myself THE repository for all information about the respected, and not so respected, members of society.

You may not believe this, but I'm aggrieved to say there are some misguided souls who describe me as a purveyor of spicy speculation, a source of salacious rumour and even an instrument of wicked gossip. In short, these unfortunates accuse me of being no better than a common tittle-tattle.Nothing can be further from the truth as those who truly know me will attest. They will point to my willingness to provide individuals in all walks of life with the opportunity to unburden themselves to me, and my determination to share whatever I learn with whomever I believe will value it most.

Sometimes, the process of acquiring information can prove extraordinarily difficult, especially if there's a carefully guarded secret at the heart of the matter. And sometimes, whatever is obtained may not be of immediate use but has to be stored and ripened as it were. Here's a case in point.

What I'm about to tell you happened some twenty years ago. I'd heard a whisper, nothing more, that Charles Dickens, then an annoying upstart author, was pursuing Miss Ellen Ternan, a London stage actress, at least that was how she described herself. But, thanks to his tight little circle of friends and especially Miss Georgina Hogarth, that marvellous woman who for some strange reason thinks it her duty to protect Dickens's literary standing and keep his private life... well... private, no one knew what was really going on. Unearthing details of the liaison was more difficult than finding deep-reef oysters in the burning sands *of the Sahara, but perseverance pays in my line of work. This is what I discovered.*

I learned from a stage-hand who witnessed these events, that it all started when Dickens decided to put on an amateur production of The Frozen Deep, *a drama by his new friend, Wilkie Collins, a real degenerate if ever I saw one, indeed rumour has it he enjoys the pleasures of a ménage a trois, but let me not be the one to spread such unsubstantiated gossip. Collins is a good novelist, at least his tales have recognisable plots, unlike Dickens's stream of unbelievable incidents and peculiar characters. This particular play was full of weeping women anxiously awaiting the return of their men-folk engaged, naturally, in a perilous Arctic expedition.*

Yes, not very imaginative, but the point is that Collins and Dickens, fancying themselves as actors, had determined to play the two male leads and were looking for actresses to play the waiting ladies. Enter Mrs Fanny Ternan and her two daughters, Ellen and Maria, between engagements and perfect for the parts. The play was performed in August of forty-nine at the Free Trade Hall in Manchester. Dickens was thirty-seven, Ellen, or Nelly as she was called, eighteen, a difference of almost two decades. The fool was smitten immediately.

After the performance, Mrs Ternan took her daughters off to Doncaster for their next engagement leaving Dickens distraught beyond measure. Acting more like a love-sick schoolboy than a middle-aged father, he persuaded Collins to accompany him on a walking tour to... where else but Doncaster. No doubt Dickens spent more time in fervent pursuit of Miss Ternan than on invigorating hikes through the Yorkshire Dales, and the romance, if that's the right word for their illicit liaison, blossomed over the next few months.

By the following May, Dickens's separation from his wife, Catherine, was complete. In less than a year, the Dickens household had been torn apart by a teenaged stage performer.

There, what do you think of that? Miss Hogarth would have a heart attack if she knew I'd told you this. I've been waiting ever so patiently for the right moment to share my findings with the delightful lady, but I've a feeling that something else is going to turn up which will make what I now have doubly valuable. We shall see.

Chapter Eight: Seeking Professional Assistance

Dunston was an orphan from early childhood. His mother died giving birth to him, and the timid little creature she'd brought into the world found itself in the care of a hard-drinking, loutish father. With that parent's death before Dunston had reached his sixth birthday, the diffident, insecure child was placed with a great aunt on his father's side. She was a kindly woman in her way but with no children of her own, she had little idea of what to do with the newcomer, soon deciding he'd be best off in a boarding school.

Dullsbury's Evangelical Academy provided Dunston with an acceptable education but it came at a cost. He was the shortest, fattest boy in his age group, and had been routinely bullied and ridiculed for twelve, long years. From there, he'd been shunted off to the boredom and isolation of keeping the books for a shipping company, a soul-destroying line of work he was obliged to endure for twenty years. By the time he left, he'd withdrawn into a solitary existence which, with only occasional interludes, would be his lot for the rest of his life. Reconnecting with Miss Georgina promised to be one such interlude.

Ever since receiving from her the unpublished fourth and fifth instalments of *The Mystery of Edwin Drood* and the treasure of treasures, the virginal, never-read, at least so he's been told, sixth, Dunston had pored over them nonstop, eyes burning into every word. What a glorious assignment. Did he give any thought to that fiddle-faddle about the novel holding the clue to the author's death? A little… enough to conclude it was a dead-end, just as he'd suspected.

Still, Miss Georgina being Miss Georgina, he'd thought it wise to solicit a professional's opinion before reporting back to her. Assuming it was as negative as his own, it might provide a shield to ward off any unpleasantness that might otherwise come his way. With this in mind, Dunston had travelled up to London early Monday morning, and now stood in the Scotland Yard office of Inspector Line – someone Miss Georgina held in high regard and therefore perfect for his purpose – with a satchel containing the three unpublished instalments clutched tightly to his chest.

The inspector's office, ascetically furnished with a plain oak desk and a bare-bones bookcase, every inch of its shelf-space occupied by well-thumbed case files, looked like the workplace of a man who was part monk, part bloodhound, a summary description that captured the policeman perfectly. His facial features, befitting someone who bore the name Line, were, well… linear. The head was angular and carried with a military bearing, but what most struck the beholder was the right-angled alignment of the nose, a kind of facial plumb-line, with the face's horizontal features – two parallel creases furrowing the forehead, straight-as-a-dye eyebrows, and spirit-levelled lips. *Line's lines*, thought a mesmerised Dunston.

Line usually chose to wear everyday clothes – today, a tweed jacket with brown elbow patches, starched white shirt and navy tie – rather than the dark blue uniform to which he was entitled as London's first Chief of Detectives. Uniform or no, the cut of the man left no doubt that he would prove unshakeable in pursuit of any villain crossing his path. And judging by his penetrating blue-eyed stare, the square block of his sturdy shoulders, and his unreadable expression, a formidable interrogator of prisoners.

'Good day, Mr Burnett, and welcome to Police Headquarters.' Inspector Line moved around his desk, greeted his caller with a firm handshake, and gestured to one of the two wooden chairs placed for visitors.

'My condolences on the loss of your uncle. Admired Mr Dickens mightily, God rest his soul. Had the great honour of escorting him through the worst slums in London a few months back when he was collecting material for his latest novel. What an eye for detail. Told him many a time he'd make a fine detective.

'Of course, there's more to detecting than simply observing, but it's the right place to start,' the inspector continued conversationally. 'Why? Well, observation is the foundation of facts, and *facts* are at the heart of the detecting business because *facts* don't lie. Criminals lie, witnesses lie, even innocent people lie, but you can always count on *facts*. Now, sir, what can I do for you?'

'Yes, well, the reason I'm here is rather… unusual.' Unusual, if not downright embarrassing, Dunston fretted, caught as he was between the imperative to serve Miss Georgina and his doubts about her fanciful notion that someone in Rochester sneaked into Gad's Hill Place and poisoned England's most prestigious novelist like a rat-catcher exterminating vermin.

'Let me assure you I've heard everything in my years on the force,' the policeman remarked. 'Not much can surprise me no matter how unusual you may think it.'

'In that case, I'm emboldened to proceed,' a relieved Dunston said. 'The fact is, I'm hoping I can enlist your assistance in a purely *personal* capacity, in following up your investigation of the burglary at Gad's Hill Place.'

'Not sure what else I can do,' the inspector said. 'I already examined the study and didn't find anything. Someone had obviously entered through the window, but there was no evidence at the scene apart from the empty drawer. Lock was jimmied and the drawer was half open and a little out of true where it'd been forced. Had to give it a good shove to close it. Beyond that there was nothing to go on and no suspects, at least not then.'

'Um, yes, quite so,' Dunston said. 'But, you see, the stolen papers included Uncle Charles's notes on the second half of his current novel, and Miss Georgina, that is, Miss Hogarth, believes the… er… *robbery* was committed to discover what Uncle planned for the rest of the story because, according to her, the… um… *burglar* feared some damaging revelation.' He'd chosen his words carefully, determined not to let any reference to his uncle's murder creep into his explanation.

Line shook his head. 'Very interesting, and very ingenious I daresay, but there's a much simpler explanation. As I said, we had no suspects at the time, but now we do. Been several burglaries throughout Kent recently, work of a well-organised gang. They take only the most valuable objects – paintings, fine silver and gold plate, exquisite jewellery and such like. That's why Scotland Yard was called in. Fellow by name of Dinky Dryker is the ring-leader. The break-in at Gad's Hill Place was most likely one of his.'

'But, if I've understood you correctly, inspector, *facts* are the foundation of any police investigation,' Dunston said with an inquiring look. Line nodded cautiously. 'And, the facts in this instance are first, nothing of value was taken from Gad's Hill Place, and second, priceless pieces are being stolen by a gang operating throughout the county. These facts, inspector, are hardly proof that the break-in at Uncle's was the work of this gang. Your conclusion is largely guesswork, if you don't mind me saying so, and could... ahem, be wrong.'

'Ye-es... you're right. I suppose it is a bit... speculative.' he conceded. 'But, based on twenty-five years' of policing experience, it's a good place to start,' he added. 'Still, we should consider the possibility that the notes were the motive behind the burglary of your uncle's house. Thank you for bringing this to my attention and, I assure you, I'll follow up to the best of my ability.' Assuming the interview was over, Line stood. Dunston remained seated. 'Is there something else, Mr Burnett?'

'Actually, there is.' The inspector sat back down. 'You see, Miss Hogarth, also believes the first part of Uncle's novel may contain some hint as to how the story is to unfold, and this might point to the villain who violated Uncle's study.'

'By Jove, Miss Hogarth must have given this much thought.' The inspector could barely keep his amusement from showing.

'Indeed, she has,' Dunston continued, the inspector's scepticism totally escaping him. 'The novel is *The Mystery of Edwin Drood*. Have you read it?'

Chapter Nine: The Mystery of Edwin Drood

'The Mystery of Edwin Drood? Of course, I've read it,' the policeman replied enthusiastically. 'It's very popular in the Yard. The lads club together to buy each month's instalment and then pass it around so, yes, I've read all three. What a powerful opening scene in that old woman's opium den, spitting image of the one I took Mr Dickens to in Spitalfields. Caught it perfectly, he did, right down to the last detail, including the man smoking himself into oblivion.

'Now, what was his name? James, no, John, John Jasper, as I recall, choirmaster at Cloisterham Cathedral by day, drug addict by night. Fellow has an unhealthy fancy for Rosa Bud, fiancée of the Edwin Drood of the title, and is scheming to eliminate his rival and clear the way for himself. Jasper is related to the Drood family, so whenever Edwin visits Cloisterham to see Rosa, he stays with Jasper in his lodgings in the Gate House, totally unaware of his host's murderous intentions, rather like the spider and the fly. There, have I got it right?'

'Yes, excellent summary,' Dunston acknowledged. 'Perhaps, inspector, I could ask if your detective instincts were struck by… anything unusual… a clue perhaps?'

Put on his mettle, Line's brow furrowed in thought. 'Well, I did wonder about Rosa's engagement ring. What was it, diamonds set in gold?'

'Rubies and diamonds,' Dunston corrected. 'In a Tudor-rose design.'

'Yes, that's it. Devotes a lot of space to the history of that ring, does Mr

Dickens. Tells us how, several years earlier when Rosa was still a child, her mother drowned in a boating accident. Her husband gently removed the ring from his dead wife's finger and entrusted it to his lawyer friend, Hiram Grewgious, with instructions to pass it to Edwin when he came of age. The young man was to give the ring to Rosa on their engagement, their parents having long ago planned their betrothal, but *only* if they were truly in love. If not, the ring had to be returned to the lawyer. All rather melodramatic, but I suppose it was your uncle's way of telling the reader to keep an eye on the ring so I assume it'll play a major role later in the story.'

Line sneaked a glance at the clock on the wall. Time and crime wait for no man, was one of Line's favourite admonitions to his officers.

'Anyway, Mr Burnett, that's what I remember and, if it's a fair reflection of what Mr Dickens has written so far, then it's not enough to point to any possible perpetrator of the burglary. So, I'm afraid Miss Hogarth's theory, even if right, doesn't help very much.'

Line stood for the second time. Dunston remained seated for the second time.

'Yes, Mr Burnett.' The inspector's words were followed by a long sigh, seeping out of him like gas softly hissing from a perforated pipe.

'Inspector, I have three *unpublished* instalments.' Dunston tapped the leather satchel on his lap.

'Three unpublished instalments? Really?' Flabbergasted, the inspector plunked down on his chair more like a sack of wet sand than one of the Yard's finest. 'And do they shed any light on the burglary?'

'I read them yesterday and made copious notes, but haven't reached any definitive conclusions.'

'I see.' The policeman pulled an official Metropolitan Police Casebook from one of the shelves and prepared to make his own notes. 'And what do these instalments tell us about Mr Edwin Drood and his mystery?'

'Not sure I'm the best rapporteur for your purposes. But I'm willing to try.' Dunston was doing himself an injustice. He lived and breathed every word of his uncle's novels and was more than capable of outlining the rest of the Drood mystery, albeit not with the novelist's flair, the uncle's

36

prose marvellously rich, the nephew's oral communication the dreariest commonplace in comparison.

'Very good. Please proceed,' the inspector said.

'Well, the story resumes with Rosa and Edwin meeting three days before Christmas,' Dunston began. 'The young couple are having doubts about the pending nuptials and in a touching scene they agree to be as brother and sister, not man and wife. They kiss a farewell kiss, but Jasper, lurking close by, mistakes it for the kiss sealing their betrothal.'

Line picked up a pencil stub, licked the lead and scratched a note. 'What about the ring? Does Edwin give Rosa the ring?' he asked.

'No. Edwin recalls Grewgious's instructions to return the ring to him if the marriage plans are abandoned, so it stays in Edwin's breast pocket. Rosa writes to Grewgious, now her guardian, informing him the marriage has been called off and he replies saying he'll be in Cloisterham two days after Christmas to see her and collect the ring from Edwin.'

More licking and scratching from Line's side of the desk.

'The next significant event,' Dunston continued, 'is a Christmas Eve dinner in Jasper's Gate House. Moments before Edwin's arrival, Jasper is seen holding a long, black scarf, a potential murder weapon if ever there was one. We're told nothing else about the evening's events except that Edwin goes for an after-dinner stroll... and doesn't return. The next morning, a frantic Jasper raises the alarm. Edwin is missing, and, as the days go by, feared dead.'

'Hmm, interesting.' The policeman spoke without raising his eyes from his note-taking. 'Pray continue.'

'Well, some time later, Jasper learns of Edwin and Rosa's parting. He turns ghastly white, shrieks, and falls to the floor unconscious, and is, in Uncle's words, *nothing but a heap of torn and miry clothes.*'

'Ha! Fellow's committed murder for no reason.' Another lick, more scratching. 'Had he known of the couple's separation, he could have courted Rosa without killing his young rival.'

'Indeed,' Dunston agreed. 'We come now to the sixth instalment – seen incidentally by no eyes but mine, and of course Uncle's. In the last chapter, Jasper returns to the opium den.'

'I'm not surprised. The fellow's clearly addicted to the drug,' the inspector remarked. 'Mr Dickens recounts several instances when Jasper becomes disoriented, almost passing out. Happens in the cathedral the day after his first visit to the opium den and later in the Gate House. Partial blackouts like those are typical of long-term users.'

'I see, I didn't know. Anyway, the old woman has learned how to mix the opiate so that Jasper talks freely while drugged. In a very telling scene, she asks him about Edwin and he mumbles he's done it hundreds of thousands of times in his dreams *but now it's over.*'

'Sounds like a confession to me.' A lick of his pencil stub and another note appeared in the casebook.

'Quite. That's all, I'm afraid,' Dunston concluded.

'An absorbing little mystery, Mr Burnett.'

'I'm pleased you think so. You see, I was hoping the additional instalments would pique your curiosity enough to persuade you to apply your detective expertise to Uncle's story as though it were a *real* case and see what light, if any, you can shed on the burglary.'

'Hmm, an intriguing proposal. Alright. I have my notes, but I will of course need to read the three new instalments myself and see what they tell us. From what you've said, Mr Dickens has given us the makings of a very fine mystery… and, truth be told, I'm keen to see if I can solve it.'

'Thank you, inspector,' Dunston said as he passed him the satchel. 'I look forward to hearing your findings. Shall we say Friday afternoon?'

'Friday it is, sir.'

Chapter Ten: Sleeping Beauty

Dulcet could see that Miss Georgina was thoroughly dismayed when she'd reported the loss of the master's signet ring on Saturday. Even so, the mistress did not upbraid the maid in the slightest. Her only concern was for the girl's wellbeing. Dulcet was packed off to bed, a flood of sorrys still issuing from her mouth, and instructed to stay there until told otherwise. Typical of miss. Always forgiving; always caring.

Although Monday evening was pleasantly sunny, Dulcet's cramped, narrow-windowed garret was as gloomy as ever, her blanketed outline barely visible on the small bed. She shifted restlessly and began to turn on her side. A swift intake of breath, a low groan, a fluttering of eyelids, and she gingerly resumed her original position, flat on her back.

Soft footsteps climbed the stairs to the attic in Gad's Hill Place. They stopped at the first of the meagre bedrooms. The latch was soundlessly lifted. The door swung inward inch by furtive inch, the gradually widening gap illuminated by a single candle. Its soft glow hovered for a moment, seemingly undecided, then advanced stealthily into the room, drawing with it a figure, indistinct, intangible.

The flickering flame moved towards the unsuspecting shape on the bed. Another slight flutter of the eyelids as the candle's halo came to rest on the delicate features of her face, but no sign of anxiety disturbed the smooth brow or brought a cry to the soft lips. Its job done, the candle withdrew to the upturned wooden box serving as a bedside table, its light now giving human substance to the erstwhile ghostly greyness of its bearer.

'Dulcet,' Isaac whispered. 'I couldn't answer when you was talking to me in the trap after them pikeys attacked you 'cos I ain't had much to do with girls and don't know what to say to 'em. But I can talk to you now when you're asleep like this. I know you can't hear me, but leastways I can say what I wants to say.'

He paused, coughed to steady his vocal chords, then continued as quietly as before. 'Don't know rightly how to put this, but I swear I would've rescued you from twenty rogues, nay, from a hundred cut-throats, I'm that...' much swallowing and throat-clearing, 'fond of you.'

He'd barely finished inching the last three words out of his mouth, much like a sommelier unwillingly drawing the cork from his last bottle of a prized vintage, when the lips of the sleeping beauty curved in a tiny smile. Isaac's eyes widened in shock. He blinked once, looked hard, blinked a second time and fixed his gaze on the mischief-causing mouth. Motionless, exactly as it had been. He glanced at the fluttering flame, then back to the face, seeing the play of shadow and light flitting from one feature to the next. The candlelight, only the candlelight.

'Dulcet,' he resumed after a few minutes, 'on me eighteenth birthday, I swore I'd take ship for Australia, and would've gone right then except for...' He licked his lips and then, as if making a decision about how much to share with the young maid, said softly, 'Except for Ma. She's real sick, and needs my help, and I couldn't leave her. Took this job with Miss Hogarth so I could support her. But if Ma passes away, and I fear her passing will be soon, then I'll be off.

'See, the colonies will give me the chance I've never had here. But life there is difficult and desperate, no place for a lovely young girl like you. You have to understand this 'cos I don't want no mix-up 'twixt us. I've tried my best to be honest 'cos you're a... a fine person and I'll always be fond of you wherever I end up in this world.'

Following this outpouring of what were surely his innermost feelings never before revealed to a single person, awake or asleep, he gulped, paused for a second and then grazed the maid's forehead with his lips. He collected the candle from the bedside table and let its light lead him out just as it led him in. He closed the door. The latch fell into place leaving the tiny bedroom in silence.

In the near-dark, one eye half opened. All was still. The eye revealed itself in full. The other followed suit. The sleeping beauty might be beautiful but asleep she was not. Again the tiny smile curved her lips but as it did a small frown settled on the just-kissed brow. Dulcet knew now the challenge facing her if she was to win her true love. Convinced, as only the deeply in love could be, that she would succeed nonetheless, the smile returned, the face relaxed, the eyes closed.

Chapter Eleven: The Biography Sweepstakes

Exactly as Uncle described it. Dunston was admiring Number 58, Lincoln Fields Inn, Holborn… and Number 57 since the two residences occupied a single structure with a pair of curved steps leading to adjacent but separate entrances. The entire building with its elegant, multi-windowed, Georgian-style façade became, in Dickens's hands, the chambers of Mr Tulkinghorn, the sinister, calculating lawyer in *Bleak House.* Dunston's interest lay in the current owner of the even-numbered half, Mr John Forster, Dickens's closest friend and literary agent.

Having done due diligence to his assignment for Miss Georgina with his visit to Scotland Yard on Monday, Dunston had stayed in London to attend his uncle's funeral at West Minster Abbey on the following day. He'd been pleased to see that the author had been placed to rest in Poets' Corner in the South Transept amidst the immortals of English literature – Chaucer facing the grave, Shakespeare to the left, Dryden to the right. Wednesday, then, was his first opportunity to begin his investigation in earnest. Even though Forster, neither family nor novelist, was not on Dunston's list of suspects, he'd chosen him as his first interviewee because he'd known Dickens better than any other man.

Dunston was greeted at the front door by Forster himself. 'Dunston Burnett! Well, well, haven't seen you for I don't know how long. How are you?'

'I'm quite—'

'Excellent, excellent.' Forster ushered the new arrival into the drawing room. 'Wilkie Collins just popped in,' he continued. 'Trust you don't mind.'

Wilkie Collins. Now there was a prime suspect. Uncle's disciple and an accomplished novelist in his own right, Collins was high on Dunston's suspect list – the protégé eliminating the mentor to clear the field for himself, a classic motive.

'Far from—'

'Good. Then that's settled. Collins, pour the man a glass of sherry.'

With a nonchalant nod in Dunston's direction, Collins did as he was bid and then returned the decanter to a small table set between two stylish armchairs facing the fireplace. He re-seated himself in the nearer of the pair, and casually gestured Dunston toward the other. Forster remained standing, occupying centre-stage in front of the mantelpiece.

The room was light and airy with a pair of large windows overlooking the forecourt, the soft pastel colours of the walls and curtains adding to its luminosity and serenity, an effect sharply at odds with the formidable figure of the owner. The dark frock coat, aggressive stance, resolute chin, intense eyes, lowering brow and full-head of iron grey hair, mirrored Forster's temperament – always opinionated, usually overbearing and frequently rude. All of this hid other facets of his character – loyalty to Dickens, support for good causes, his business acumen, and his own literary expertise as editor and reviewer. A complex man, then, beneath his austere exterior.

'Now, Dunston, tell us what brings you to Mr Tulkinghorn's lair, ha, ha. Fire away, my boy.'

'Well, you see, I've come to you, sir, because you were Uncle Charles's most trusted confidant. So I—'

'Correct. I commend you. I can say without fear of contradiction,' Forster said in a tone that brooked no disagreement, 'that I was closer to Dickens than any other man, dead or alive.'

Collins peered at Dunston through moon-shaped spectacles. 'Perhaps you should move on,' he said lazily.

'Yes, let's hear what you have to say,' the host added.

'I've been thinking,' Dunston began cautiously, 'about a tribute to Uncle and—'

'A tribute. Splendid,' Forster said approvingly.

Encouraged, Dunston pushed on. 'And what could be more fitting, I thought, than for me, his nephew, to write his biography.'

'POPPYCOCK!' Forster boomed. 'Dickens *must* of course have a biography. But it has to be by someone who knew the man throughout his career, shared his triumphs first hand, participated in his literary creations, was his friend and advisor, someone who can write with the elegance and grace merited by such a grand undertaking. I don't know who that someone might be,' he said disingenuously, 'but it's not YOU!'

'Forster, old chap, if you don't mind,' Collins interjected, clearly not in the least perturbed by his host's outburst. Pasty-faced with a full beard, he was the image of the Bohemian he actually was. 'Mr Burnett,' he said, 'given the excellent observations Forster has made, it seems to me that a fellow author, someone who's worked closely with your uncle would be best placed to paint the most informed portrait of the man. I have in mind the special understanding such a person would have of Dickens's thinking, his creative impulses, his methods of composition and so on. I'm not sure you, Mr Burnett, have any claim to such knowledge.'

Collins smiled as he saw Forster nodding vigorously.

'Of course,' he resumed, 'I'm actually the *only* writer your uncle ever collaborated with, so...' He left his sentence hanging like the empty sherry glass dangling loosely from his hand.

Forster eyed Collins shrewdly. Collins returned his gaze. The message that flashed between them, unspoken but apparently clear to each, said, 'Yes, we may be competitors in the Dickens biography sweepstakes, but the immediate task is to eliminate Dunston Burnett. And in that we are comrades in arms.'

'My boy, I esteem highly your suggestion that a biography of Dickens is a most worthy enterprise,' Forster began, 'but as you must realise such a task requires access to background material. Letters from the author for instance. I still have every letter he ever wrote to me, more I suspect than any other person on the planet. What letters do you have, young man?'

'I—'

'Ha! None!' Forster exclaimed belligerently. 'Just as I expected. Well, that's unfortunate because Dickens didn't keep *any* of the letters written *to* him. Burned all of them. Twenty years' worth. Letters from the likes of Thackeray, Tennyson, George Eliot. Threw the lot on a bonfire ten years ago. Absolutely inexcusable, the man should've been burned along with his papers, as I told him. And d'you know what's worse? Of course you don't. What's worse is that for the rest of his life, as famous as he was, he didn't keep a *single* letter he received. Quite monstrous.'

That's odd, Dunston thought. If Uncle burned all his letters a decade ago and didn't keep any incoming post after that, how can Miss Georgina have thought there were some personal letters among the items stolen from his desk drawer? He must have kept *some*.

'Now,' the schoolyard bully continued, plainly not satisfied that Dunston's biographical ambitions had been fully crushed, 'while you've been off goodness knows where for the last twenty years, I've been at the man's side day and night. John Forster, and *only* John Forster, has read in draft each of Dickens's great works. Even his latest piece about that fellow Drood, not one of his best, I grant you, but I'm the *only* one to have seen the fifth instalment, the last penned by his hand. What do you say to that, young man?'

'Actually I've seen the s—'

'I recall,' Forster carried on as though Dunston hadn't opened his mouth, 'one of our last exchanges most vividly. "Forster, old chap," Dickens said, "need your opinion on the ending for Drood." He wanted the *Forster Blessing*, as he used to call it, on how the villain of the piece, this John Jasper, was to be brought to justice.'

Dunston sat up. Was he about to learn the solution to the Drood mystery? He leaned forward, all ears like the classroom swot hungry for another helping of educational enlightenment.

'It all revolves around the diamond and ruby engagement ring that Edwin is supposed to give to Rosa Bud. That doesn't happen. The young couple separate, and the ring stays in Edwin's breast pocket, but Jasper, unaware of this, remains intent on doing away with his rival. When Edwin goes for a stroll after a Christmas Eve dinner, Jasper follows him in the darkness, wraps his long black scarf around the young man's neck and pulls it tight.

'He hides the body in the Sapsea family sepulchre in the cathedral grounds, and hurries to the nearby stonemason's yard to fetch the quicklime – "quick enough to eat your bones," as Dickens says – that will remove all trace of his crime, except for the engagement ring still in Edwin's breast pocket. And *that* is the key, the ring, of course, being impervious to the corrosive power of the compound. Its distinctive Tudor-rose design allows the identification of Edwin's decomposed body and that in turn leads to Jasper's capture.'

Dunston couldn't believe his good fortune. He'd learned the conclusion to the Drood mystery without any effort on his part. Miss Georgina, though, might not be so pleased when she hears this, he fretted; nothing in what Forster said to even hint at Uncle's murderer.

'Didn't strike me as a very original denouement, rather amateurish as I told him in no uncertain terms,' Forster continued. 'Poor fellow was quite put out. To give him his due, though, he claimed he had, and these are his own words, *a very curious idea* for the final chapter. Apparently, Jasper confesses to the murder in his prison cell as though speaking about the actions, not of himself, but of another person. Rather flimsy, not at all up to his usual standards, I fear.'

Collins, evidently bored with proceedings, languidly signalled his host to get on with his Dunston-squashing campaign.

'Now, it's your turn, Dunston. Let's see how much *you* know about the Drood mystery.' Forster was moving in for the kill. 'As I'm sure you've guessed, Cloisterham, the cathedral town in the story, is based on Rochester.'

Dear Lord, Miss Georgina was right. 'Well, I—'

'And, according to the story, Jasper lives in the Gate House. Now, there are three premises in Rochester that could have served as a model – College Gate abutting the High Street, Deanery Gate adjoining the cathedral, and Priory Gate within the cathedral precincts. A good biographer would know which of these was the inspiration for Jasper's Gate House. So, I ask you, which was it?'

'I don't kn—'

'Then let me tell you,' interrupted London's paramount interrupter. 'NONE OF THEM! And why is that? Because Dickens had IMAGINATION!' Forster bellowed. He was working himself up into a fully-fledged tantrum. 'And you, sir, missed that vital point entirely!' he scolded.

'But I-I—'

'BOSH!' Forster's index finger jabbed the air like a Roman short sword stabbing at Dunston's biographically treacherous heart. 'I'm making a point for your edification, my boy. You should be grateful. I'm doing my best to prevent you ending up a disgrace to England, to Mankind, to the Almighty, AND a disgrace to ME!' Forster thundered. 'Take my advice, young man, drop this nonsensical idea, forget your miserable proposal, and leave my house.'

'Beg your p—'

'LEAVE!'

'I—'

'LEEEAVE!' Forster drained his sherry in one practiced swallow, much as he expected Dunston to be drained from his presence. And that was exactly what happened. Collins took the bewildered man by the arm and shepherded him from the room.

'Burnett, don't take Forster too seriously,' Collins commiserated once they were outside. 'His bluster's just that, rather amusing really.'

'Yes, quite… thank you. But Jasper's lodgings and the three gate houses… quite distressing,' Dunston moaned.

'Don't worry yourself. In fact, that was rather mischievous of Forster,' Collins said. 'Dickens certainly had imagination but he also had an eye for detail and probably took bits and pieces from all three lodgings for Jasper's residence. He was always taking material straight from real life. Take the opening scene in the Drood novel, the one in the old woman's opium den. Dickens captured the atmosphere so realistically because he visited one in Spitalfields – Thrawl Street, I believe – with some inspector or other before he started writing the book. *That's* how anxious he was to make sure his fiction was true to life.'

'Well, thank you for the explanation and for your kindness.' What a considerate fellow, Dunston thought. Couldn't possibly be a murderer. 'I bid you good-day, Mr Collins.'

Dunston slowly made his way down the steps from Number 58. Glancing about for Nick, his manservant, he suddenly found himself flat on his back, arms and legs flailing like a belly-up tortoise.

'Beg pardon,' muttered a well-built man, handsomely dressed in a royal blue, velvet jacket, white cotton shirt, impeccably knotted cravat of steel-grey silk, and flawlessly tailored, tan trousers. He carried himself with confidence and assurance, patrician from head to foot, the head part topped with thick, black wavy hair and side whiskers, the foot part displaying a pair of knee-high, leather boots, emphasising his long legs.

With the merest backward glance at the man he'd just bundled out of his way, he hurried on. He jumped into a waiting hansom, rapped on the roof with his cane, and was on his way without a further thought for the still prostrate Dunston.

'Sir, you alright?' Nick helped his master to his feet.

'What impudence. Hardly an apology,' was the grumbled reply. 'Who was that fellow?'

'Couldn't tell yer, tho' the cabbie called him Lord Lavelle. Only had a quick peek at him as he bowled you over, sir,' Nick continued, 'but could swear I seen him someplace before. Makes no sense. Where'd the likes of me run into a gent like him?'

Chapter Twelve: The Athenaeum Club at its Best

*h, you're back. Excellent timing because I've just turned up a real gem.
Despite my best efforts, it was proving extremely difficult to learn
anything about this Lord Lavelle. Nobody had any inkling of his
background, even though he was a common topic of conversation in view of
his pursuit of Lady Moffet, one of London's wealthiest widows. But then, there's
always the Athenaeum Club. What a glorious institution, a fertile field of intimate
exchanges, off-the-record discussions, and whispered confidences, all conveyed in
a manner that says to the world this is of the utmost secrecy, absolutely hush-hush,
not for your ears... unless, of course, you're a member in good standing of the
Athenaeum Club, in which case, listen and you shall hear.*

*The club, abutting Pall Mall, looks across Waterloo Place. The portico with its
extravagantly expensive frieze copied from the Parthenon (where else?) and statue
of Pallas Athene (who else?) is crushingly ostentatious, but that's what the members
– all known for their scientific, literary or artistic accomplishments – consider
decoration befitting a meeting place for such distinguished persons as themselves.
Alas, my nomination has yet to be accepted, some minor administrative detail I
imagine, so I was pleased to receive a lunch invitation from that extraordinary
port-imbiber and bon-vivant, the rich-as-Midas Earl of Toxington.*

*Lunch over, we repaired to the smoking room and relaxed our over-stuffed bodies
in a pair of over-stuffed, leather armchairs. The earl, suffering from yet another
attack of gout in his big toe, had his right foot resting on a stool, and a decanter of
port, surely the cause of his discomfort, stationed at his elbow. As a young man,*

he'd been a keen hunter, riding to hounds at every opportunity, but as age and drink took their toll, he'd degenerated into a more or less permanent fixture at the club, an inveterate gossip, fascinated by scandals of boardroom, bedroom and courtroom alike, and especially those involving all three in one delicious mess.

The earl was drifting off into a postprandial nap, when one of his semi-somnolent remarks snapped me to full alert like a raw recruit jumping to attention at the command of the drill sergeant. At last, here it was. The nugget of information I'd sought so desperately being delivered, without my even asking, by a half-drunk, half-asleep peer of the realm – the Athenaeum Club at its very best. This is what transpired.

Earl: Can't believe the nerve of that charlatan Lavelle.

Me: Lavelle? Charlatan?

Earl: Why of course. Real name's Nobby Scrivins.

Nobby Scrivins! I had it! I'd struck a truly rich vein.

Me: Nobby Scrivins?

Earl: Yes. Used to be under-groundsman on my estate in Warwickshire. Good-looking fellow in a dark sort of way, with a real gift of the gab, especially with the women. And that was his ticket to the good life. Took advantage of the squire's daughter... and the squire for that matter. Should've given the blighter a good thrashing to my mind, but the squire was a timid sort of fellow. Silly sap paid Scrivins to clear off and keep away from the girl. Anyway, that little episode opened up a new career for the scoundrel. Widows with a little money are his specialty.

Me: But how did you find out he's masquerading as Lord Lavelle?

Earl: Ha! That's the best part. Received a dinner invitation from Lady Moffet. Lord Moffet was a good friend of mine in my horse-riding days, but he's been gone best part of two years, rest his soul. Anyway, first guest I'm introduced to is none other than Nobby Scrivins, although according to Lady Moffet, he's Lord Magnus Lavelle, her new admirer with estates somewhere in Ireland, or so he said. Magnus Lavelle, indeed. Such a phony-sounding name. Teased him mercilessly all evening, but didn't give him away. Then, over port, after the ladies had left, had a quiet word with him. Don't give a damn if he goes around pretending to be a lord, but I wasn't going to allow any harm to come to Lady Moffet. Rascal obviously had designs on her, but by the time I'd finished with him, he knew that particular game was up.

Me: Hmmm... thought he was after that actress, Ellen Ternan.

Earl: Yes, been chasing her ever since I put a damper on his Lady Moffet venture. Can't imagine, though, how he expects to profit from a common stage performer like Miss Ternan.

Well, I could. Thank goodness for blabbermouths like Clatterbuck. He's Dickens's lawyer and one of my most reliable sources. I knew from him a smidgen more about the 'common stage performer' than did his lordship. If what Clatterbuck told me is right, Dickens, what an old fool he is, plans to leave the little gold-digger a tidy sum in his will, ten thousand pounds if you can believe that, making her an excellent prospect for our pretend-lord.

After a few more glasses of port for the earl, the decanter failing to find its way to me, I bade him farewell. After all, I had what I wanted. All I needed now was a little time to decide how best to use it. Perhaps a courtesy call on the delightful actress? Alerting the lady to her new paramour's real background may be a small service she'd find of value.

Chapter Thirteen: A Wife's View

Whatever happened to Aunt Catherine's bosom? So pondered Dunston as he greeted his uncle's former wife for the first time in twenty years in the parlour of her house in Gloucester Crescent, Regent's Park. He didn't pose the question aloud although his eyes betrayed his thought. Her once splendid breasts had glided downwards and sideways to such an extent that only Catherine's corset knew where bosom ended and waist began, the demarcation between the two being much like the equator, invisible to the eye but understood to be there.

He recalled a full-bosomed woman with long black hair usually captured in a knot at the back with a profusion of curls either side of her face. She had a tendency to tilt her head downward and lower her gaze, perhaps unconsciously admiring her own bust, in a pose that veiled the smouldering promise in her brown eyes but added a heavy-lidded sultriness to her allure. She moved with languid grace further accentuating the sensuousness so appealing to his uncle.

His present inspection revealed a round-cheeked face, lustreless eyes, a heavy neck disappearing into a formless expanse of chest, dull hair pulled back in a tight bun mostly hidden under a drab, crocheted cap, and chubby arms ending in plump hands and fingers evidently drawn all too frequently to the box of assorted chocolates resting on the table beside her chaise longue. The resulting excess pounds aged her well beyond the fifty-five years she'd spent on God's earth. Clearly incapable of scrambling in and out of Uncle's study window, Dunston mentally crossed her off his list of suspects despite her powerful motive.

Her parlour was moderately to well furnished, designed, it seemed, to ensure the least effort in transferring chocolates from box to mouth. Her well-cushioned chair and the immediately adjacent side-table were perfectly placed for this purpose, and both in turn positioned at precisely the right distance from the open, marble-mantled fireplace to ensure maximum warmth for Catherine when the coals were lit in winter while exposing the chocolates to minimum risk of melting.

After Wednesday's debacle with the overbearing Forster, Dunston had spent Thursday refining his interviewing technique. He'd equipped himself with a notebook, a nice touch he thought, and much to his surprise and relief, Friday morning's visit got off to a smooth start.

'Well, nephew, a biography. Yes, a wonderful idea, I suppose,' Catherine said with no outward sign of interest. 'I don't know how I can help, I'm sure, but I'll try. Where shall I begin? Let me see.Well, you know, my husband was a difficult man to live with. Always complaining about this and that, and always making it out to be my fault,' she said with neither malice nor much of anything else in her voice. She selected a chocolate, settled it in her cheek and sighed contentedly.

'The man had such an ego,' she resumed. 'Called himself *The Inimitable*, you know. Well, he did have a point. Nobody could write like Charles.'

Pleased that Aunt Catherine was willing to talk about Uncle Charles despite the break-up of their marriage, Dunston held his peace, letting her continue at her own pace. Remaining silent was clearly the key to successful interviewing.

She paused, inserted another chocolate and closed her eyes, delving into its sweet depths with her tongue to determine its filling. Her eyes opened with delight when she discovered one of her favourites.

'Now where was I? Ah yes, Charles. What energy and ambition he had. Worked too hard for his own good if you ask me. Still, he did have to provide for all the children. And he did love them in his own way, I suppose. After every birth, he'd have the initial of the child's first name engraved on the inside of his signet ring. Never saw the inscription myself, but Charles was very proud of it. Having that ring on his finger, he used to say, meant the children were always with him. Called it his Progeny Ring.'

Hmmm, the ring stolen by the tramps, thought Dunston. Miss Georgina must be devastated that Uncle's memento of his children has been lost.

'And we had so many... children that is. Charles was always fond of... how shall I put it? Let me just say he liked his *cooked dinner* every night if you know what I mean, and the babies popped out almost one a year.' She peeped at him from beneath her eyelashes, trying for a coquettish look, but succeeding only in making her bloated face even more like a puffed-up blowfish.

'Of course, all that stopped when he took to sleeping in his dressing room.' She sniffed, put her handkerchief to the corner of her eye with one hand and sent the other in search of chocolate reassurance. 'All because of that *vixen*.' The butter-fat tabby spat the last word out, showing some spirit for the first time.

'Vixen?'

'That little... actress.'

'I'm not sure I follow, Auntie.'

'Ellen Ternan. His... inamorata. His paramour.'

Actress... Ellen Ternan... paramour... Uncle Charles? Dunston had been painfully aware of the rumours that had flared up when the novelist separated from his wife. Poisonous headlines had spread like toxic flames racing through sun-dried bracken, but to him they were just the sort of unsubstantiated nonsense those scurrilous broadsheets thought it their business to print.

Now, without any warning, an important constant in his world for more than twenty years had been shattered in a matter of seconds. His long-admired hero who made married bliss and the joys of home and hearth an article of faith throughout his novels, the man he'd placed on a pedestal, this paragon of Christian virtue, had a... paramour. An actress!

Catherine, apparently oblivious to her nephew's stunned silence, was becoming more agitated – a chocolate disappeared, and another – and more voluble.

'Of course, I knew about his interest in women, especially young ones, and more so the older he got. But that little minx! Put on such a show for

Charles and the fool fell for it hook, line and sinker. Didn't know what hit him. The little money-grubber got everything that should have come to me. He even gave her my emerald brooch. His engagement gift to me. Little slut wore it everywhere to spite me. But that was just the start. The latest is the bequest. It's really too much to bear. *Ten thousand pounds* according to that sieve of a lawyer, Clatterbuck.'

'Ten thousand pounds!' exclaimed Dunston heatedly. How could Uncle behave like that? he asked himself. Especially when in story after story sinners invariably met their downfall – like Nancy, a fallen woman, beaten to death at the hands of Bill Sykes in *Oliver Twist*. 'That's terrible, Auntie. Seems Uncle had one moral code in his novels, and another in real life.'

The chocolates were now disappearing at a startling rate.

'You're right,' Catherine said as distinctly as her truffle-gorged mouth allowed, 'but that didn't bother Charles. All he cared about was his precious reputation and how any kind of scandal would affect his book sales. In the end, he packed the little tramp off to the continent.'

She smirked, evidently savouring this rare triumph over her rival.

'Thought nobody knew, but his frequent cross-channel visits made it all too obvious he had a little nest with that strumpet somewhere in France. And *strumpet* is exactly the right name for her, let me tell you. I hear she's taken up with another old goat. Wasn't satisfied with having only Charles on her string. Oh, no. Not enough for her. And this one's a lord – Lord Magnus Lavelle.'

'Lavelle? How extraordinary.'

'Ah, you know him?'

'Not really, just happened to... bump into him. Rather ill-mannered in my view.'

'All airs and graces, is he? I know the type. Probably doesn't have a penny to his name, one of those impoverished, ne'er do well aristocrats out to make as much easy money as he can off his title. He and that trollop make a fine pair,' she said maliciously. 'I swear they'd have done away with Charles to get their hands on her legacy if he hadn't died and saved them the trouble.'

'You mean... murder?'

The myriad questions about his uncle's liaison that had popped up in his mind like the quills on a beleaguered porcupine's back were suddenly swept aside by a new thought – ten thousand pounds... ten thousand *motives* for murder. His uncle might, much to Dunston's dismay, have been a philanderer, but he was still a literary colossus, and still his uncle, and Dunston's determination to find his killer was unwavering.

He wrote furiously in his notebook, his pace matched only by Catherine's accelerated transfer of confectionary from table to mouth. But then, suddenly, the last chocolate was gone. The box empty. The hand, operating like a well-oiled metronome, continued up and down until understanding sank in, and the robotic motion ground to a halt.

Catherine, her stress-relieving panacea exhausted, began to weep gently but her tears meant nothing to the intrepid investigator so intent was he on what he'd just heard. Lord Lavelle. A suspect of the first order. And Ellen Ternan. A willing accomplice? Dunston was focused on only one objective, learning whatever he could about the pair.

'Um... Auntie, do you happen to know where this Lord Lavelle lives?'

'Somewhere in Ireland...' sob, sob, 'but spends most of his time in some fancy hotel in Mayfair.'

'And Miss Ternan? Where does she live?'

'Still in Pec...' more weeping 'Peckham, I suppose. That's where Charles installed her when he brought her back from France, the perfect little hideaway for his concubine. A quiet backwater in easy reach of his bachelor quarters in Wellington Street. The beast even paid for her house...' sniffle, sniffle 's-signed the lease as Mr T-Turnham, no, Tringham, that's it, typical of him to hint at her real name. Loved his little jokes.'

The spigot was now open to the full, and tears were cascading down her round cheeks like twin waterfalls. Dunston, finally realising all was not well with his aunt, decided he best withdraw.

'Yes, well, Auntie, thank you for your insights. Most—'

'N-nephew,' she spluttered through her tears, 'g-go... please, go.'

'Of course. Glad I found you so—'

'Dunston, leave... please leave,' Catherine moaned.

Chapter Fourteen: Inspector Line Reports

Later that day, Nick turned the rented hansom into Whitehall. The afternoon was pleasantly warm and dry as it had been in London for the last week or two, a happy circumstance it might be thought.And so it was, except for one unfortunate consequence. The thousands of horse-drawn carriages, carts and wagons criss-crossing the great metropolis had, once again, reduced the granite surface of the roads to grit. Clouds of dust rose from the heavily-trafficked streets, clinging to clothing, lodging in hair, wigs, beards, even penetrating nostrils and worst of all congesting lungs.

Arriving at the headquarters of the Metropolitan Police Force, Nick jumped down, opened the carriage's wooden half-door and helped out his begrimed master. The building's public entrance was through Great Scotland Yard, the genesis of the headquarters' name, and it was here that Dunston presented himself for his second meeting with Inspector Line. The desk sergeant escorted him to the inspector's office, knocked on the door, opened it, ushered him in and, saluting smartly, left.

'Ah, Mr Burnett. Please take a seat.' Dunston did so. 'Back to hear what a policeman makes of the evidence Mr Dickens has presented so far, correct?' He raised his eyebrows inquiringly.

'Actually,' Dunston replied, 'that won't be necessary. You see, I came to tell you I already know the ending.'

'What? You already know what happens,' the inspector exclaimed, obviously taken aback and perhaps a trifle put out. 'How, may I ask?'

'From Mr Forster, Uncle's literary advisor. Uncle told him how it ends, and he in turn shared it with me.'

'And what did Mr Forster have to say, if you don't mind my asking?' Eyes glinting, Line looked ready to pounce at the first sign of sloppy thinking.

'Not at all,' Dunston said. 'Apparently, Jasper places Edwin's body in the Sapsea family burial tomb in the cathedral grounds and fetches quicklime to remove all evidence of his crime. But he's unaware that the diamond and ruby engagement ring that Edwin was supposed to give Rosa, is actually in Edwin's pocket. The ring is impervious to the corrosive and when it's discovered, it leads to Jasper's capture.'

'That's it?' the policeman blurted. 'Not very exciting to my mind. Exactly what the author's led the reader to believe. No surprises. Nothing. Very unlike Mr Dickens if I may be so bold.'

'Yes, indeed. Mr Forster had the same reaction and informed Uncle Charles in, I suspect, his usual forthright manner,' Dunston said. 'The interest of the novel, Uncle told him, was to lie in the murderer's confession in his cell. According to Mr Forster, the villain describes what happened as though speaking about the actions of another person.'

'Really? It may surprise you, Mr Burnett, but every murderer I've ever sent to the gallows insisted his crime was committed by someone else. I told you on your last visit, everyone lies to the police but, as you can imagine, murderers are among the biggest liars. What a weak ending. Not likely to generate any interest in the Yard, if you don't mind me saying so.'

The policeman fell silent, his fingers tapping the official Metropolitan Police Force Casebook lying on his desk, evidently mulling whether to share a real detective's observations with his curious guest or simply bring the interview to a close. The former, it emerged.

'Frankly, I'm not at all convinced by Mr Forster's version of the story's conclusion. I'm trained to study facts, and one critical fact casts considerable doubt on Mr Forster's interpretation.'

'Critical fact?'

'Non-fact really. Let me tell you what struck me as odd in this little adventure.' He opened the casebook and glanced at his notes. 'It's the ring. Absolutely *no* evidence it was in Edwin's breast pocket when he was murdered,' he declared with a sharp, downward motion of his open hand as though slicing straight through the flimsy offering. 'Yet this is vital to the solution according to Mr Forster.'

'I'm not sure I—'

'It's like this, sir. The ring's supposed to be in the tomb with Edwin's body. The quicklime causes the corpse to decompose but leaves the ring untouched and this somehow leads to the capture of Jasper. Well, that can't happen if the ring is *not* on Edwin's body.'

'Not on his body? But what makes you think Edwin didn't have the ring?' Dunston was totally at sea.

'Imagine you're Edwin Drood. You've been entrusted with this ring, valuable in both price and sentiment, and instructed to return it to the lawyer, Grewgious, if the marriage to Rosa Bud is not pursued for any reason. You and Rosa decide to be as brother and sister, not man and wife, and the ring remains in your breast pocket as a result. Do you follow me so far?'

'Indeed, I do. Pray continue.' The amateur was hanging on the professional's every word.

'Very good. According to the novel, this parting of the ways occurs two days before Christmas. Rosa, mindful she should inform Grewgious of this development, writes to him suggesting he collect the ring from Edwin on his next visit to Cloisterham, scheduled for the day after Boxing Day, a full *four* days after the young couple decides to separate. I ask you, as Edwin Drood, what would you do with such a precious object if you expected it to be in your care for this length of time?'

The inspector stared intently at his visitor and was clearly gratified by his response.

'Why, I'd place it somewhere safe,' Dunston replied.

'Exactly. Probably somewhere in your room in Jasper's lodgings. You certainly wouldn't leave it in your pocket, but this is precisely what has to happen in Mr Forster's version *if* it is to be on Edwin when Jasper dumps the body in the tomb.' The policeman held both hands out in front of him, much as a conviction-minded prosecutor at the Old Bailey might after he's spellbound the jury with his closing argument.

'Astounding. I congratulate you. A remarkable piece of detective work,' the totally convinced juror gushed.

Line did his best to look modest but succeeded about as well as an armless contestant in a greased pig competition, though to be fair, it was a matter of professional pride for him, not personal vanity.

'Thank you, Mr Burnett, but I'm afraid that is all I have for you. I've knocked a hole in Mr Forster's account of the conclusion, but, sorry to say, I haven't been able to come up with a plausible alternative.' The policeman shrugged his shoulders.

'Inspector, you underestimate your contribution. Wonderfully illuminating, I assure you. Mr Forster's seemingly authoritative description of the mystery's outcome closed my eyes to a major flaw, but your analysis has opened them again, and for that I will forever be in your debt.'

'Then, Mr Burnett, if there is nothing el—'

The inspector's sentence was cut off by a sharp rapping on the door, followed by the appearance of a blue helmet atop the round, be-strapped face of an anxious-looking, young constable.

'Sorry to interrupt, sir, but the lads in Kent reported seeing one of Dinky Dryker's gang,' he said. 'Feller going by the name of Stingo Pete on account of his liking for brandy and porter. Seen hanging 'round a country house in Higham.'

'Gad's Hill Place?' Line cast a sideways glance at his visitor.

'Aye, that's the one, sir.'

'Very good. Make sure the boys keep an eye on him.'

'Yes, sir.' The young policeman saluted and quickly exited, glad no doubt to be out of his superior's office.

Line smiled at Dunston. 'Dryker's mob, the gang I mentioned on your previous visit. Looks like they're going to have another crack at your uncle's house. Must've been interrupted first time round. Explains why nothing valuable was taken.'

Dunston nodded. But doesn't explain why Uncle was murdered, he thought. Nor why the Drood notes were taken.

'Be assured, I haven't forgotten Miss Hogarth's theory about the notes to the Drood story,' Line said as though reading Dunston's mind, 'but given what the constable reported, I'll make sure my men in Kent watch Gad's Hill Place for the next few days.' Line stood to signal the visit was concluded. 'Here, take my casebook, you may find it useful. And this.' He handed Dunston the leather satchel with its precious contents. 'Fascinating reading, sir.'

Dunston took the satchel and turned to go.

'Oh, almost forgot to mention one other thing,' Line said. 'Remember I told you I escorted your uncle through some of the worst areas in London last September? Well, your uncle's description of Jasper in the novel's opening chapter reminded me of the young gent he and I saw in a particularly squalid hell-hole in Spitalfields, in Thrawl Street if memory serves. Fellow was on his feet but doped to the gills. Crossed my mind, your uncle may have used him as his model for the murderous John Jasper. Thought you might be interested.'

'Indeed, inspector, thank you. You've been most helpful. Good day.'

Chapter Fifteen: A Glimmer of Light

Dunston returned to Strood from London late Friday afternoon and went straight to the library in Woods View House, anxious to write up the results of his interviews.An hour later, the task completed, he was disheartened to see an even longer list of his uncle's possible killers than when he'd started. Surely, the process of investigation as practiced by the great Inspector Line eliminated suspects one by one until only the guilty remained. Not so in Dunston's case. For him, it was one out, and *two* in; he'd removed Aunt Catherine, but *added* Lord Magnus Lavelle and Ellen Ternan.

He struggled to make sense of what he'd learned, but twilight had come and gone with no noticeable progress. The hands on the grandfather clock crept forward finally coming together at midnight as though in prayer, seemingly imploring the Almighty to inspire the intrepid investigator to one more glorious effort. But it was not to be. Dunston rested his head on the desk, closed his eyes and slipped into the Land of Nod, and he was still in the depths of that fair country's softest mattress when Nick eventually found him and assisted him to his proper bed.

The next morning, the slumbering man, enmeshed in a tangle of bedsheets and pillows, shifted uneasily. He raised his head and gingerly opened his eyes. What a strange dream, thought the waking Dunston. Whatever did it mean? He rubbed his eyes, trying to recall what had bothered him.

It was the ring! How could it switch from one thing to another? One minute, it was a plain, twelve-carat gold ring with a string of letters – Greek,

Arabic, Roman, impossible to tell which – inscribed on the inside. The next minute, it was transformed into sparkling diamonds and blood-red rubies, set to perfection in an exquisitely crafted Tudor-rose design. When the sun shone on it one way, it was nothing but a commonplace gold band. Turned another way, the sunlight illuminated the most sublime arrangement of diamonds and rubies ever to adorn a ring.

The gold band was surely Uncle's signet ring with the engraving on the inside exactly as Aunt Catherine had described it. And the other was just as surely the diamond and ruby-encrusted engagement ring at the heart of the Drood mystery. But how could an *actual* ring and a *fictional* one interchange like that? A complete muddle of fact and fiction.

Hmmm… fact mixed up with fiction. Could Miss Georgina be right after all? Dunston wondered. Could Uncle's real-world murderer be lurking in the pages of the Drood story as she claimed? When Dunston first read the six instalments, nothing of value to his inquiry into his uncle's murder had jumped out. Nor had Forster's version of the mystery's solution shed any light on it either. But perhaps Line's theory about the ring *not* being on Edwin at the time of his murder might open up more promising avenues. Hmmm… best take another look at Mr Edwin Drood and his little mystery before reporting to Miss Georgina.

Breakfast, usually a leisurely affair, disappeared in no time at all and Dunston hurried to his splendidly spacious but incongruously under-curtained, under-furnished and under-carpeted drawing room. The library had not proved particularly fertile ground yesterday, so today it was the drawing room and his favourite armchair.

Whoever designed the elegantly contoured room had undoubtedly visu-alised rich, velvet draperies, ornately carved tables, sumptuously upholstered chairs and sofas, and plush Kashmiri carpets. The reality was quite different: ill-fitting, drab curtains; a much-used and well indented armchair lost in the centre of the room; a badly stained and slightly uneven side table; and a threadbare rectangle of dingy carpet. And yet like an old man's slippers warming on the hearth, the sparse furnishings conjured up a sense of comfort and cosiness that the room could never have realised in all the imagined magnificence of its creator.

Before entering, he informed Nick he was not to be disturbed, adding to himself, *until I've solved this silly Drood mystery*. After all, how long could it take? Should be through by lunch if he put his mind to it. But once he'd added the views of Mr Forster and Inspector Line to his own summary, it was only too clear that, instead of a neat trail of evidence leading straight to the murderer, Dunston was faced with a confusion of conflicting clues.

The problem was the ring. Line's analysis was convincing. Edwin would surely have placed the damn thing somewhere safe in his room in the Gate House. But if it wasn't on the young man's person when Jasper dumped him in the tomb, how could its gold and precious stones – that weren't there – resist the corrosive power of the quicklime and ultimately cause the murderer's downfall? And yet, it was highly unlikely Uncle Charles would have told Forster, his long-standing associate, that the ring was the vehicle leading to Jasper's exposure had he not meant this to be the means of his capture. How could the inspector's analysis be squared with what the literary agent had been told?

Lunch is history. Dinner fast approaching. Headway zero. Dunston felt as though he was trapped in the convoluted coil of Hampton Court Maze unable to escape its baffling dead-ends and full-circle loops. He was getting nowhere. He needed a fresh approach, a new perspective. Was there something else in his interview notes that could point him in the right direction?

Well, there was Forster's cool reaction to Uncle's outline for the remainder of the story. That would certainly have stung the author... or would it? Hmmm... not if that was *exactly* the reaction Uncle was looking for. Could the novelist have deliberately fed his confidant a *boring* version, while secretly planning a radically different outcome, something much more electrifying as Line suggested?

It would be so in keeping with the delight Uncle took in teasing and hoodwinking his friends with all manner of pranks and jokes, always amusing albeit sometimes bordering on the malicious. And what better way to have some fun at the expense of his puffed-up adviser than to respond to the man's lukewarm assessment with the *real* ending. Nothing would please him more than to watch Forster's face when he presented the new, thrilling version, a version in line with what he'd already shared but with a sly, plot-shifting variation that exploded into a gloriously un-boring denouement. Uncle would dine out on the hoax for weeks, setting the Athenaeum abuzz with hilarious tellings and re-tellings of Forster's come-uppance.

Dunston could picture the novelist craftily dangling the bait in front of the butt of his trickery and then laughing to himself as Forster bit. Given the prominence of the ring in the first half of the novel, simply mentioning that its gold, its rubies and its diamonds could withstand the corrosive effect of quicklime would be more than sufficient to cause his dupe to conclude the ring was on Edwin when Jasper dumped his body in the tomb. Uncle Charles dropped strong hints and let Forster fill in the blanks and draw exactly the *wrong* inference.

Yes, now it was beginning to make sense. Forster was fooled. Uncle had a second outline up his sleeve all the time. And if so, his murderer, if he was hiding anywhere in the Drood story, was to be found in Uncle's *real* vision for the conclusion, not in the intentionally tepid offering fed to Forster. All Dunston had to do now was figure out how his uncle *really* intended the plot to unfold.

He began sorting through what he knew, trying to fashion the pieces into what he hoped would become the crowning glory to his uncle's story, the Forster-bamboozling, surprise ending. In his imagination, he was Sir Christopher Wren visualizing the *pièce de résistance* for St Paul's Cathedral, the magnificent dome that dominated the London skyline. Dunston already had the foundations in place – the six existing instalments. The story would have to follow exactly the path Uncle had laid out so far, from Jasper's unwholesome obsession with Rosa, all the way to his confession to the old woman in the opium den.

And he had the keystone, the centrepiece that locked everything in place – the location of the ring, not in Edwin's pocket as in Forster's account, but in Edwin's room at the Gate House as Line theorised. That was the switch, the redirection that would transform the story from the dullness feared by Forster into the dazzle Uncle's readers expected. Dunston was beginning to see how the ring could play its expected part in Jasper's capture *without* being in Edwin's pocket, but where was the dazzle? What was the denouement that would turn the story on its head and astound the reader just as the dome topped the cathedral and amazed the visitor?

Twenty years ago, Charles, an astute observer of people, had said, 'You know, Dunston, ninety-nine percent of your silly brain cells are nothing but worthless dross,' a cutting remark, but typical of the sharp-tongued way the great author spoke to his nephew, 'but the other one percent – pure gold.' Unexpected praise indeed from the master novelist and very much on the mark. He was referring to Dunston's uncanny ability to leap from A to C and even to D, when everyone else was struggling to make the tiniest connection between A and B. Not all of his 'flashes' hit the bulls-eye, but when they did...

It was late in the evening before a flash from his one per cent of cellular gold finally flared in his brain, not a fully formed construct by any means, nothing as nicely rounded as Wren's masterpiece, no more in fact than a glimmer of light at the end of a long tunnel, but a glimmer all the same. Dunston smiled.

Chapter Sixteen: Plum Pie

Dulcet was coming down the stairs from Miss Georgina's room after delivering her lunch tray just as Isaac was coming in from the stables. What an opportunity. With Cook busy in the scullery in the basement, she had him all to herself.

It was Saturday, a full week after the assault by the two vagabonds, and Dulcet had resumed her customary duties. Her left shoulder and hip were still bruised but the stiffness had gone and the remaining soreness was bearable. Anyway, neither illness nor injury was considered an excuse for neglecting one's duties in any respectable establishment as Cook was quick to point out. In her view, 'the young'un may be black an' blue but ain't no reason she can't pull her weight,' and that was the end of the matter.

'D'you like plum pie?' Dulcet asked.

'Course I do,' Isaac replied. 'Who don't?'

He was right. Plum pie was a universal favourite, and an especially renowned offering at Gad's Hill Place. The master used to say that Cook's rendition was pastry from Heaven's Own Oven sublimely paired with the Garden of Eden's choicest plums, a harmony of flavours not to be missed on any account.

Any uneaten pie was always returned to the kitchen to be dispensed at Cook's pleasure much as Queen Victoria bestowed knighthoods on those who had performed a special service for Her Majesty. Of the pies baked on her return from London after the master's funeral, only three slices remained. She'd taken pains to hide them from covetous eyes until she had time to decide if anyone had pleased her sufficiently to warrant some of this divine dessert. Or perhaps she'd sample them herself, as she frequently felt obliged to do, to ensure they met her exacting standards.

'Well come with me and lets see if I can find you a nice big slice,' Dulcet said, knowing full well the precise location in the pantry of the hidden leftovers.

Two minutes later, Isaac was sitting at the wooden table in the servants' hall, formerly the coach house, abutting the right side of Gad's Hill Place, his mouth stuffed with stewed plums and flaky pastry. Judging the moment right, Dulcet, like a stalking tigress, closed in on her prey.

'How's the pie?' she asked innocently.

'Mmmm,' was all Isaac could manage through a fully occupied mouth.

'Glad you like it. You know what Dad says?'

Having never met 'Dad', all Isaac could do was shake his head.

'Well, he says they have these lovely plums in Australia, biggest and juiciest and sweetest ever, just perfect for making pies. If ever I goes to Australia, I'd make you the very best plum pie you ever tasted.'

She watched Isaac digest this information along with another sizable piece of pie. Still thinks I was asleep when he told me he was going overseas, Dulcet guessed, and, being a man, he's made no preparations whatsoever regarding what to say to me when I'm wide awake. Well, Australia and, more to the point, my presence in Australia, are now on the table. That should get his attention. And indeed it did. With a panicked look spreading across his face, Isaac shrank into his shell like a hermit crab seeking safety.

Undeterred, Dulcet moved in for the kill. 'D'you know what else Dad says? He says Australia needs young people 'cos there's so much land, not like here. And most of all, they need young couples, young *loving* couples to build homes and start... families.' This brought a slight blush to her cheeks while the stable-boy decided to inspect the pie-dish with avid interest. Got him, she thought, very pleased with herself. 'Wouldn't that be a wonderful life?'

DING, DING! DING, DING! Miss Georgina's bell jingled and jangled at exactly the wrong moment for Dulcet. What terrible timing. She had no choice. She must answer the summons at once.

'Have to see what miss wants. Won't be long. Stay here,' and with these words she left the one-sided conversation dangling at this most critical juncture and hurried up the stairs to her lady's room.

The hermit crab released a long sigh… and reached for the last slice of pie. Before he was half way through it, a breathless Dulcet dashed back into the servants' hall.

'Isaac, Miss Georgina wants to see you.'

'Me? What's she want me for?'

'Don't know. She didn't say. You'd best go.'

Isaac swallowed the last piece of crust with some difficulty, straightened his jacket, wiped his sleeve across his mouth to remove any tell-tale crumbs and, in his turn, hurried up the stairs.

Needing a breath of fresh air, Cook climbed the stairs from the stale smelling scullery to the ground floor and made her way to the backyard. And there he was. Lounging against the garden wall in that debonair way he had.

'What a man,' she sighed.

Truth be told, Stingo Pete was a skinny young fellow with long brown hair flowing from beneath a wool cap, a loose fitting jacket covering a grimy, open-necked shirt, and heavy hob-nailed boots. His brown eyes, sparkling with charm, and his mischievous smile nevertheless managed to produce an overall rakish effect that might appeal to a certain type of woman, and Cook, forty, fat and fading, was definitely that type.

He waved casually and sauntered over to the noticeably excited woman. She fluttered her eyelashes, producing an effect similar to a rabid bat flapping its wings. Stingo Pete smiled. This was not his first visit to Gad's Hill Place. As scout in Dinky Dryker's gang, his job was to find out all he could about each house's valuables, a task made easy in this case by virtue of a little flirting with Cook. She imagined Pete had come back to resume his amorous overtures, not suspecting for even a second that his interest actually lay in the size of any bequest she might have received from her master.

'Afternoon to you, my lamb. This beautiful day's all the more beautiful for the sight of you, my dear,' he began. He gave her his most seductive and, judging by past experience, most appealing grin. 'Like an angel sent from heaven, you are, if you don't mind me saying so.'

'I don't mind,' she said coyly. In fact, Cook, all of a dither, seemed to be on the point of collapse in anticipation of what Pete might say next... or do. She gestured him into the now-empty servants' hall.

'Well, my flower, great pleasure for these eyes of mine to see such rare loveliness, an English rose if ever I saw one.'

The bat wings flapped at a rate rarely achieved by any living creature, rabid or otherwise. He stepped a little closer, reached out to caress her well rounded shoulder and whispered in her ear, 'Word has it you was up in London, my petal.'

This was greeted with a little whimper, totally at odds with Cook's usual town-crier bellow. 'I was. Poor master. We all had to go up for the funeral. In West Minister Abbey,' she boasted.

'Blooming shame his passing like that. Still, I'll wager he left a little something for such a treasure as the fair cook of Gad's Hill Place, eh?'

'Can't say. Will ain't been read yet, but master was always generous,' she simpered, her apron almost bursting as her chest swelled with pride.

He leaned in to plant an exploratory peck on her cheek only to encounter the considerable obstacle of Cook's vast bosom. He stood on tip toe, bent his upper torso over her mammary ramparts and strained to deliver the kiss. In this delicately poised position, Cook suddenly pulled him on to her, and landed a loud, wet kiss on his surprised lips. A helpless Pete was stranded on her ample bust, beached like a whale on a sand bar.

At length, with the thrill of the kiss dissipating, Cook returned Pete's feet to the firmness of the hall's paving stones, and said primly, 'Oh, you Devil! What a nerve taking advantage of me so.'

The Devil, still gasping for breath, could only stare in astonishment at Cook's inverted summary of events.

'You young fellers are all the same. After only one thing. Don't think I don't know. But I knows something else what you men like... *pie*, and I've got three slices of the best plum pie ever in the pantry. Come.'

Plum pie. What a remarkable dish it must be. Vital to both Dulcet's and Cook's romantic ventures, but, sadly, in extremely limited supply.

With Pete in close attendance, Cook went back down the stairs and swept into the kitchen intent on procuring the last pieces of pie for her paramour, only to be brought to a halt by the sight of Dulcet sitting at the table, crying her heart out.

'Lawks! Whatever's the matter, Dulcie? Why're you taking on so?'

She put her heavy arm around the girl's shoulders and gave her a motherly squeeze. Dulcet didn't move, didn't speak, didn't even register Cook's presence. She just sat there, staring blankly through her tears at a letter resting on the table, left there by Isaac after seeing Miss Georgina. Cook, bursting with curiosity, abandoned the girl to her weeping, and picked it up.

'Dear Miss Hogarth,' she read aloud. 'Ain't had much practice at letter writing, but Mam's fading fast and wants to see Isaac afore she passes. He's her only son and her favourite of us children. If you can spare him, would it be alright for him to come home and say his farewells to Mam? Respectfully, Isaac's sister, Ruthie.'

Cook put the letter down and turned to the sobbing girl.

'Don't cry so, lovey. Real sad about Isaac's mother, but death comes to us all, and for her it may be a happy release,' Cook said, only for more tears to stream down Dulcet's cheeks. 'Come on, girl, not the end of the world, now is it.'

'You don't understand,' the maid mumbled between sniffles and gulps. 'Course I'm sad 'bout his mam, and he's right to go to her, but I'm afeared he'll decide to go off to them colonies and never come back.' Eyes and nose were wiped with apron, sleeve, hanky and whatever else was at hand. 'It's his mam what've kept him here. Once she's gone, he'll be gone as well.'

'Ah, sweet on him, are you? Well, if he loves you, he'll come back for you. And if he don't, he won't, and good riddance to him, I say.'

This piece of wisdom cake, as Cook called it, activated a fresh flood of tears that flowed freely down the wretched child's face.

'There, there. You stay here and collect yourself,' she told Dulcet, eager now to resume her own romantic interest. She turned to the waiting Pete. 'I'll just pop in the pantry and fetch the leftover pie for you.'

Under normal circumstances, mention of the pie, now resting comfortably in Isaac's belly, would have left Dulcet quaking at the prospect of Cook's wrath. Not so today. Today, she was oblivious to everything around her, until an explosion of rage and fury penetrated even her cocoon of distress. Cook had discovered the empty pie-dish.

Dulcet, still weeping, edged out of the kitchen.

Chapter Seventeen: A Visitor

Typical English weather – cloudy, dull and wet. The fine drizzle was enough to keep casual strollers off the street but evidently not enough to deter the figure walking purposefully along Linden Grove. The brim of his hat was pulled well down, reasonable enough given the weather, but the way he held the collar of his cloak over his face, only his eyes visible, seemed an excessive response to the light misting.

His gait and posture suggested a young man but judging by his attire not a wealthy one, his cloak too shabby for a gentleman, and his hat, a hand-me-down by the look of it, too large for his small head. So what was a commoner doing in Peckham's most select residential area on a Sunday morning?

Rat-a-tat-tat. Rat-a-tat-tat.

'Oh, dear,' Molly muttered. 'Why do callers have to come on Midge's day off?'

Sundays were one of the few chances Midge, the parlour maid, had to get away from Windsor Lodge and her mistress's sharp tongue. As scullery maid, Molly was at the bottom of the pecking order in the household, a blessing that kept her well clear of miss... except on Sundays. Then she was on the front line. And here it was, not even nine o'clock, and already someone was at the door and she'd have to find out who and then tell miss and probably get it all wrong and miss would scold her like only miss could.

Molly had to struggle to gain a foothold on the lowest rung of the intellectual ladder, but, unlike Midge, her looks in no way compensated for her mental shortcomings, and spinster and scullery maid she'd remain for the rest of her days. She dried her hands, set her cap, and exited the kitchen.

She scurried to the front door, opened it and peeped out.

'Letter for the lady of the house,' the bundled-up visitor said. 'Have to deliver it straight to her hand.'

Molly had never encountered this particular situation before in her relatively short experience of filling in for Midge. She gaped blankly at the young man, her mind apparently just as blank.

'Go tell her, you silly cow,' the muffled voice growled.

Silly cow? Whenever her father called her that, a fist or boot followed in short order and Molly clearly had no wish to be treated to either by this fellow. She shut the door and rushed off to find miss.

'Miss, visitor!' she screeched at her mistress who until this moment had been enjoying her morning tea in the parlour.

'Yes, well I rather gathered that. Who is it, you silly cow?'

Silly cow! If she was alarmed before, Molly was now visibly petrified, her foot shooting off the ladder's bottom rung, all pretence at coherent thought vanishing. 'Letter... with a man, Miss.'

'Man with a letter, is that it? Then you'd better show him in.'

The hapless visitor was about to knock again when the door opened and Molly, speech escaping her, silently beckoned him in and scampered off towards the parlour, leaving him to follow. He strode after her and though slight of build, pushed her aside with ease and barged into the parlour slamming the door behind him. Miss Ellen Ternan, Dickens's kept woman, started at this violent entrance but before she could say a word the intruder raised his hand for silence, discarded his hat and cloak, turned and stared boldly at her.

She'd dealt with all manner of men during her days on the stage and in most cases her charms had stood her in good stead. She smiled a practiced smile, exactly the right blend of female trepidation and womanly allure, a combination that had disarmed many a man and it seemed to work as well as ever in this instance.

'That's right, miss. No need for alarm,' he said quietly. He continued to stare at her with an intensity bordering on rudeness. 'Just needs to talk to you.'

'I see.' She already felt in control. 'And what brings you to Windsor Lodge, young man?'

'Come to you 'cos chance have placed a certain piece of information my way and I'm here to explore the lie of the land.' He thrust his right hand into his jacket pocket as though to reassure himself its contents were safe.

Ah… opening gambit for a little blackmail? Well, whoever you are, you'll have the devil of a job with me. Such were her thoughts but her words conveyed no trace of her thinking. Sweet and charming as only an actress could be, she said, 'And what, may I ask, is this information that's so important?'

'All in good time.' He continued to appraise her, his eyes closed to the heavy-handed opulence of the parlour's furnishings, sparing nary a glance for the exquisite Chinese silk of the sea-green curtains, the ornate sideboard overloaded with a hodgepodge of expensive Staffordshire figurines and Wedgwood bronzes, or the magnificent, upright piano adorned by a solid gold candlestick. His gaze remained fixed on the demurely clad woman.

In a tailored, grey cotton morning dress, her only adornment an emerald brooch resting on the swell of her right breast, the lady of the house probably considered her attire quite drab, but drab could not hide the curves of the well-fleshed figure. Was lust what concentrated the visitor's attention? Or extortion as she suspected? Whatever lay behind the unrevealing eyes, he continued his inspection in silence.

She too could play the waiting game, but today the staring contest was so oddly disturbing she was first to break off.

'Well… perhaps you'd like to tell me your name.'

'My name? Ha! That's a good 'un.'

More silence. She watched him as he seemed to debate how best to proceed. Then, he straightened his spine, lifted his head and fixed his expression. He's ready, she thought, steeling herself for battle.

'Like I said, come to you today 'cos of what I found. It's… well, it's something been kep' hidden too long,' he began in a husky voice. He watched her, obviously trying to gauge her reaction.

She was much too savvy to reveal any emotion. Denial was her best course of action.

'Really? The best newshounds in London have searched high and low for gossip about me and found nothing. And do you know why? Because there's nothing to find. There, young man, what do you say to *that*?' she said defiantly.

He viewed her through narrowed eyes, listening to her denial, a look of exasperation or perhaps disappointment creeping across his face. Then, his expression hardening, he drew an envelope from his jacket pocket. He opened it, extracted a single sheet of notepaper and thrust it at her.

Cat-eyes, green as the emeralds in her brooch, marked how the letter in his outstretched hand shook, and how the envelope slipped unnoticed from the trembling fingers of his other hand. Ha, nervous as a spooked filly, she thought as she took the letter. Unfolding it, she began to read. Not a muscle moved as she quickly scanned the copperplate writing. Not a tremor of lip or flutter of eyelid as she came to the end. Nothing, even though she was staggered.

How did this scum find out? No use worrying about that now. She must think. She was not going to allow this piece of slime to disrupt her plans. As soon as she had the ten thousand pounds in her hand, she'd be off to Italy or Switzerland and this little guttersnipe was not going to get in her way. Only one sure way to put this extortion-minded genie back in its bottle.

The young villain pointed to the letter. 'What do *you* say to *that*?'

She laughed a full-throated laugh designed to convey her utter disdain for his pathetic attempt to extract money from her. Delivered perfectly, it had the intended effect, her would-be blackmailer looking increasingly unsure of himself, a lost little boy.

'This,' she thrust the letter back at him, 'is worth less than a dog's turd. Let me tell you why. I–DON'T–HAVE–A–SINGLE–PENNY–TO–MY–NAME!' she spat at him, the words stinging like slaps to the cheek.

'Ha! Surprised you, you lump of shit. Thought I was sitting on a nice nest egg, didn't you? Yes, Dickens provided for me, but it's all gone. Every single penny. So even if that silly story in your precious letter were true, it would still be worthless, Mr Flimflammer, because *you can't suck blood from a stone.*'

The ruffian, thrown by her barrage, stuffed the letter in his pocket and took a step back, a confused look on his face. Confusion, though, swiftly gave way to a sullen coldness. Damn! The greedy maggot's not going to give up. Better cork this blackmailing genie's bottle so tight he'll *never* be able to crawl out.

'Creditors and debt collectors are after me like dogs after raw meat, already carving up the pittance he left me in his will.' A performer born and bred, she was now fully into her role of penniless cast-off. 'My jewellery, my clothes, this brooch, they'll sell off the lot, and I'll still owe money all over the place. The house, that's on the block too.' There, she thought, that should put paid to his scheme to bleed me dry. She laughed at him again. But that was the last time she'd laugh at him.

The candlestick gracing the upright piano was there solely for decoration. Made of pure gold, it had a tiered pedestal for stability, with a long shaft designed to hold a single candle. The only time the lady of the house had looked at it was when she bought it, a purchase based entirely on its exorbitant price. Today, it drew her eyes. Or perhaps she sensed her unwelcome guest glancing in that direction and simply followed suit. Whatever the sequence, the candlestick suddenly found itself the centre of attention.

Swiftly removed from its customary position, it experienced that unpleasant, stomach-lurching sensation as it was swung backward and upward seemingly propelled by its heavy base. Reaching its apex, it abruptly reversed direction, rushing downward, accelerating as the weight of the stand pulled it on, faster and faster, until it shattered Miss Ellen Ternan's skull.

Chapter Eighteen: The Envelope

The Lord giveth and the Lord taketh away... and sometimes, the Lord giveth again. Ha! Ha! Sums up yesterday afternoon perfectly. I'd travelled down to Peckham to share with Miss Ellen Ternan the disquieting news about Lord Lavelle and his designs on her. I was pretty sure the imposter knew about her expectations. After all, I'd found out about the ten thousand pounds easily enough from Dickens's blabbermouth lawyer, Clatterbuck. Fellow leaks information by the bucketful. What a gift to mankind.

The Lord, as in God, not Toxington, although they're the same in this instance, had seen fit to bless me with the truth about Lavelle – or should I say Nobby Scrivins? – but what the Lord giveth, the Lord can taketh away and, sad to say, He tooketh away the little actress.

Yes, when I got to Windsor Lodge, the poor woman's carcass was being carted away on an open wagon like a side of mutton, her head covered with a bloodied cloth, but the emerald brooch she always wore, was clearly visible. The Lord had taken the one person who would most value the information I'd so assiduously gathered. But then the Lord giveth again. And my goodness, did He giveth. Here's what happened.

Since I'd come all that way, I thought I should at least find out how the lady died. My knock was answered by a nicely rounded little charmer called Midge. She was quite willing to tell me what she knew which unfortunately wasn't much, at least to begin with.

'No, sir. Didn't see nothing,' she informed me. 'Wasn't even here. When I got home, found Molly hiding under her pinny, and miss dead in the parlour so I fetched the police. That's all I knows.'

I was about to take my leave when a new thought came to mind. 'My dear, one last question, and I'll be on my way. Did the intruder leave anything that might point to his identity?' A simple question, but for the first time she shut up like a clam and looked everywhere except at me. Ha! The little minx did find something. I wonder what? Something valuable, no doubt. A cigarette case? A watch? Something she could pawn. I was sure of it.

'Let me explain who I am,' I continued as though nothing had happened. 'I'm a special investigator sent by Scotland Yard to look into your mistress's murder. If I report that someone withheld evidence from the police, that someone will be in very serious trouble. Do I make myself clear?' The silly girl was obviously scared but not yet ready to open up. 'Very well,' I said. I took out the little black book I always carry with me in case I need to record some interesting snippet of news. 'Now, young lady, what's your full name?' Well, that did the trick.

'Very sorry, sir. It's Midge Elvey, and I did find something right next to miss's head,' she replied.

I was dying to know what she'd found but thought it wise to play my part to the full. 'And why didn't you give this something to the police?'

'Never asked me.'

'Very well.' I put away my notebook. 'I think you've acted in good faith so I won't have to arrest you, provided...'

'Provided what?'

'Provided you immediately hand over what you found,' I responded with all the threat of officialdom I could muster in my voice.

She turned on her heel and darted off along the passageway faster than a ferret chasing a rabbit down a burrow. She was back in a flash and before she could change her mind I grabbed what she held in her hand. An envelope. A crumpled, blood-spattered envelope. How disappointing.

'Is this all?' I demanded.

'Yes,' she replied but I sensed she was lying.

I inspected the envelope. Oh my goodness! Could this be? I looked at it again, my mind whirling with possibilities. How odd. And how interesting. This could prove more valuable than any trinket the intruder might have dropped. I had to get hold of the letter it once enclosed.

I shoved the envelope in her face. 'This is a vital piece of evidence. I'll deliver it to the police as soon as I leave here but, make no mistake, they will be very upset when they see that the letter is missing. Where is it? I must have it. It's the only thing that can save you.'

She was as frightened as a cat-cornered mouse by this time and I felt sure the letter would soon be handed over, but to my surprise she continued to insist she hadn't found one. She thought the envelope must have fallen to the floor when the murderer took the letter out to show her mistress. Then, once she'd read it, he'd returned the letter to the safety of his pocket, overlooking the envelope. He'd be much more careful with the letter than the envelope, she reasoned, and I had to concede she had a point.

'Very well. Now listen carefully. I'll make sure this envelope reaches the police without mentioning your name. That way you will be safe as long as you keep your mouth shut. Do you understand?'

'Oh, yes, sir. Won't breathe a word. Cross me heart and hope to die. Thank ye kindly, sir.' The stupid wench was genuinely grateful to me.

With that I took my leave, but as soon as I was at a safe distance, I examined the envelope more closely. It was a business envelope, addressed in a man's hand to Charles Dickens. The sender's address was faded but I could still make out it was from his solicitors, Clatterbuck and Jorrin.

All of this I'd seen immediately. But what had really intrigued me was the postmark – the envelope was dated May 3, 1850. That's impossible! The story of Dickens burning all his correspondence ten years AFTER the date on this envelope, was known throughout the literary world. Only something of unusual importance could have escaped that irreverent bonfire. What could matter so much to Dickens that he'd saved this particular envelope – and presumably whatever communication it once contained – from the flames?

Chapter Nineteen: Opus Interruptus

Dunston spent most of Sunday at Woods View House inching his way ever closer towards yesterday's glimmer of light and the solution to the Drood mystery. By late evening, he finally understood how his uncle planned to expose Jasper by means of the engagement ring and astonish poor old Forster with the real surprise ending.

His task now was to set everything down on paper and see whether his vision of Uncle's conclusion yielded a clue to the novelist's murderer. But first he wanted to play the scenes through his mind one more time to make sure he'd stayed true to the story as recounted in the first six instalments. He sat in his favourite chair in the drawing room, closed his eyes and envisioned the opening scene in his continuation of *The Mystery of Edwin Drood*.

Eleven months after Edwin Drood's Christmas Eve disappearance, news of a reward offered by that fuddy-duddy lawyer, Grewgious, for any information regarding the priceless ruby and diamond ring entrusted to Edwin Drood, was spreading through Cloisterham like dandelion seeds carried on a stiff breeze. It mushroomed through an ever-expanding network of relatives, friends and tradesmen, and in no time at all reached the ears of John Jasper.

The engagement ring! He'd forgotten about it, but once reminded, he could think of nothing else. He searched Edwin's bedroom but didn't find it. What if, Jasper fretted, Edwin had the damn thing in his pocket when I laid him in the tomb? Did I search the body? Damnation! I can't remember. Everything about that night is so hazy. And even if I did search him, would my fingers, trembling with fear and opium aftereffects, have found it? Probably not. This could be disastrous. The ring would survive the corroding effect of the quicklime and if it was discovered...

Jasper traced through the possible consequences. The presence of the ring with it's distinctive Tudor-rose arrangement of precious stones would convince everyone that the corpse was Edwin's even if the body itself was too decomposed for identification. And since he, the cathedral's choirmaster, was one of the few who had access to all the precinct keys including that to the Sapsea sepulchre, suspicion might fall on him!

Still, all this presupposed someone opened the tomb in the first place, and why should anyone do that? Nobody knew the ring was there. Or Edwin's remains. So why would anyone open it? Nobody had any earthly reason to do so. I'm safe, concluded a much relieved Jasper. Days passed, and with them all his remaining fears.

Eyes still closed, Dunston smiled, pleased with the imagery so far, and excited about what was to come. The groundwork laid, time to see the unexpected denouement that Uncle had in store for Forster.

Three days before Christmas, Thomas Sapsea, mayor of Cloisterham passed away in his sleep, his heart, severely damaged at birth, finally ceased beating. His death was of no interest to Jasper, he never liked the man, but then his own heart suddenly stopped in mid-beat when he remembered the jackass's wish to be interned beside his deceased wife in... the Sapsea family sepulchre. The tomb would be opened! And if the ring was found there...

Jasper, frantic with worry, his nerves at breaking point, steeled himself. He knew he had to go back into the tomb and find the ring... and soon. The funeral was set for Christmas Day.

Midnight on Christmas Eve, one year after Edwin Drood's disappearance, John Jasper, dressed in black from head to foot, stood once more in front of the tomb, the final resting place of his rival for Rosa's hand. The lock turned easily, just as it did last time. The heavy door slowly swung open, creaking eerily. He shone his lantern into the gloom, searching for the glint of diamonds or the burn of rubies.

'NO, NO!' Jasper staggered back as though struck. 'It cannot be!' What had he seen? What had caused this violent reaction? 'NO, NO, stay away from me, Devil

that you are!' he shrieked at the figure slowly but steadily gliding towards him. The apparition stared at him, an odd mixture of hate and pity burning bright in its demon eyes.

'Yes, John Jasper, it is I,' said a much alive Edwin Drood.

Dunston opened his eyes, very pleased with himself. Yes, that should shake up old Forster, he thought. And, what's more, it doesn't deviate in any way from what Uncle had told the reader in the completed half of the novel. With the creative juices still flowing through his veins, he grabbed his quill keen to set down on paper what he'd just pictured in his mind.

After ten minutes of busy jotting, he was finished. But then, much to his consternation, he saw that when pen met paper, the swiftly flowing narrative of his imagination had turned into a boring, epigrammatic, facts-only account of events. The word-stingy title of each scene – *Gossip about Grewgious's Reward*; *Jasper Haunted by Ring*; and so on – was followed by two or three short sentences as dry as the dullest in his well-thumbed copy of *The Fundamentals of Bookkeeping*.

Ink was evidently the scarcest of commodities in the nephew's world. Not so in the uncle's. The master would have milked the story for all its worth, making the reader's eyes dance across the words just like the tittle-tattle about the reward waltzed from one neighbour to the next, building the tension, step by nerve-wracking step, until finally stunning the heart-in-mouth reader with the spine-tingling vision of entombed Edwin Drood returning from the dead.

Uncle was right, Dunston had to admit. He'd never make a successful, or even a passable, novelist. But exquisite prose was not the point of the present exercise; its purpose was to unearth Uncle's killer. That too, though, went unfulfilled. At least so far. He'd write up the rest of his version of the story's ending tomorrow and, with luck, that would yield some sort of clue so that he'd have something to report to Miss Georgina.

Late the next morning, Nick, night-eyed and saggy-tailed after a long evening in The Falstaff Inn in Higham, found his master still at the breakfast table.

'You ain't going to believe this, sir,' he said.

'Not now,' his master replied. Still thoroughly disheartened by yesterday evening's pathetic attempt to turn his vision into tolerable prose and his failure to unearth some hint about his uncle's murder, the unhappy-looking man swirled coffee in his cup, not drinking.

His master's grumpy demeanour didn't have the slightest effect on Nick who began reporting his news regardless.

'Seems Lord Lavelle, fellow who bowled you over, was down in our neck of the woods. Thought you might be interested.'

INTERESTED? Nick's seemingly innocuous announcement pierced Dunston's testy crust with the force of a javelin launched by Olympia's most powerful athlete. The ill-mannered peer was near the top of Dunston's list of suspects, and here, for the very first time, he might be privy to some information about him. And, what was more, information that placed him in the vicinity of Gad's Hill Place.

'What?… Lord Lavelle?… Here?'

'Yes, sir. In the pub.'

'Really? How d'you know?'

'This bloke was in the Falstaff last night earwigging with the landlord, and I caught a mention of Lord Lavelle,' Nick explained. 'Can you imagine that, sir? Turned out the prattle-box was the landlord's brother, Joe, down from London for a visit. Anyways, I joined 'em and Joe told me he spotted his lordship last time he was in the pub. Lavelle had a low-brimmed hat pulled down over his face and was sat in a corner, but Joe recognised him right enough 'coz he'd been paying regular visits on Lady Moffet. Joe's her ladyship's handyman, see?'

Dunston impatiently waved his hand, urging his manservant to get on with it.

'Turns out this lord, highfaluting feller Joe said, was after her ladyship's money, but he just disappeared into thin air after one of Lady Moffet's dinner parties. Bunch of big-wigs was there and Joe reckoned one of 'em warned him off.'

Hmmm. Looks like Lavelle switched horses and went after Miss Ternan when his Lady Moffet venture fell apart, thought Dunston. Then, aloud: 'Er, when exactly was Lavelle at the inn?'

'Hard to say,' Nick replied. 'From what I could make out, must've been sometime in early June, around the time of that break-in at Gad's Hill Place', he added, making sure his master saw the connection.

'Indeed. And what did our lordship do?'

'Don't know. Drank his pint, I suppose. Landlord thought he was waiting for someone 'cos he kept looking at his timepiece but no one showed up. Then, 'round eleven o'clock, he checked the time once more, finished his ale, threw a few coins on the table and walked out without a word.'

'Is that all?' Dunston asked, disappointed

'Afraid so, sir. Sorry about that. But,' he continued quickly, 'got something else what might interest yer. Talking with Joe and the landlord 'bout Lavelle helped me remember where I'd seen him before. He was coming out of Ma's early one morning, late September last year, after a few pipes by the looks of him.'

'Coming out of Ma's? Pipes? What sort of enterprise are we talking about?'

'Well, Ma's in the… medicine business.'

'And what medicine, pray, may that be?'

'That would be… um… poppy juice, sir. Very beneficial, so I'm told.'

'Poppy juice? You mean opium?' The master was shocked to imagine his manservant spending his formative years in an opium den, and his mother's to boot.

'Er, yes, sir. Nothing wrong with opium, though. Nothing in the Ten Commandments 'bout opium. Thou shalt not kill. That's in the Bible. Thou shalt not steal. That's in the Bible. But don't say nowhere, Thou shalt not have a pipe or two of opium. So the Lord don't have no quarrel with it, 'sfar as I can see. Nor the law. In fact, Inspector Line was there 'xact same night as Lavelle. With your uncle as it happened. Ma said he was looking for real-life partic'lars for his latest book. So, seems to me—'

'WHAT?' Dunston leaped to his feet, his entire five feet two inches quivering from head to foot like a dog shaking off rainwater. 'This den, is it in Spitalfields?'

'That's the one, sir. Thrawl Street to be 'xact, back of The Saracen's Head. You know it, then?'

'N... not exactly.' Dunston slowly sank back to his chair, as he grappled with Nick's astonishing news. It plopped into a mental whirlpool of disconnected recollections swirling around like driftwood until gradually the vague beginnings of what it meant emerged from the watery turmoil.

Thrawl Street, Spitalfields. The place kept cropping up. It was where Wilkie Collins said Uncle visited a *real* opium den, the original for the opening scene in *Drood*. And it was where Inspector Line mentioned he and Uncle encountered a young gent, doped to the gills, the *mould*, Line speculated, for Jasper, the mystery's fictional addict. Now Nick's report – he saw his *lordship*, much the worse for wear, coming out of his Ma's opium den. All in Thrawl Street. Jasper... Lavelle? Could they be one and the same?

Had Dunston stumbled across the link between the novel and Uncle's murder? If so, it had nothing to do with some clue hidden in his uncle's unwritten denouement as Miss Georgina suspected. The key was actually right there in the *first chapter*.

'Nick, make haste! Prepare the carriage at once. I have to see Miss Georgina.'

Chapter Twenty: Bluebell Hill

'We are the forgotten, we are the dregs,
But we're Kings of the Road an' none of us begs.
Say so, oh my brothers-
We say it is so!
If the Kingdom's not offered-
We'll take it, ho ho!'

The gang gave voice to their anthem with an enthusiasm stoked by liberal quantities of rum and ale. On most summer evenings, Bluebell Hill with its soft turf underfoot, occasional patches of springtime bluebells lingering in the woods and splendid vistas over the River Medway, was the choice site for casual strollers and lovesick sweethearts from Strood and Rochester. Not so this Monday.

Clouds from the English Channel had blotted the dipping sun's light, making dusk unusually dark even at this relatively early hour. That by itself might have kept the locals from venturing up to the brow of the hill. If not, the rowdy singing, more like wild caterwauling, and the foul oaths flooding down the hillside would certainly have done so.

Snatcher rested on his haunches, his mate Nobbler by his side. As newcomers to the gang, nobody knew much about them except that they were a team, with Nobbler, the brawniest brute ever, clearly the follower, and Snatcher, despite his slender build, the one with the brains and the natural leader. They had a simple but effective method of operation – Nobbler frightened the living daylights out of some poor soul while Snatcher relieved the terrified victim of all valuables. Snatcher's task rarely called for force but he wasn't averse to slicing off a finger or two if the rings looked worthwhile.

Snatcher watched as the gang's leader, Dinky Dryker, strutted into the circle of men around the campfire, the twilight accentuating the ghostly pallor of his face, the bleached whiteness of his hair, and the disquieting pink of his eyes.

'Aye, that's some fine singing, lads. Better than any church choir I ever heard. Like bleedin' angels, you are,' he said.

Despite the best part of an hour's drinking and singing, the score or so of ruffians he was addressing, fell silent and eyed their leader. Those familiar with the Albino never used his nickname – Pinky – to his face. Those unfamiliar with him only ever made that mistake once.

'Right, lads. Think you all know we're having this meeting 'cos of what Stingo Pete reported 'bout the peelers. But 'fore I comes to that, jus' remember what this mob was like only a month ago and how far we've come with my hand on the tiller. With our scouts like Pete picking the best targets, our cracksmen, tops in the business, and our fences in London, we're ten times richer than we was.I've divvied up the swag, so you all know how well we've done. And we're in the clear. None of our boys nabbed, and the bluebottles as baffled as the dumbest buffle-heads in England... leastways up to now.'

'Get on with it!' came a yell from the back of the crowd where the speaker was well out of sight. No point getting into Dinky's bad books.

'Aye, cut the flam!' another voice snarled, also from the safety of the rear.

'Alright, alright. Just shut your rattletraps, will you?' He raised his hands for silence before continuing. 'So, lads, a profitable month. But, I been thinking how even tho' we done very nicely here in Kent these last few weeks, maybe time have come to move on to new pastures. Pete thinks the scufters have their eye on him, and I don't see no reason why we should press our luck here when there's plenty of juicy pickings elsewhere.'

The mob fell silent, the news not at all welcome. Kent had been a good hunting ground, so why leave? Dinky was being challenged. Snatcher could see that Dinky knew it, and didn't like it. Some of these rogues would slit his throat just as soon as he'd slit theirs. He waited to see how the master crowd-manager would handle this silent mutiny.

'So, here's what we'll do. We'll move out of Kent tomorrer. Everyone on the road by sunrise. We'll meet up on the weekend outside Gloucester, you all know where I mean. Best you travel separately or in pairs so the crushers can't follow us. Then, lads, we'll take our pick of the best houses in the west country.' This went some way to appeasing the gang. Next, came the clincher.

'And since this is our last gathering here, I got a special surprise for you.' Dinky paused and then shouted: 'REAL TROLLS… FROM LONDON.'

This was greeted with the loudest roar of the evening from the women-hungry mob along with the crudest boasts of what each would do with his doxy.

'That's right, lads. Not any old draggletails but some real class from the big city. Should be here within the hour, so plenty of time for one more chorus. Come on, lads!'

The singing resumed, the men well pleased with the prospect of harlot-flesh straight from London.

As darkness settled on Bluebell Hill, the robbers remained clustered around the campfire waiting for the strumpets, except for Snatcher and Nobbler who had wandered off a ways and were busily trying to attract the attention of Stingo Pete. Eventually, he sauntered over and sat cross-legged beside the similarly seated pair.

'Everythin' alright, mate?' Snatcher inquired. He appraised Pete carefully. He hadn't had much to do with him. Bit of a loner, Pete.

Pete in his turn, eyed Snatcher just as warily.

'Not too bad, thank ye. How's your gristle stick?' he asked, nodding companionably at Nobbler.

'Don't rightly know.' The beefy lump's hand slipped inside his pants.

'For Gawd's sake! Save it for later, will you?' Snatcher yanked Nobbler's hand away from its intended objective and cuffed him roughly across the face. The behemoth didn't even blink. Pete smiled at their antics.

'So what can I do for you fine gents?' he asked in a more business-like tone.

'Well, could use a little help and you may be just the man for us,' Snatcher replied in like manner.

'Oh aye. How's that, then?' Pete asked cautiously.

'Understand you was checking out the lay of the land at that house on Gad's Hill,' Snatcher began.

'So, what of it?'

'We're looking for this young lad we think works there. We got a score to settle with him afore we heads off for Gloucester,' Snatcher explained.

'Going to give him hell of a larruping,' the human gorilla clarified. 'Won't know his head from his arse by time I've finished with him.'

'And what did the young feller do to get you all riled up?' Pete probed.

'We was at the top of the rise, right before you reach Gad's Hill Place, finishing off a piece of business when he butt in,' Snatcher replied.

'I see. Nobbler was walloping some unwary passer-by all to pieces while you was filching whatever you could get, and this lad got in the way,' Pete said with a laugh. 'Is that it?'

'Well, more like we was helping a poor lass carry her purse when this damned Jack-o-dandy drubbed us with his whip. With his whip, mark you. Seems to me he needs a little lesson.'

'Sounds like the stable-boy at Gad's Hill Place, a measly muffin-face, name of Isaac.'

'Isaac, you say.' Snatcher salted the name away in his memory bank.

'Aye. Real dandyprat, he is. Shouldn't be any trouble for you boys, but you've missed your chance. He's gone home, wherever that is, to see his dying ma.'

This unexpected news put an end to the pair's plans for revenge, and the conversation came to a stop.

A few minutes of silence and then, 'Bet that busty cook told you that, right?' Snatcher asked.

'How d'you know 'bout her? If I finds out who's been talking 'bout me, I'll make 'em regret it, sure as my name's Stingo Pete.' He reached for his knife in the time-honoured manner for resolving disputes among the Kings of the Road.

'Whoa! No need to get all twitchety. No harm having a little bit on the side with the wench, tho' from what I hear she's more than a little bit. Ha! Ha! Good for you, if you asks me. But Dinky wouldn't be too happy if he knew how you spend your time when you're supposed to be scouting the house,' Snatcher said slyly.

'True enough, no harm done,' Pete replied quickly, clearly not at all anxious to incur Dinky's bloody brand of wrath.

'Suppose the lad'll be back sometime,' Snatcher mused, beginning to see a new possibility. 'P'r'aps you can help us after all. Maybe you can find out from the lov'ly cook when he's 'spected back then me and Nobbler can have a little welcoming party for him.'

Snatcher watched Pete thinking the matter through, no doubt deciding on his best bargaining strategy.

'If you think I'm going to hang 'round here,' Pete began, 'with the peelers on the lookout for me, you're as crazy as me Aunt Bertha and she thought she was the Virgin Queen. Off with his tadger! she used to yell if a bloke as much as glanced at her. Nah, don't think I can help you. Sorry lads.'

'Aye, bit of a carriwitchet, I grant you. But maybe we can make it worth your while.' Snatcher recognised Pete's opening gambit for what it was. 'We'll set you up with four sovs from our cut of the loot, two now and two after you've sweet-talked that cook of yours into telling you when Isaac's coming back. Soon as you've seen her, you can be on your way and catch up with the other lads. What d'you say?' He studied Pete closely, trying to gauge whether or not he'd have to sweeten the deal.

'Let's see the colour of your blunt, then.'

Got him. Snatcher held out two coins and Pete grabbed them greedily.

'Well, now lads, nice doing business with you. Bad luck that little bugger messed up your dealings with the lass and her purse.'

'Didn't mess up nothing,' Snatcher snapped heatedly. 'Me and Nobbler knows how to handle our rig and don't you forget it.'

'Alright, alright, no need to yell. My mistake. What d'you get then? Cash?'

'Weren't no cash,' Nobbler replied before Snatcher could stop him.

'Ha! Gems was it? Or a nice piece of silver? Or gold?' Pete paused. 'Tell you what, whatever it was, I could fence it for you, if you like. Give you a better deal than old Dinky any day.'

Snatcher eyed him shrewdly. 'That's nice of you but let's sort out Isaac first, then we'll see.'

Chapter Twenty-One: Brown's Hotel

G eorgina studied her... her what?... neighbour?... collaborator?... no, her *companion*, perfect for Dunston. Not much to look at; no gift for small talk whatsoever; and far from a smart dresser, but still...

She noticed that his cravat wasn't sitting properly. It had ridden over the collar and looked decidedly uncomfortable. She leaned across the carriage and fiddled with his necktie, her body swaying with the train's motion. She patted the collar and resumed her seat. No, not quite right. The operation was repeated. Yes, much better. She smiled at him; he smiled at her; and their journey to London continued in contented silence.

The previous day, Georgina had listened carefully to Dunston's explanation of the Lavelle-Jasper connection, and immediately decided they should share his discovery with Inspector Line. Hence today's visit to Scotland Yard. They'd agreed, though, to stay true to their pact with Dr Frank Beard to keep Charles's murder quiet for a full month after his death. Their discussion with the police would therefore be confined to Lavelle's part in the burglary, with no mention of the murder, even though Old Testament retribution – a life for a life – was dear to Georgina's Scottish heart.

On arrival at police headquarters, they were escorted into Inspector Line's office. He welcomed the odd pair warmly, invited them to sit and listened intently as Georgina explained the reason for their visit.

'I take my hat off to you,' he said graciously when she'd finished. 'Never thought your theory about the burglar lurking in the Drood mystery made much sense if you don't mind me saying so, Miss Hogarth. And of course Dinky Dryker and his gang seemed like a more promising line of inquiry, but… I take my hat off to you. What you and Mr Burnett have found out about Lavelle points to both opportunity and motive: he was in the vicinity of Gad's Hill Place on the night of the burglary, and no doubt concerned that Mr Dickens's portrayal of Jasper as an opium addict, already evident in the first chapter, would be damaging to him.'

Georgina acknowledged the inspector's compliment with a smile.

'Yes,' she said. 'I imagine Lavelle waited in the Falstaff until dark, walked up to Gad's Hill Place and broke into the study. Whatever he read in those notes was sufficiently worrying that he stole them.'

'Looks that way,' Inspector Line agreed. 'Now, let me share some news with you. It so happens, we've been keeping a close watch on Lord Magnus Lavelle ever since the Earl of Toxington had a quiet word about him with the Commissioner of Police last Friday. Seems the fellow was bothering Lady Moffet and the Earl was concerned because the blighter's *not* a lord.'

'What? Not a lord?' Georgina and Dunston exclaimed in unison.

'No, complete fraud. Real name's Nobby Scrivins, used to be grounds-man on the Earl's estate.'

'Well, that's another reason why he'd break into Gad's Hill Place,' Georgina pointed out. 'He must've been frantic Mr Dickens would reveal something about Jasper that would expose him as a sham as well as an addict.'

'Indeed, miss,' the inspector agreed. 'What puzzles me though is that the man's a confidence trickster, not a burglar, and most criminals stay with what they know. True, some change their line of business and Lavelle had good cause to change his. Still, it's a big jump…' The inspector let his sentence trail off, evidently considering how best to proceed.

'Well, now,' he said at last, 'we have the beginnings of a case against our fake lord, but nothing I'd call hard evidence. No one saw him at Gad's Hill Place even though he was in the area, and we don't know for sure that Mr Dickens based Jasper on him. We need something more concrete. Let me see what I can do and then tomorrow I'll have a word with him.'

The next day, Line stationed a burly constable – tall pot hat, billy club and handcuffs attesting to his readiness to deal with any eventuality – outside the door to Lavelle's suite in Brown's Hotel, Albemarle Street. He knocked loudly and, when invited, entered with Georgina and Dunston in tow, Georgina having cajoled the inspector into allowing them to accompany him.

Lavelle was attired in a fashionable, full length, floral dressing gown, his unshaven chin and remains of a lavish breakfast on a side table testimony to his leisurely life style. He suavely invited Georgina and Dunston to sit in a pair of comfortable looking armchairs, and settled himself on a well upholstered sofa. His lordship didn't even acknowledge the inspector who, by default, was left to stand.

Line ignored the slight and opened the interview with an abruptness presumably designed to throw the imposter of balance.

'You, sir, are the man I saw.' He pointed an accusing finger at the lounging figure.

'What d'you mean? Where d'you see me?' the man blustered, but it was clear the policeman's unexpected and intimidating assertion had unsettled his quarry, a small crack already appearing in the clay of the charlatan's façade.

'Opium den in Thrawl Street. Last September. Saw you with my own eyes.'

Lavelle relaxed at this clarification, his lordly mien restored in a flash.

'Opium den, was it? Far as I'm aware there's nothing in the laws of God or man,' he said, unwittingly using the same defence as Nick, 'to suggest a gentleman can't indulge in an opium-aided dream once in a while.'

'Right you are, but burglary's another matter. Both the Lord and the police have something to say about that.'

The sudden switch in Line's attack had immediate impact, the phony lord's mask crumbling around the edges like dried-out plaster of Paris. He licked his lips nervously, swallowed and struggled to recapture his blustery tone.

'B-burglary? What have I to do with burglary?' And then, building up steam as his confidence returned, 'I find your questions and your manner totally unacceptable. I'm not accustomed to being treated like this and I fully intend to report you to your superiors.' He jumped up, glaring at Line. 'I bid you good day.'

'Not so fast, Nobby Scrivins,' Line said with another abrupt shift in his offensive, all the while keeping his face as expressionless as sandstone worn smooth by wind and rain.

For a second, Lavelle was too stunned to react. Then he slowly slumped to the sofa, his lordly veneer fracturing more noticeably.

'I'm not… that's not my… I mean, who's this Nobby Scrivins?'

'Used to be grounds-man on the Earl of Toxington's estate but now he's sitting right in front of me.'

The policeman's implacable, rock-like demeanour as much as his words was plainly unnerving the rogue.

'Alright, alright. What if I am Nobby Scrivins? Nothing says a man can't go by another name if he wants.'

'Right again, sir. And to be perfectly honest I don't care what name you use. But I do care if you rob Gad's Hill Place.' For the first time, Line's voice had a menacing edge to it.

'Gad's Hill Place? Never heard of it,' the trapped man managed but not with any conviction.

'Not what Dinky Dryker says.'

'Dryker?' cried Lavelle, signs of panic beginning to show. 'You'll never get hold of him.'

'That's where you're mistaken. He's sitting in one of the Yard's holding cells at this very minute, and he's been more than willing to tell us how one of his gang helped you break into Gad's Hill Place.'

Lavelle paled. The inspector had played his man perfectly.

'I'm arresting you for burglary. Let's see what you took.'

The fraud hesitated for a moment but with Dryker in police hands, the game, as he obviously realised, was up. He stood, wrapped his dressing gown around him and stalked into the suite's bedroom with a scowl darkening his face. When he returned, he thrust a manila envelope at the detective.

'There, the notes to the Drood mystery. Let's see what you make of them,' he said with a sneer as though he'd scored a minor triumph.

Knowing Dunston's interest in the conclusion to the novel, the policeman handed the envelope to him.

Dunston looked at the inscription written in his uncle's hand on the front of the envelope: 'Drood Notes'. Dunston had them. He eagerly pulled out the dozen or so sheets of writing paper, and scanned the top one. Blank. Next. Blank. He flicked through the remainder. Blank. 'They're blank!' he screeched. 'Not a single word.'

'Dickens was past it,' Lavelle snarled. 'And that wad of nothing proves it. He didn't have a clue how to finish his silly story. I didn't need to break in at all,' he whined. 'Should've known the old fool was spent.'

Line had little sympathy with Lavelle's griping. Professional to the core, he set about tying up the loose ends. 'What was the name of the gang member who helped you break in?'

'How should I know? Didn't ask, and he didn't say.'

'What did he look like?'

'Smallish, I suppose, bit on the skinny side but strong – opened the window easily enough and forced the drawer.'

'Did you take anything else?'

'Nothing. I was only interested in the Drood notes. That's all I took.'

The inspector, apparently judging he was speaking the truth or as close to the truth as a life-long liar ever came, ordered him to get dressed. Lavelle headed into the bedroom without a murmur, the haughty man-of-leisure who'd treated the policeman with such contempt at the start of the interview now nothing but a whipped cur anxious to do its master's every bidding.

'Remarkable,' Georgina said, with a quizzical lift of her eyebrows. 'Am I to take it you located, captured and arrested this Dinky Dryker *and* got him to confess about the burglary all in the space of the few hours between the time we left you yesterday and this morning?'

'Ah, Miss Hogarth. I'm glad I was interrogating Lavelle and not you,' he replied with a smile. 'Have to confess I stretched the truth a little. As I told you, our bogus peer had no experience as a burglar and, while it's all very well to talk about breaking into this building or robbing that house, in fact it's not at all easy. So someone helped him.'

97

'I see, an interesting point, but where does it take us?'

'Well,' Line said, clearly enjoying himself. 'Dryker and gang had been robbing houses throughout Kent, so it seemed likely that Lavelle paid him to have one of his gang help with the break-in. Dryker's men had the experience and were right on the spot. So you see, they were involved, just as I suspected,' he pointed out.

Georgina smiled at the inspector's transparent attempt to establish that even if he hadn't hit the nail squarely on the head, at least he'd not flattened his thumb. What she said was, 'Very clever indeed. And, inspector, a feather in your cap to find and arrest this Dryker so speedily.' She arched her eyebrows again.

'Thank you, miss, but that's not exactly what happened. Fact is, I've no idea where Dryker is. My men suspect the robbers have already moved on to their next hunting grounds, so, to be honest, I fear we may never catch Dryker. But our friend Lavelle wasn't to know that, and now that he's kindly handed over the envelope and confessed into the bargain, we have the hard evidence to arrest him for burglary. A touch of misdirection I'm afraid, miss, but when it comes to dealing with scum like this fellow, I'm not averse to a little deception,' the inspector admitted, although it sounded more like a boast than a confession.

'What a neat and effective ploy. You really fooled—' Georgina broke off abruptly as the duped confidence trickster, dressed in his day clothes, reappeared.

'Fooled who?' he asked, sensing he was the butt of some kind of joke.

'We were talking about Lady Moffet and how you tried to fool her,' the detective said quickly. 'Lord Toxington put an end to that little caper, and now that your arrest, your addiction and your masquerading as a lord will all be made public knowledge, you'll have a hard time fooling anyone else.'

'Damn you to Hell!' Lavelle cursed.

'That's enough! You'd best come with me.' And with that, Line escorted him out of the suite and into the waiting arms of the constable.

Chapter Twenty-Two: Surprising News

Dunston entered the drawing room at Gad's Hill Place. He'd been invited by Georgina as they were parting company after returning from London, to call on her today, Thursday, for afternoon tea.

She greeted him with a smile. 'Dunston, I'm so glad you've come.' She was dressed in mourning black again, as she would be for the next two months, but otherwise seemed to be in good spirit.

While the pair settled themselves, she on the green sofa, he on a cane-bottomed easy chair, Dulcet brought in the tea tray. As soon as the tea was properly steeped, Georgina served them both and launched into what she obviously wanted to say.

'I can't thank you enough, Dunston. You have been magnificent. Spotting the connection between Charles's fictional *Jasper* and the real-world *Lavelle* was brilliant.'

Blushing and beaming in equal measure, Dunston was left speechless by such high praise from the much-esteemed Miss Georgina.

'A truly remarkable insight, Dunston,' Georgina continued. 'As I'm sure you noted at the time, Frank was not too sanguine about waiting a whole month after your uncle's death before notifying the authorities that Charles had been poisoned, but now, I can write and reassure him we made the right decision. He'll be very pleased to hear that Lavelle is under arrest for the burglary. And even more pleased to know that when we inform the police of the real cause of Charles death, we can tell them that the prime suspect is already under lock and key. We've done their job for them, Dunston,' she concluded proudly.

Dunston saw an opportunity to enhance his standing even further in Miss Georgina's eyes and finally finding his tongue, said, 'I've unearthed something else which, I believe, greatly strengthens the case against Lavelle. You see, besides his fear of being exposed, Lavelle had another reason for wanting Uncle dead.'

'Another reason? What?'

'The bequest – ten thousand pounds, that's a lot—'

'Bequest? Ten thousand pounds!' Georgina exclaimed.

'Um, yes, so Auntie said. To… um… Miss Ellen Ternan.'

Silence. The loudest silence Dunston had ever heard. He was unsure how much Miss Georgina knew about Uncle's… entanglements, so he'd not mentioned the bequest before. Why ever did he bring it up now? He should have left it to Clatterbuck and the reading of Uncle's will.

'How could Charles do this?' a stunned Georgina railed. 'How could he leave all that money to some… some *harlot* from the stage?'

'I don't know, but Auntie thought the… er… young lady may have ended the… um… liaison with Uncle and taken up with Lavelle.'

'Lavelle?'

As this new wrinkle pierced the anger-chill that had sprung up around her, Dunston, to his relief, detected a shift in Georgina's mood.

'Hmmm, maybe you're right, Dunston. Ten thousand pounds is a powerful motive… so perhaps Lavelle poisoned Charles to hasten the inheritance on its way to the hussy, and then to him when they married. Is that what you are saying?'

'Exactly,' Dunston agreed. 'He'll have a wedding ring on her finger as soon as he—'

A gentle tap-tap on the door stopped Dunston mid-sentence. 'Telegram, miss,' Dulcet announced on entering the drawing room. She handed it to Georgina and with a quick curtsey took her leave.

Georgina opened the envelope and glanced through the short message.

'Oh, my goodness,' she gasped, and thrust the telegram at Dunston.

He scanned the first few lines. Just a routine inquiry from Mr Clatterbuck, as far as he could see. Evidently, the lawyer hadn't received the revised will he'd left for Uncle Charles's signature, and the reading was scheduled for tomorrow afternoon at Gad's Hill Place. Dunston looked at Georgina. Why was she so agitated? He returned to the telegram. *Saddened to report*, he read, *only new beneficiary—*

'WHAT?'

It was the next few words that left him gasping in his turn: *...bludgeoned to death, June 19.*

The *only new beneficiary...* that must be Ellen Ternan. Dead. Not just dead, murdered. The morning's second silence descended on the room, its suffocating stillness stealing speech from hostess and visitor alike.

Dunston watched Georgina, sensing that her Christian remorse over the death of any child of God, a pillar of her faith, was quickly giving way to a feeling of relief, satisfaction almost, that the actress was no more. Charles's reputation was safe from that quarter. If some riffraff from the vixen's theatre days, or a jilted lover, saw fit to do away with her, well, that was plainly of no concern to Georgina.

For him, it was the timing that caught his attention. Uncle was poisoned and then ten days later his kept woman was battered to death – surely the murders of man and mistress must be connected? But Lavelle had no reason to want Ellen Ternan dead, quite the contrary, and anyway, according to Line, he was already under police surveillance when the actress was murdered, so he couldn't be her killer. Did that mean he wasn't Uncle's killer either? Dunston wasn't sure, but he sensed some deeper mystery behind the two deaths.

Dunston had bid Georgina goodbye shortly after the telegram's arrival and returned to Woods View House. Late afternoon found him back in his favourite chair in the drawing room, mulling over how the telegram's surprising news fitted with what else he knew. He accepted that Lavelle burgled Uncle's study, and he accepted that Uncle used Lavelle as his model for Jasper, but did Lavelle murder his uncle? As Inspector Line said, Lavelle, a confidence trickster by trade, didn't have the wherewithal to manage a burglary, so how could he pull off a murder? Perhaps Dunston had been too hasty in pegging him as his uncle's killer.

Maybe the Drood mystery was hiding another clue, he mused, so why not finish his continuation of the novel and see if anything else turned up? Persisting with Sunday's technique – visualise first, draft second – he closed his eyes and pictured the events leading up to Edwin's incarceration in the tomb and his 'return from the dead' exactly one year later.

The hour was approaching midnight on Christmas Eve as Edwin left the Gate House for an after-dinner stroll. He'd just reached the cathedral precincts when something wound around his neck and jerked him backwards. Jasper, dressed head to foot in black, pulled the two ends of his black scarf as tight as he could about his rival's throat. When he felt Edwin go limp, he gave the scarf one final tug, released his grip and let the body slump to the ground.

Breathing hard, he dragged his victim the short distance to the tomb, unlocked the door and manhandled him in. Next, he must fetch the quicklime. Nerves taut as violin strings, hands trembling, he stumbled out of the tomb. The stress of what he'd just done was taking its toll, but it was the aftereffects of his latest opium intake that severed him from reality, the narcotic's toxic darkness engulfing him like a tide of molten lava. Long before he reached the yard where the corrosive was stored, he sank to the ground, his mind slipping away, sliding into the blackness of the night.

Several hours passed before Jasper recovered his senses and found himself back in the Gate House. The absence of Edwin, the black scarf still in his hand, and the repeated dreams of the entire killing exactly as he'd planned it, convinced him he'd actually doused Edwin with quicklime, locked the tomb, and made his way home. He couldn't remember exactly what happened, but until he saw Edwin alive exactly one year later, Jasper believed himself a murderer.

Back in the tomb, Edwin, only half-strangled, was coming to. Panicked and disorientated, he staggered out of the tomb's open door – the key still in the lock – and fled Cloisterham, making his way to the safety of Mr Grewgious's chambers in London.

The next day, Edwin, Grewgious and Detective Datchery, a retired policeman and Grewgious's partner in crime or rather in justice, held a war council in the lawyer's chambers. Edwin hadn't seen who attacked him, but all three suspected Jasper.

Datchery, a sombrely dressed, well-built man in his late forties, his dark hair tinged with flecks of grey, was the natural leader. 'Our job now,' he was saying, 'is to prove that Jasper was indeed Edwin's attacker. I don't know how we'll do that yet, but I want you, Edwin, to stay out of sight while we try. And you, Grewgious, must go to Cloisterham, lock the tomb door and return the key to the vestry, everything must appear normal until we figure out what to do. Since Rosa requested you attend her, you have the perfect excuse to visit. Edwin insists you tell her that he's alive, so I suppose you must, but make sure she understands she has to behave as though she believes him still missing, and fears he's dead. At all costs, we must not alert Jasper that we're after him.'

Detective Datchery spent the next ten months in Cloisterham spying on Jasper to no avail, but then in October, Jasper led him to the opium den in Spitalfields. A few coins and the old woman who prepared the smokers' opium pipes was willing to alter the mix she gave to Jasper so that he'd talk freely while drugged. Grewgious and Datchery were right there and heard the semi-conscious man's damning words – 'Done it hundreds of thousands of time in my dreams but now it's over.' They were certain then that Jasper was Edwin's attacker, but they still didn't have any real proof.Something else had to be done.

Datchery was responsible for the first part of their plan to trap Jasper. He slipped into Edwin's room in the Gate House while the choirmaster was occupied in the cathedral, and stole the engagement ring. He knew from Edwin exactly where the young man had put it for safekeeping after the break-up with Rosa.

Then, it was Grewgious's turn. In November, he publicly offered a reward for information about the ring, an announcement intended to make Jasper start wondering where it was. The choirmaster immediately searched Edwin's room but when he didn't find it, he feared it must've been in Edwin's pocket when he dumped him in the tomb.

The honour of closing the trap around Jasper fell to Mayor Thomas Sapsea. Only Edwin's attacker would fear the ring being found in the Sapsea family sepulchre. The mayor's task was to die, or at least 'die enough' to convince Jasper the tomb would be opened. The mayor's make-believe heart attack forced Jasper's hand.Desperate to find the ring, he walked straight into their trap.

On Boxing Day, two days after Edwin's reappearance, the three conspirators – Datchery, Grewgious and Edwin – were once again in Grewgious's chambers, this time congratulating themselves on Jasper's capture. They'd been joined by Rosa, who was siting on a sofa, holding hands with Edwin. If absence made the heart grow fonder, 'death' had proven ten times more effective, and the young couple were renewing their courtship, brother and sister long forgotten, man and wife on the horizon.

Detective Datchery had just finished explaining to Rosa, who, much to her annoyance, had been kept completely in the dark regarding the plans for Jasper's entrapment, how they tricked him into re-entering the tomb, the proof they needed for his arrest.

'So there you have it, my dear The bait was the missing engagement ring,' he concluded.

'But where is the ring now?' asked the perplexed innocent, the perfect foil for the worldly-wise Datchery.

'Right here.' With a flourish of his hand, Datchery magically produced the ring of diamonds and rubies from his pocket like a conjurer plucking a white rabbit out of a top hat.

Grewgious, a silent bystander thus far, stepped forward, hand out, and said, 'I'll take that, if you please, Detective Datchery.'

The ring was passed to him but all four knew it would not remain long in the lawyer's possession. All four understood it would be passed to Edwin and this time it would end up on Miss Rosa's charming finger, exactly where it belonged.

Dunston skipped dinner, a rarity for him, and spent the next hour in the library, putting down on paper the just-imagined events leading to Jasper's downfall. His write-up completed, Dunston reviewed his efforts. As before, he'd somehow managed to transform the cleverness of the Datchery-Grewgious ploy into a series of pithy, disjointed jottings. Still, he consoled himself, the denouement, if not the writing, was worthy of Charles Dickens.

This is how Uncle Charles would have concluded the novel.

What exquisite fun Uncle would have had hitting Forster over the head with this. All perfectly consistent with what he'd told him about the concealment of the body in the tomb and the discovery of Jasper's crime by means of the ring, but all so different. Same with Edwin's disappearance. Uncle mentioned a long black scarf to Forster, true; he described Jasper dumping the body in the tomb, correct; and he referred to the quicklime, correct again. *But he never said Edwin died.*

He sat back in his chair, well pleased with himself. A job well done. The Drood mystery solved. But then he remembered that the point of all this work was to find a clue to his uncle's killer. On that, there was nothing. He reread his jottings from start to finish. Nothing. Nothing that he could report to Miss Georgina.

Could there be something else in the Drood story? Something he'd missed? What was it Forster said about Uncle's 'very curious idea'? Something about Jasper's prison cell confession. Something about him describing the murder as though observing the actions of another person. But that didn't make any sense. By the time Jasper was jailed, he was well aware Edwin wasn't dead, so how could he recount a murder that he *knew* never happened? Did Uncle have in mind some opium-induced dream of the 'murder'? Or something totally different?

Chapter Twenty-Three: A Tender Moment Of Treachery

P lum pie. The words roll off the tongue so enticingly, the palate tingling in anticipation of the delicate pastry and succulent fruit. What a dish. Food holds premier place in the courting rituals of rural England and of all possible dishes, the delicacy of choice for most romantic overtures is plum pie. But there are plum pies and then there are **PLUM PIES**.

Yesterday, Cook had created an offering that surpassed all previous efforts. In fact, it was the third such creation in the five days since Pete's last visit. Unsure when, or even if, he would come back, she'd been obliged to have a fresh pie permanently on hand in view of the well-known fact that peak plum-pie consumption occurred within two days of baking. The first two pies had already been dumped in the pigsty to the delight of its occupants who now looked down their snouts at anything that didn't rise to the heavenly heights of one of Cook's masterpieces.

Third pie lucky. It was Friday morning when word reached the kitchen in the basement of Gad's Hill Place that a skinny fellow was lounging around the servants' hall. Cook smiled happily, already anticipating Pete's delight with the plum pie – baked exactly one day, seven hours and thirty-six minutes ago, and consequently in prime eating condition – and the manner in which he would express his gratitude. The very thought made her feel 'all overish', quite gave her the 'dithers' in the legs. These physical complications notwithstanding, she grabbed the dish and hurried up the stairs.

'Mind me pie, you silly mot!'

Dulcet, also on her way upstairs, was brushed aside on the narrow staircase, squeezed against the wall by a hustling, bustling Cook.

'Keep out of the way, you little monkey. Pete's waiting for me.'

'Sorry,' the maid said. 'Miss rang for me.'

Cook pushed past her, secretly pleased Dulcet would be occupied elsewhere giving her, and Pete, a free hand. She puffed her way upstairs, scurried down the passage to the right, burst into the servants' hall and there he was, sitting at the table. Pete looked as debonair and dashing as ever to her boggling eyes. What a man. Everything about Pete, his clothes, his limbs, his movements, even his speech, had this disarming looseness that thrilled her to the core.

He doffed his hat and bowed.

'Ah, the beauty of this beautiful morning have been increased a thousand-fold by your presence, my precious. The county of Kent is blessed to have you as its crowning glory.'

'Oh, Pete. You say the nicest things. But come, you don't have to bow to me. Sit here by me and let me show you what I've got for you.'

Cook sat at the table and patted the wooden bench beside her. Pete was evidently uneasy about getting too close given his previous experience, but he'd already spotted the pie dish resting in her lap and dutifully took his place on the patted spot.

He eyed the pie. 'Ah, I sees you knows how to please a man.'

'Indeed, I do,' she replied. She smiled archly, running her hand over the swell of her breast as though brushing off some crumbs, although none were visible. Sufficient attention having been directed to her bosom, her hand continued towards the pie. She placed the bait ceremoniously on the table and cut him a slice.

The piece of pie disappeared down Pete's throat in short order. No looseness about his actions when it came to such serious business. A second followed in rapid succession. Pete let out a long sigh, his eyes closed. When he opened them, he found Cook had closed hers, pursed her lips and opened her arms.

Cook obviously had in mind a little firkytoodle, her name for a bit of a kiss and cuddle. He moved closer to the spinster, slipped his left arm round her hefty shoulder, slid his right hand inside the top of her straining apron, and scrunched his face in preparation for the kiss he was clearly expected to deliver.

Dulcet, having followed Cook up the stairs, turned left into the drawing room where she found her mistress seated on the sofa, the day's post on her writing tray.

'Yes miss?'

'Isaac's sister has written again,' Georgina said.

'Isaac's sister? Oooh! What'd she say? Is he coming back? Oh! Beg pardon, miss. Forgot meself,' the lovelorn girl said.

Georgina had become quite fond of the new maid, such a natural spirit, full of goodness. 'I don't know, Dulcet. I haven't read it. Knowing your... *interest* in the young man, I thought you should read it first. Here.' She handed the unopened envelope to the maid.

Dulcet took it and with trembling hand removed the enclosed letter.

Georgina felt for her. The girl had reached the first crossroads of her young life. If the letter said Isaac was returning, she'd be ecstatic, a new life beckoning. But if it said he'd already left for Australia, she'd be devastated, the future holding nothing but despair and painful memories of what might have been. Dulcet began to read.

Georgina watched her eyes edge left to right across the first line, each word carefully mouthed to make sure she had it right. The eyes moved down a line and the process was repeated. When she reached the fourth line, Georgina saw a tear glisten in the girl's eye. She waited in silence. The maid finished reading and looked to her mistress.

Cook's lips had barely made contact with Pete's when matters were brought to an abrupt halt by Dulcet's sudden entrance.

'Cook, another letter... from Isaac's sister.' Dulcet stood in the doorway, her face as white as the sheet of paper clutched in her hand.

'Dulcet! Be off with you! Can't you see, I'm busy. Pete is… um… well, he's savouring my… my offerings,' Cook said.

'Now, now, my angel,' Pete cooed in Cook's ear, as he extracted his hand from under her apron with obvious relief. 'Let the little girl get whatever it is off her chest,' he whispered. 'Let her read the letter. Then I can savour your *offerings* some more,' he murmured so only she could hear.

'Very well, missy. Read the letter. But be sharp 'bout it. Pete's appetite have been whetted and I don't want him kep' waiting. Get on with it, Dulcie.'

Pete smiled. Dulcet might be about to deliver the two sovereigns' worth of information he was seeking and, if so, he could kiss Cook goodbye and be on his way.

'Oh, thank you,' Dulcet said in a tiny, grateful voice. 'I don't have nobody else I can tell. I'm so—'

'Get on with it, child,' Cook ordered.

'Yes, Cook. This is what it says: "I'm writing to tell you Ma have passed away and our Isaac's… *all set to return.*" See, he's coming back,' she exulted.

'Is that all?' demanded Cook impatiently.

'Bit more,' she said. 'Listen, "He'll be back at Gad's Hill Place next Wednesday, late afternoon or early evening. He asked me special to write that he hopes Miss Dulcet is well and what he've thought a lot about plum pie and Australia. Makes no sense to me but he said I had to write it." That's the end.'

The maid looked up, clutching the treasured letter to her bosom. 'I'm that excited. Isaac asked special for me to be mentioned in the letter. Miss Dulcet, he called me,' she said, twirling and whirling faster than a spinning-jenny's spindle. 'And he'll be back Wednesday.'

She pranced over to Cook and Pete, put her arms around both and planted loud, juicy kisses on their cheeks.

'Alright, alright, Dulcie. That'll do,' Cook complained, more amused than angry, although the mention of plum pie had caught her attention. 'What's that about my plum pie, then, young lady?' she asked in a more challenging voice. She recalled only too well the empty pie-dish on Pete's last visit.

'Not *your* plum pie,' the maid replied hastily, 'I was telling Isaac 'bout the wonderful plums in Australia, that's all.'

'Humph! A likely story. Be off with you, you little hussy,' Cook said sharply but with a small smile to soften her words.

As soon as Dulcet was gone, Cook closed her eyes, opened her arms again and pursed her lips ready for Pete to resume his savouring. He apparently had different ideas. He had exactly the information he needed to claim those two gold coins from Snatcher. He looked at Cook, her eyes shut tight, and shuddered. He looked at the door and without another word silently took his leave of Kent's crowning glory.

Chapter Twenty-Four: A Very Curious Idea

Dunston had gone to bed Thursday night wrestling with how on earth the jailed Jasper was supposed to own to murdering Edwin when the alleged victim, far from being dead, was happily planning a future with his adored Rosa. But when he woke on Friday morning, he recalled the attention his uncle had paid early in the novel to the accident – rather melodramatic in Inspector Line's opinion – that befell Mrs Bud, Rosa's mother.

He reread the passage. Yes, just as he thought, Mrs Bud drowned in a boating mishap. Why did Uncle include this incident? It did allow him to introduce the engagement ring but that could have done in any number of ways. No, Uncle wanted to draw attention to her drowning because, Dunston sensed, the tragedy was to play a major role later in the novel.

This insight prompted another. He was mentally sifting through possible developments of the boating accident when the golden one percent of his brain-cells suddenly leapt unbidden yet spectacularly from A to D. A was the drowning; D was what Jasper saw when he made his confession. At last, Dunston understood his uncle's 'very curious idea'.

Before putting pen to paper for the final chapter, he decided it might be best to reread his account of the preceding scene, the one in Grewgious's chambers. To his horror, he found it worse than he'd remembered – a chronological listing of terse, mind-numbing entries from which slumber was the only escape for the reader. The nephew was definitely not the uncle.

The master would have dredged every ounce of drama from the reunion of Edwin and Rosa, his words leaving the reader limp with delight.

How did Uncle Charles do it? Well, he obviously didn't sit and imagine characters and incidents and then, only when it was all clear in his mind, begin to write because that was exactly what Dunston had done to no effect. No, Uncle was a *natural* writer, his mind and pen working as one, his thoughts flowing seamlessly from brain to paper. Dunston would never match the master in this regard, but he could try.

He set aside his sequential technique, freed his mind, and picked up his quill. And then it happened. Energy suddenly surged from brain to hand and the quill took off as though propelled by some Druid wizardry. Skimming and spinning across the page, it left an ink trail of words that captured to perfection everything he'd imagined. For the first time in Dunston's writing experience, vision and composition were fused.

The Cell

The heavy iron key turned in the lock, the cell door swung open and Datchery entered, followed by Grewgious. The stench of vomit, shit and piss hung in the air like a densely woven shroud. The men gasped, hands flying to cover nostrils. Jasper, dressed in grey shirt and pants, standard garb for a convicted felon, was seated, head bowed, on a sparse mattress covered by a coarse linen sheet, his cot nothing but a few planks on a rough wooden frame.

The cell, narrow, windowless, with a low, vaulted ceiling supported by oak rafters and a single cross-beam, had no amenities other than a crude hole in the ground, undoubtedly the source of the nauseating stink. No evidence of food was visible, only a jug of water on the floor.

Jasper looked up but showed no interest in his visitors or even any awareness of their presence.

'The dream,' he moaned wretchedly, 'the dream is back.'

'What dream?' Datchery asked.

'THE DREAM!' the prisoner screamed. 'The dream that's haunted

me. *From the beginning.'*

'You mean of Edwin?'

'Edwin? No, not that dream. The old dream. It's back. It haunts me, terrifies me, leaves no escape from the horror of that day, the heartbreak of that deed.'

'What dream are you talking about, man?'

'The old dream. How many times must I say it. The old dream is back. It won't let go. AHHHHH!'

Jasper straightened, shaking his head violently from side to side.

'I see it! I see it!' he cried.

He jumped to his feet, staring about wildly, twisting and writhing before collapsing flat on the cot, groaning. His whole body shook and then stiffened until he was ramrod-rigid, more like a corpse in full rigor mortis than a living being... except for the eyes, wide open, rolling crazily in their sockets.

The two men exchanged looks.

'Perhaps we should leave,' Grewgious said.

'Yes, we won't learn anything from him in this state,' Datchery agreed. And then, 'Hold on, though. Look. He might speak yet.'

Jasper's face was still stiff as a clergyman's collar but his eyes had closed, the eyeballs moving rapidly beneath the lids. He was dreaming. In an oddly ethereal, faraway voice, he began to speak as though relaying events seen from a distance.

'What a beautiful day. I see the river. The sun sparkles on the water, reflecting off the ripples from each dip of the oars. I see the grown-ups in the approaching boats. Mr and Mrs Bud, and Mr and Mrs Drood, all laughing, enjoying their day in the sunshine. The children, Rosa Bud and Edwin Drood, playing with a hoop on the bank. A third youngster, several years older, standing a little apart, watching Mrs Bud's every move, his gaze covetous, possessive, unnerving in its intensity.

'The first boat glides to shore and Mr Bud helps his wife to disembark. The Droods are close behind and in no time they too land and leisurely follow the Buds across the meadow towards the shade of a chestnut tree

where a picnic lunch has been laid out. Everyone is very happy. Mr Bud is in especially high spirits. "Drood, old chap," he says, "fancy a rowing contest after lunch? I'll race you to that little island, the one about a mile upstream. What d'you say?" "You're on," Mr Drood replies in good humour.

'There's lobster salad, cucumber sandwiches, a handsome veal and ham pie, mince pies for dessert, champagne for the ladies, cider for the gentlemen and lemonade for the children. Quite a feast and everyone falls to with a hearty appetite. With one exception. The young lad doesn't eat a thing. Instead, he wanders back to the river.

'He gets into Mr Bud's boat and sits on the middle seat, bent over as though searching for something. He stays in this position for a good ten minutes, his hands occupied with some task or other. At length, he sits up, looks all around and satisfied nobody's watching, stands, closes his pocket knife, jumps ashore and returns to the still-lunching party.'

Jasper paused as though admiring the youngster's daring.

'What do you make of that?' Grewgious asked in a whisper.

'Hard to say. But the lad's the young John Jasper,' Datchery replied.

'What?'

'Yes, I'm sure. The Jasper before us is dreaming about himself as a youth. He's related to the Droods, don't forget, so it's not surprising he was at the picnic. Quiet, he's going to speak again.'

Still in the dream-level of sleep, Jasper picked up the narrative where he'd left off, his lips barely moving, his voice, the merest murmur, a gossamer sound-wave reverberating eerily off the cell's stone walls.

'Yes, there they are, still at lunch. Everyone's enjoying themselves, except the youth. The poor lad's too agitated to eat even a morsel. Mrs Drood tries to tempt him with a mince pie. No, he cannot eat. His stomach is churning with the knowledge of what's about to happen. He takes a glass of cider to placate her and drinks as she watches him attentively. At last, she returns to the others and he slinks away to the coppice at the top of the hill. He sits with his back against a yew tree, watching and waiting.

'*The wait is a long one. Why can't they get on with the boat race? A half hour slips by, and the lad begins to feel drowsy. The warm sun and the cider on an empty stomach are having their effect. His eyes close, but he shakes himself awake. He mustn't sleep now. Too late, Morpheus has him in his soporific embrace. His eyes close again and his head droops to his chest.*'

Jasper's head followed suit.

'I suspect we'll have to wait a while if we want to learn what happens next,' Datchery remarked.

'Why d'you say that?' Grewgious asked.

'Because, if I'm right, today's Jasper is reliving the sleep of yesterday's Jasper exactly as it happened on that fateful day. Are you game to wait?'

'You needn't ask. Of course I am.'

It was a full hour before Jasper even rustled. He sighed as though waking from an afternoon nap, still drowsy, still relaxed. But not for long. His eyes started moving rapidly underneath his lids and the far-off, other-worldly voice resumed the story.

'*Distant cries for help from the river pull the youngster from sleep. His plan is working. He hears what sounds like splashing in the water but he's too far away to be sure. Best wait a few moments and then walk casually down to the mooring. But he can't wait. Before he knows it, he's rushing down the hill hurling himself forward, driven by some inexplicable compulsion like a lemming plunging to its death.*

'*As he approaches the water's edge, out of breath, heart beating, he sees Mr Bud's boat, half-submerged, lying in shallow water two or three yards from shore. Good. And there, right on the river bank, he sees the adults, crowded around.... what? A body? Yes! His plan has succeeded beyond his wildest dreams.*

'*He can't make out what's happening in all the confusion. Someone's kneeling over the prostrate form on the grass blocking his view. He edges closer, his eyes burning into the back of the crouching man, willing him to move. Why won't the fool get out of the way? Who is he? It looks like... NO, it can't be!*

'He rushes forward, desperate for a better look. The man half-turns. HIM! Then who... who's laid out on the bank? The lad, frantic, pushes his way through the ring of adults. NO! NOOOO! But there's no mistaking the horror that greets his eyes – Mrs Bud, laid out on the grass, her husband, on his knees beside her, gently removing a diamond-and-ruby ring from her lifeless finger.

'Mrs Bud, the woman he desired with all his heart, dead. He can't believe it. Half crazed, he watches without really seeing until men, called from the village, gently lay her dear body on a blanket, grasp the four corners and with a shout of Heave-ho lift their limp burden. His eyes follow them as they disappear over the brow of the hill with their precious cargo. He can't reach her now but he vows to find her, wherever they take her.'

The dream was over. Jasper, thrashing and twisting during the last part, gradually relaxed, until he was just lying there, asleep.

'Young Jasper killed Mrs Bud,' an ashen-faced Grewgious murmured.

'Yes, he did,' Datchery replied. 'He damaged the bottom of the boat with his knife expecting that the next person to use it would be Mr Bud, the man standing between him and Mrs Bud. But he lingers at the picnic while poor Mrs Bud takes his boat for some reason. Perhaps she and Mrs Drood were going to show their husbands that women could row as well as men. Whatever the explanation, Mr Bud's boat sinks or half-sinks and his wife drowns.'

'We had our suspicions about young Jasper,' Grewgious said, 'but I feared we'd never learn the truth... and certainly not in this manner. The way he recounted it, so callous, so premeditated.'

'Premeditated is the right word,' Datchery agreed. 'Premeditated but to little effect. Just as the adult Jasper botched Edwin's murder, so the young Jasper botched the murder of Mr Bud... and worse still, killed the woman he was obsessed with.'

'You know, I expect this tragedy is what led to Jasper's opium addiction,' Grewgious said. 'He was probably given laudanum to help him sleep. Once the medicine was withdrawn, he turned to other sources of the

116

drug.'

'Most likely,' Datchery replied, 'but that's not all. Mrs Bud's death also led straight to Jasper's fixation with Rosa. Think about that last pledge he made – to find Mrs Bud, wherever they took her. Well, he could never find Mrs Bud again. But he could find the next best thing, Rosa, her daughter.'

'Ah, yes. You're right,' Grewgious said, resignation and sadness in his voice. 'The child grew into her mother's exact image and Jasper transferred his obsession from one to the other. And poor Edwin became the obstacle keeping Jasper from Rosa, just as Mr Bud had been the obstacle keeping the young Jasper from Mrs Bud. Madness repeating itself.'

'Come, this little visit has taken its toll on you,' Datchery said. 'We're done here.'

Chapter Twenty-Five: A Ruse in the Making

I cannot take my eyes off the envelope I'd acquired from Miss Ellen Ternan's maid. What could've mattered so much to Dickens that he saved it, and presumably its contents, from the Gad's Hill Place bonfire of 1860 when he was supposed to have burned all his correspondence? Well, consider what was happening at the time the envelope was posted twenty years ago.

Start with that first meeting of Dickens and the delightful Miss Ternan in August of 1849 which I've already mentioned. Next, recall that the actress was noticeably absent for several months in the first half of the following year, but known by everyone to be in France. And finally, we have this envelope, postmarked May of that year.

Now, I've never sired a child, but even I know this timetable allows nicely for the process of procreation. I'd long suspected that their sordid union produced an illegitimate child, so did Dickens keep this envelope's letter because it contained news of the birth? Or, more likely, since it was from Clatterbuck's office, arrangements for the infant once it entered the world? What a find that would be. Long rumoured, but never proven. Until now. And whom did the good Lord choose to be the bearer of this shattering news? ME. Yes, the Lord has given me a truly wonderful gift.

With great difficulty, I stop myself from getting too carried away. After all, I only have an envelope with a date. Hardly conclusive proof... except for one key fact. Someone thought the envelope's letter of such consequence they confronted Miss Ternan with it and in the ensuing argument or struggle struck her dead. A routine *business communication was hardly likely to result in such a violent outcome. No, it had to be something that would ignite murderous passions, and what could be more explosive than accuser facing accused with evidence of a long-hidden love-child.*

It doesn't take me long to decide how best to use it. It's exactly what I need to win a particular lady's hand. Or is it? Is the envelope sufficient for my purpose? Without the letter, what is it worth? Then, it occurs to me that if she sees me with the envelope, she will automatically conclude I have the letter and, if I play my cards right, could be led to believe it contained proof of Dickens's illegitimate offspring even if in reality it was nothing more than a bill from his solicitors. Yes, having the envelope should be more than sufficient.

Chapter Twenty-Six: Georgina's Verdict

The day after drafting the Drood mystery's final chapter, Dunston realised something was still missing. He was a dedicated student of all his uncle's works and knew the master delighted in revealing on virtually the last page some unexpected connection among the characters and delivering that final surprise so loved by readers... and authors.

That Esther Summerson was the illegitimate daughter of Lady Dedlock and Captain Hawdon, the secret that ultimately drove her ladyship to suicide, was only disclosed towards the conclusion of *Bleak House.* That John Rokesmith was actually John Harmon, heir to a substantial fortune and presumed drowned at the start of the story, was not revealed until the end of *Our Mutual Friend.* That the lady in the portrait on display in Mr Brownlow's house was Oliver's mother only emerged in the forty-ninth of *Oliver Twist's* fifty-two chapters. *The pattern was repeated time and time again.*

Dunston saw several possibilities along these lines in *The Mystery of Edwin Drood,* but one stood out like a lighthouse beam on a stormy night and he'd grabbed his quill and immediately started drafting Part II of *The Cell.* Two hours later, Dunston, steaming like a saucepan on the boil, laid his pen down and dispatched Nick to Gad's Hill Place with a note requesting permission to visit Miss Georgina that afternoon.

Georgina, still in mourning clothes, received Dunston in the drawing room. After presenting her with his continuation of the Drood mystery, they seated themselves at the round table. She read, he watched. She turned a page, his eyes followed. She furrowed her brow, his eyes squinted. She pushed aside a loose wisp of hair, his eyes widened. Finally, she reached the second part of the last chapter, penned only yesterday. This was what she read.

The Cell: Part II

Datchery took Grewgious by the arm and called to the turnkey to open the door and let them out. But events in the cell were not yet concluded.

'Is that you Grewgious?' a waking Jasper asked, 'or am I still dreaming?'

'It is I,' the lawyer said.

'Ha! It really is you.'

The prisoner turned towards Datchery and after studying him carefully said, 'And you, where have I seen you before? Hmmm, you were there... after the drowning. You're that nosey policeman, always asking questions. Detective... um... Detective...'

'Detective Datchery, sir, Edwin Datchery.'

'Edwin? Same as—'

'Yes, sir, same as my son.'

'What? You're Edwin Drood's father?' Jasper asked, taken aback.

'Datchery, come. Let it be.' Grewgious grasped the other's arm.

'No.' Datchery pulled away. 'I want him to know the whole story. I want him to know why I tracked him down like the rabid cur he is. Listen, you wretch. Edwin was born out of wedlock to a lowly chorus girl and her devoted policeman. His mother, always sickly, died giving birth. Distraught beyond reason, the father disowned the infant. Grewgious, a close friend, handled the adoption. He found foster parents, the Droods, and decided on the child's name – Edwin, my given name.'

'You dog! What kind of man abandons his son?' the murderer demanded.

'I'll tell you what kind of man – a failure, heartless, full of hatred towards an innocent baby. But that was then. With time I realised what a terrible mistake I'd made. I pestered Grewgious to keep me informed

about the lad's progress. That was how I learned about Mrs Bud's drowning, a tragedy indeed, but for me the most wonderful moment of my life, because that was when I was reunited with my son. Then, after you almost strangled him to death, I was there to help him and set our little trap for you.'

'Damn your eyes!' the prisoner cursed.

'Blame yourself, fool. You've put the Tyburn tippet round your own throat just as surely as you put the scarf round Edwin's. Once the hangman's finished stretching your neck you'll roast like a pig on a spit in Hell's unquenchable fire for all eternity.'

'Hell holds no fears for me. Rather the Hell of the hereafter than the living hell of my dreams,' the inmate moaned.

He stared venomously at his tormentors, but little by little hatred gave way to unease... and then terror.

'The DREAM! It's coming BACK!' He threw himself on the cot, screaming and grabbing his head. The two men exchanged glances and without a word left the cell and the raving man.

But events in the cell were still not concluded.

The linen sheet might be coarse but it was as strong as when first woven. The cross beam might be old but it was sturdy. The turnkey, on his rounds early the next morning, was made all too aware of the physical properties of both. One end of the sheet – torn into lengths, the strips knotted together – was tied tightly around the beam, the other just as tightly around the neck of John Jasper, Choirmaster of Cloisterham Cathedral.

Georgina finished reading and looked at Dunston, an odd expression on her face. 'Dunston,' she said. Not a very illuminating remark for the apprehensive listener. 'Dunston,' she repeated.

Her one-man audience beseeched her with his eyes to say more. What did she think of the story? Did it conclude well? He silently begged her to pronounce and end his misery.

'Dunston,' she said for the third time, 'I don't know what to say. I'm beyond words.'

Dunston took this as a positive sign and the tension dropped several notches, but he wanted more.

'This is most remarkable, Dunston,' she said, and flashed him a special smile. 'You've stayed faithful to the story as Charles outlined it to Mr Forster yet added astonishing layers of excitement and marvellous twists of misdirection. I salute you. Truly masterful. Indeed, the master himself would have been proud to have penned this.'

Dunston coloured. 'Oh... yes... um... delighted you like it.'

'So clever,' she resumed. 'The ring in Jasper's Gate House – brilliant.' The special smile flashed again. 'And Edwin's survival – exactly what the novel needed.' One more special smile hit its target, now crimson with pleasure.

'You know, I now understand a remark Charles made to me just two days before he died. I said to him that I hoped he hadn't really killed poor Edwin Drood. And do you know what he replied? "I call my book the *Mystery* of Edwin Drood, not the *History*," which I took to mean that Edwin's history would not be fully told in *this* novel, that he had a future beyond this tale and must therefore live.'

'Fascinating,' Dunston gushed. 'So you think I'm on the right track.'

'I have no doubt. And what a stunning concluding chapter. Adult Jasper describing in his dream the murder committed by young Jasper finally makes sense of Charles's "very curious idea", something that had left me totally baffled ever since he mentioned it. And the chapter ties everything together so neatly – Jasper's opium addiction and his obsession with Rosa, both stemming from that tragic day at the river, and, best of all, Datchery's resolve to be Edwin's protector, the detective making amends for abandoning his son.'

'I'm so pleased you think so.' Dunston said.

'And as if that wasn't enough,' Georgina continued, 'the prose in that last chapter is so rich and elegant, a vast improvement over the um... jottings in the preceding chapters.'

'I know. I can't explain it but the words for the scene in the cell just appeared on the page almost before I'd thought them. Never happened to me before,' Dunston confessed. 'It was as though Uncle was guiding my hand.'

'Well, I'm sure it took hours of hard work and deep thought to conclude *The Mystery of Edwin Drood* in such an absorbing fashion. I congratulate you most warmly and thank you with all my heart,' she said. 'To be frank, I thought I'd set you an impossible task but you have succeeded beyond my wildest dreams.'

Dunston was thrilled with her reaction, until he saw a small frown pucker her brow, nothing much, but then the furrow deepened and he realised something was bothering her.

'What is it?' he asked.

'This is the conclusion as Charles himself would have written it, I'm sure. I congratulate you and thank you.' She hesitated. 'Still, there's one small point, such a trifle, it's hardly worth mentioning.'

'Please, don't hold back on my account,' the fiction-detective declared full of the confidence that came with solving the great Drood mystery.

'Well, it's a bit of um... a let-down that your ending doesn't shed any additional light on Lavelle's role in burgling your uncle's desk and taking his life. That was my hope when I received your note but... nothing, your conclusion adds nothing to what we already know.'

Dunston stared at her. She was right of course. He'd realised it himself in the carriage on his way to Gad's Hill Place. He'd hoped that she might spot some clue that had escaped him. But no, it was not to be. How disappointing after all that effort. Hours of work to no avail... unless...

He looked at his draft in Georgina's hand, still open to the last page. That final chapter... there was something else in that scene in the cell, something intensely personal to his uncle. He'd felt it when the quill was flying across the page. It wasn't only Uncle's elevating influence on his prose; it was more like he was sending words through Dunston's hand into the mouths of his characters, or at least one of them. And then, when the character spoke those words, it was as though they were coming straight from Uncle's mouth. Was Uncle speaking for himself through that character?

Should he share his suspicion with Miss Georgina? He looked at her.

Knowing she could be as prickly as a Scottish thistle when something didn't turn out as she'd hoped, he said, 'I fear you're right, Miss Georgina. It doesn't provide any further evidence against Lavelle. I'm so sorry.'

Chapter Twenty-Seven: The Drawer

Dunston returned to Woods View House and went straight into the drawing room. He sat in his favourite chair and glumly mulled over the disappointing ending to his meeting with Miss Georgina. He still sensed that the final chapter of the Drood novel – *The Cell* – contained a vital piece of information about his uncle, but he'd searched Saturday evening and again this morning to no avail. Like a butterfly, this germ-of-an-idea had fluttered tantalisingly close once or twice to that nucleus of brain cells – that golden one-hundredth of his full complement according to his uncle – that could project beyond what the eye saw, only to float out of reach, leaving him grasping at thin air.

Worse yet, David Copperfield sprang up in the elusive insect's place. There was young David hard at work in a Thames-side bottle-labelling warehouse; and there he was again, visiting spendthrift Mr Micawber in the King's Bench Prison. What in the world did David Copperfield have to do with Edwin Drood other than both being brought to life by Uncle's quill?

Enough, he said to himself at breakfast. Focus on facts, not wild fancies. What did he actually *know*? Well, the two parties to the illicit liaison, Uncle and Ellen Ternan, died within ten days of each other. Surely no coincidence. A single murderer, then? On the other hand, there was the manner of the murders. His uncle's killer had come prepared with the strychnine, whereas Miss Ternan was bludgeoned to death. The first premeditated, the second more like spur-of-the-moment violence. Two very different murders, then… and two different murderers? Dunston ran his hands through his hair in frustration.

He'd resume his interviewing strategy, he decided, beginning with some of Uncle's leading rivals – George Eliot, Anthony Trollope, Edward Bulwer-Lytton. But first, he'd write up for his own records, an account of Lavelle's arrest for burglary, the one success to date. He entered the library and sat at his desk. He discarded his jacket, rolled up his sleeves and began to write.

Nick entered. 'Coffee, sir,' he asked.

'Not now. Busy,' was his master's dismissive reply.

Nick, evidently curious about what was keeping his master so 'busy', sidled around the desk until he was looking over the writer's shoulder. Like a watchful tutor checking a pupil's composition, he read a couple of lines, enough to see that his master was wrapping up the Lavelle business. Whistling softly, he sauntered out.

Dunston was on his second page when he sat up with a start. How strange. Something wasn't right. He scrutinised the last few lines to see what was bothering him, the intuitive one percent of his brain cells working furiously. And there it was.

Miss Georgina said the burgled drawer had contained Charles's notes for the Drood mystery *and* some letters. Lavelle swore he took *only* Charles's plans for the rest of the novel, nothing else, and Inspector Line said the drawer was *empty* when he examined it. Goodness me. He knew what had happened. He must share this with Miss Georgina at once.

The front door at Gad's Hill Place opened to Dunston's knocking and he was greeted by a smiling Dulcet.

'Miss is upstairs, sir, but I'm sure she'll be down directly she hears it's you. I'll put you in the drawing room if you'll come this way,' she said.

Nine times out of ten, no, ninety-nine out of a hundred, Dunston would go wherever directed without complaint. If asked to wait in the scullery, that's where he would willingly go.If the stable, then in the stable he would position himself without a second thought. But not today.

'Actually, I think I'd like to wait in the study.'

'Very well, sir, if that's your choosing.' She saw him into the study and popped upstairs to Miss Georgina's room.

Dunston headed straight for the desk. The drawer was slightly off centre where it had been forced shut by Inspector Line, and the wood around the lock was scratched, but that was all. He scolded himself for not inspecting it earlier, especially in view of what he now believed happened. He pulled the handle. The drawer held firm. He pulled again, a little harder and, with a dry rasp like a dying man's final gasp, it opened an inch but no more. He grasped the handle with both hands, braced his feet against the desk and pulled with all his might.

The drawer flew free, throwing Dunston flat on his back. The puffing man manoeuvred himself onto all fours, lifted his head like a hound hunting a fox and detected, not the scent of a fleeing quarry, but the fragrance of perfumed notepaper, a single sheet, folded in four, spinning gently to the floor. He picked up his find, guessing it must have been pushed behind the drawer when Lavelle rifled it, and struggled to his feet.

His first thought was to replace the drawer before Miss Georgina arrived, but he couldn't resist a quick look. He unfolded the note and began to read. A sharp intake of breath punctured his reading.

'My Goodness,' he muttered. 'Miss Georgina must *never* see this. Definitely not for her eyes.'

But to his eyes, it made clear why David Copperfield kept popping up and what his repeated appearances meant for that final chapter in the Drood story. Transfixed as he was, he still caught the sound of an upstairs door closing. Miss Georgina was on her way. He folded the note, stuffed it in his jacket pocket and hastily restored the drawer as best he could.

'Dunston, whatever are you doing in here?' she asked.

'I wanted to see the drawer,' he replied. 'I've had… a breakthrough about the burglary. You see, you said the drawer held Uncle's notes for the Drood novel *and* some personal letters.'

'True, but that hardly seems like a breakthrough to me.'

'No, not by itself, I grant you, but recall that Lavelle confessed to taking the notes but *nothing else*, and Inspector Line said he found the drawer *empty*.'

'Yes, I know, but what—' She glanced sharply at him. 'D'you mean—'

'Yes! Two robbers!' he interjected unable to restrain himself. 'The drawer was robbed *twice*.'

'Robbed twice?'

'I believe so,' he replied. 'Lavelle stole the notes for the Drood mystery, but that's all he wanted. Someone else then took advantage of the drawer being open to steal Uncle's letters.' His eyes glistened at the prospect of the praise about to be bestowed upon him by a grateful Miss Georgina.

'Ye-es, possibly,' she allowed, clearly not pleased that Dunston was reopening a matter she obviously thought had been closed with Lavelle's arrest. But then, 'Hmm, you're right about the letters... and the notes. And, I was with Inspector Line when he examined the drawer after the burglary and found it empty.'

'Not completely empty,' Dunston blurted out. A stickler for the truth, he was already pulling out the crumpled note to prove his point before he could stop himself.

'What's that?'

Oh no! The sheet of stationery he was waving in front of Miss Georgina was the *last* thing he wanted her to see.

'What? This? Oh, just a scrap of paper. Fell from the... the drawer.' He did his best to refold it and stuff it back into his pocket.

'Nonsense. It was empty, I tell you,' she said irritably.

'Yes, the *inside* of the drawer... empty as you say,' agreed Dunston. 'But this trifle was stuck *behind* it. That's why everyone missed it – the second burglar, you and Inspector Line.'

'Let me see this *trifle*,' she demanded.

Dunston gulped, but there was nothing he could do except hand it over. Georgina took it and began to read.

Windsor Lodge
  April 15, 1850

My Darling Charles:
  As always, you've thought of everything. A monthly stipend to cover the costs of a suitable home and proper care for the child—

CHILD! Like a spitting cobra's venom, the word leapt from page to eye, drawing a horrified gasp from Georgina.

Dunston could see that Georgina, her Scottish stoicism notwithstanding, was shocked to the core by what she'd just read. He watched as she slowly returned her eyes to the toxic note and its reputation-shredding contents.

...is an excellent idea.

Dare I make one tiny suggestion? It might be more convenient for you, my beloved, if the monthly payments go directly to my bank account rather than a trust for the child as you are planning. My humble suggestion would eliminate any demands on your precious time as I could, I'm sure, easily handle day-to-day expenses without troubling you. If you feel my trifling proposal has any merit, you might wish to instruct Clatterbuck accordingly.

My dearest, I send you all the love in my heart and wait only for the time we can be together once more. May it be soon!

Forever and always,

Your loving Nelly

Ellen Ternan's letter read, Georgina's look of shock changed to one of worry, or dread even. She sat down heavily on the green sofa.

Not chivalrous by nature or upbringing, Dunston nonetheless hurried to her side. He reached out to her only to stop his hand before it could touch her arm, society's emotion-stifling etiquette and her high-on-a-pedestal status effective as a thorn-hedge barricade in keeping him at a distance. The best he could do was offer his handkerchief, but Georgina, already getting a grip on herself, waved it away. She was not given to tears. Dunston silently withdrew, taking a seat in the cane-bottomed easy chair some half a dozen respectable feet away.

Propriety restored, Georgina said grimly, 'A child. Charles and that actress woman. This news is most unwelcome. The danger to Charles's reputation if a child of his, born out of wedlock to an actress, ever surfaces is incalculable. If other letters taken from the drawer and now in the hands of the second burglar, contain even the briefest mention of Charles's child—'

'Not a child anymore,' Dunston pointed out. 'A young person of twenty, given the note's date of 1850.'

'Yes, of course.'

'And male.'

'Male? Why do you say that?'

'David Copperfield.'

'David Copperfield? Whatever do you mean, Dunston?' Georgina asked crossly.

'Sorry, let me explain. Uncle based David's early life on his own boyhood,' Dunston reminded her. 'Uncle was sent to work in Warren's shoe-blacking factory when he was twelve, David to label bottles in a warehouse in Blackfriars; Uncle visited his father in the Marshalsea Prison, David went to see Mr Micawber in the debtor's prison; and so on. Uncle was so ashamed of his upbringing he rarely mentioned it, but he wanted some way of telling *his* story, some means of unburdening his soul, and David Copperfield was his vehicle.'

'I'm well aware of that,' Georgina snapped, 'but what does it have do with the child's gender?'

'Detective Datchery... in Part II of the cell chapter... *he's* the surrogate for *adult* Uncle, just as *David* was for *young* Uncle,' he explained. 'So when Datchery owns to abandoning his new born babe, it's really *Uncle* admitting *he* abandoned *his* new born babe. Uncle wanted some way of absolving himself by acknowledging, albeit indirectly, the child he'd disowned. If I'm right, then Uncle and Ellen Ternan, like Datchery and his chorus girl, had... a son.'

'I see. Very clever of you, I'm sure, but, frankly, rather flimsy. After all, that conclusion to the Drood story is only your interpretation, and while it might be exactly what Charles would have written, we can't be certain. Anyway, it makes no difference to what must be done,' no-nonsense Georgina said. 'I swore to protect your uncle's memory until my last breath so I intend to do everything I can to find this... this unwanted offspring and make certain he, or she, *never* lays a claim on Charles. And you, Dunston, must help me.'

'Of course. I'll do everything within my power to discover the whereabouts of this person,' he vowed without having the faintest idea where to start.

Chapter Twenty-Eight: The Elastic Concept Of Confidentiality

Monday morning found Dunston on his way to London once more, this time to see the only person he and Georgina could think of who might have knowledge of his uncle's offspring – Dickens's lawyer, Clatterbuck. Recognising she could not participate in a meeting on such an unseemly topic, Georgina had been obliged to trust Dunston as her intermediary, but not before impressing upon him that any issue from Charles's liaison with that 'actress woman' must be persuaded to keep quiet about its parentage at all costs.

What was for Georgina a threat of the first order to Uncle's reputation, was for Dunston an important development in his murder investigation, which, together with the twice-robbed drawer, pointed strongly to a single murderer. Ensconced in a comfy seat in the train's first-class carriage, he pictured what happened. The abandoned boy, now grown-up, tracks his father to Gad's Hill Place. He sees the window left open by Lavelle, enters the study and poisons the tonic. One of the letters he spots in the half-open desk drawer reveals that Ellen Ternan is his mother. He confronts her at Windsor Lodge and batters her to death. Yes, two murders and two different means of killing, but only one murderer, and definitely not Lavelle.

Dunston would do his best to find Uncle's bastard and limit any damage to the novelist's memory as Miss Georgina wanted. But he'd also do whatever he could to prove the misbegotten brat murdered his father and mother. The starting point for both endeavours was Mr Clatterbuck's chambers in

Lincoln's Inn.

As befitted a lawyer required to deal with the most sensitive matters in the lives of his clients, Mr Clatterbuck had acquired an air of confidentiality. It was not known whether this outward demeanour was patterned on his father, a founding partner in *Clatterbuck and Jorrin, Solicitors* and a man who genuinely practised client privacy, or independently developed to hide the younger Clatterbuck's unfortunate habit of revealing more than he kept secret. Either way, the impassive face, upright stance, and habitual dark jacket gave every appearance of trustworthiness.

He was sitting in his chair, staring at the object on his desk. The item was so inconsequential it hardly seemed worth coming to London for, but that was what Mr Dunston Burnett wanted to do.

'Hope he isn't going to be difficult,' he muttered.

He'd soon find out. His clerk knocked and ushered in his visitor.

'Ah, Mr Burnett. A great pleasure to welcome you to my law offices.' He gestured Dunston to one of the two hard-backed chairs placed for clients. 'Thought you would've been at Gad's Hill Place last Friday for the reading,' he said conversationally.

'The reading?'

'Your uncle's will. The old one actually, not the new one. I'd left the new one with him for his signature, but he never returned it to me so I imagine he decided against the amendment we'd discussed, or perhaps he wanted to add something else. No matter, doesn't affect your bequest.' His eyes directed Dunston's attention to the object on the desk.

'Bequest?' Dunston was mystified by this odd opening to the meeting.

'Yes. I confess it's not overly large, but I assure you Mr Dickens was most keen for you to have it.'

'Forgive me, Mr Clatterbuck, but I'm not following you.' Dunston looked more bemused than ever. 'As I explained in my telegram, my visit is in connection with—'

'Your bequest. Quite so, sir. And there it is.' The lawyer nodded more pointedly at the item centred on the desk, this time succeeding in drawing

Dunston's eyes to it.

'Uncle's inkpot! He left this... this treasure to me?'

'Indeed, sir. This... um.... treasure is his bequest to you.' Noticeably relieved the interview was turning out much better than expected, Clatterbuck moved on quickly. 'I'll have my clerk wrap it for you while we complete the formalities.'

'Yes... yes, quite.' The legatee was barely listening, his eyes fixed on the magnificent memento, empty now of the writer's favoured blue ink, his lifeblood as he called it, but still overflowing with memories of all his bizarre characters and their relentless buffeting in life's ups and downs. 'This is the most wonderful moment of my life,' he enthused. 'I shall cherish his gift until the day I die.'

'I'm so glad,' Clatterbuck said aloud, and then under his breath, 'Each to his own.'

The treasure having been wrapped and the requisite signature obtained, the lawyer made to show his visitor out, but Dunston remained firmly in his seat.

'I fear,' he said, 'my telegram may not have been as... clear as I might have wished.'

'In what respect, sir?' a concerned-looking Clatterbuck asked.

'Well, I'm here about the child.'

'Child?'

'Actually, young man by now... or possibly young lady.'

'The child has turned into a young man or lady, you say.' It was the lawyer's turn to look puzzled.

'Exactly,' replied Dunston, pleased the lawyer had at last grasped the reason for his visit. 'The child was born in 1850, so that makes him, or her, twenty.'

'A young person of twenty, you say.' Clatterbuck's face made clear he still had no idea what his visitor was talking about. This, he evidently decided, was one of those occasions when it was best to invoke the never-failing safety net of solicitor-client privilege. He puffed his legal cheeks, pursed his lawyerly lips, and exuding confidentiality from every pore, said, 'My dear Mr Burnett, with respect to this or that child, or this or that young person, I must remind you that all dealings with this firm's clients are *strictly private.*'

'Oh, dear,' Dunston said. 'Mr Dickens made Miss Hogarth promise to make sure his child is properly provided for,' he fibbed.

'Mr Burnett, had you been at the reading of the will, you would know that Mr Dickens made generous provision for all ten of his children.'

'No, no… not *those* children. The one I'm interested in was born… how shall I put it?… well, he was born *outside* the family.'

'What? Am I to understand there's a child… Mr Dickens's… born, as you say, outside the family?'

'Exactly, in 1850, most likely in July or August.'

'I had no idea. I was just a junior clerk then. Father was running the firm. But let me take a look in the documents room.'

Clatterbuck went out through a side door, returning in a matter of minutes with a weighty black ledger marked *CONFIDENTIAL* in large, legal-looking letters.

'This is the file for the third quarter of 1850.' He leafed through its contents. 'My goodness, you're right, there was a little boy, William by name, born in July,' revealed Clatterbuck, the bastion of confidentiality suddenly changed into a legal sieve, blithely doling out information about Dickens's most private matters more freely than a priest dispensed blessings.

'I knew it,' Dunston exclaimed. 'And is… er…. William still alive?'

'Let me see. Ahh, now this is interesting, seems he was to receive monthly payments until Mr Dickens's death, and… ha, yes, there's a note in this month's calendar, probably written by Father's clerk, saying "Final payment, June 30." That's in three day's time, so I imagine the young man is alive and well.'

Dunston was almost as excited with this news as he was with the inkpot. But would Miss Georgina be so pleased? She'd undoubtedly have considered it more convenient had Uncle's offspring failed to reach adulthood. Unfortunately, the child hadn't cooperated, making it even more important that Dunston learn the young man's full name and whereabouts.

'Mr Clatterbuck, you've been most helpful. Miss Hogarth will be delighted to hear about this… this individual and most keen to ensure that Uncle's wishes with respect to his care continue.'

'Most commendable, I'm sure.'

'Perhaps, then, you could let me have the young man's full name and address,' Dunston said. 'Then Miss Hogarth can contact him and continue the monthly payments. That is, if these details are not *too* confidential.'

'Excellent suggestion,' Clatterbuck said approvingly. 'Frankly, I don't see any issue of confidentiality here given Miss Hogarth's admirable intentions. Between you and me, one can place too much weight on confidentiality. In the abstract it's all well and good, but in reality one has to use judgement and experience to chart a sensible course through tricky legal waters. Yes, confidentiality can be safely dispensed with in this instance, trust me.'

'A splendid attitude if I may say so. I will pass the... er... person's particulars to Miss Hogarth if you would be so kind...' Dunston prompted.

'I'm afraid that's not possible.'

'I'm... not sure I understand.'

'Well, you see, the monthly payments went straight to Miss Ternan's account, so there's no mention of William's full name or his address.'

Chapter Twenty-Nine: A Proposal

After breakfast on Tuesday morning, Georgina headed for the drawing room and her monthly routine of bill-paying. She'd barely started, when Dulcet knocked and entered.

'Mr Wurmsley's here, miss.'

'Oh Heavens,' Georgina groaned. 'I'm really not in the mood for him today.' The man, an acquaintance rather than a friend, was a gossip through and through, barely on the fringe of acceptable society.

'He's on the doorstep looking ever so sorry for himself.'

'Dulcet, you're right. Where's my Christian spirit? He's called several times now and I've not received him. Show him in.'

'Yes, miss.'

The maid was soon back with the visitor in tow.

'Miss Hogarth, please forgive my intrusion,' he began nervously. 'I would never have dared disturb you were it not for a matter of some importance.'

'Mr Wurmsley. How delightful,' she said. She invited him to sit, determined to do her best to make the man feel welcome.

Re-seating herself, she studied him as he engaged her in inconsequential news about mutual acquaintances. His squat body was so concertina-ed, Georgina wondered if he actually had a spine. His protruding eyes swivelled disconcertingly, adding to his toad-like appearance. And his black hair was plastered so tightly to the skull, it looked for all the world like a hanging judge's black cap. Ugh! She shuddered. Georgina! she scolded herself, he's one of God's creatures no matter what he looks like. She smiled warmly.

She listened politely for a few minutes but patience was not one of her virtues, and, despite her genuine intent to treat Mr Wurmsley with all the decency and human kindness she could muster, she was not slow to cut him off.

'Fascinating,' she fibbed, 'most fascinating, but I believe you said a matter of importance has prompted this charming visit. Perhaps you would like to come to the point because I have some pressing matters...' She let the sentence trail, hoping he'd take the hint.

He smiled. Or rather his upper lip writhed up like a wriggling worm and then back down, the disconcerting simper disappearing almost as soon as it appeared. 'Yes, of course, quite understand,' he said with a meek nod in response to her prodding.

He slipped his hand inside his corduroy jacket and drew from his breast pocket the slightly crumpled, brown-stained envelope he'd acquired from Miss Ellen Ternan's maid. 'Perhaps, Miss Hogarth, you may find this of some interest.' He handed it to her.

She saw immediately that it was an everyday business envelope addressed to Charles. She glanced inside. No letter. She looked inquiringly at Mr Wurmsley.

'May I be so bold as to direct your attention to the postmark?'

She inspected the frank. May 3, 1850. Odd, she thought. Must've escaped Charles's bonfire. Still, apart from that, I'm not sure what's supposed to interest me in an old envelope. She glanced at him again, a little annoyed that he'd seen fit to bother her with such a trifle.

'Mr Wurmsley, certain individuals, philatelists I believe, might find some value in an old postmark, but I'm much too busy to engage in such an idle pursuit. Here, let me return your envelope.' She gave it back to him. 'If that is all you wish to say to me, I must beg you to excuse me. As I said I have some pressing matters—'

'Ah, yes, pressing matters.' Concern flitted momentarily over his frog-like features and then it was gone, much like his smile. 'Well no matter how pressing the matters, I *insist* you grant me a few more minutes of your precious time,' he said in a tone that left Georgina feeling most uncomfortable, even a little threatened. What could he mean by such behaviour?

'Thank you,' he continued more amiably. 'Before you rush to attend to your pressing matters, let's consider this envelope a little further. Third of May, 1850. What an interesting date. Almost a year after Mr Dickens met that young actress... Ellen... um, what was her name? Do you recall it, Miss Hogarth?'

Georgina grasped in a flash where the conversation was headed and she was furious. What cheek to refer to that strumpet in her presence. About to give him the sharp edge of her tongue, she bit it instead, remembering just in time her good intentions. She must be charitable even to such a socially graceless misfit. Calling on all her powers of self-control, she replied as equably as possible, 'Ellen Ternan, I believe.'

'Ah, yes. Ellen Ternan. Such a pretty thing, I've been told. What a shock her death was. As it happens, I was at her house the very day she died. A social call, you understand, but when I got there, I saw these workmen carting the poor woman's carcass away on a wagon. Quite a shock, let me tell you. Still, that's neither here nor there for present purposes. Let's return to the date. Yes, third of May, 1850. I understand that the delightful Miss Ternan spent most of that spring and early summer in France. A wonderful country, I understand. Are you familiar with the great city of Paris or perhaps the French countryside?'

The insinuation was abundantly clear to Georgina. The man knew about the child. The grubby envelope's letter must make all too clear the disastrous outcome of Charles's foolish liaison with Ellen. Georgina was beside herself. Still, she was not going to play silly games with him.

'Mr Wurmsley,' she replied, 'I have no wish to discuss France or any other part of the globe with you. Please keep that in mind, and afford me the courtesy of telling me what you intend to do with the envelope's letter.'

Wurmsley smiled again, his ruse was working. Georgina obviously believed he had the letter.

'My dear Miss Hogarth, please forgive me. I fear there may be a small misunderstanding. Surely my fault and I beg your pardon most humbly.'

'I... don't understand.' Georgina was thrown off balance by this sudden change in tenor.

'Allow me to explain,' he said, a third smile writhing briefly across his face. He waved the envelope in the air. 'An envelope as old as this one,' he said, 'is not the matter of importance that brought me to you today. A curiosity, a small reminder of the great man, a tiny piece of history, nothing more.' Georgina relaxed. 'I'm gratified it elicits some interest on your part, but, no, that is not what brings me to Gad's Hill Place... and to your side.'

He paused to let his words sink in, watching her struggle to make sense of this last remark and then consider her options – send him packing or listen to him. Finally she spoke.

'Then what, pray, is so important?' she asked.

To her astonishment, he dropped to one knee and took her hand. 'Ah, my dearest Georgina, I thought you would not need to ask, but now I'm glad you have because it gives me the opportunity to share my heart's longings with you, dear lady, mistress of my ever-lasting love, and dare I hope... *my bride?*'

The words were hardly out of his mouth when Georgina jumped to her feet knocking Wurmsley on to his backside, exactly where the toad deserved to be. Georgina was shaking, too incensed by his appalling effrontery to even speak. She glared at him, her mouth a tight grimace.

He struggled to his feet. 'Ah, I see, precious one, my proposal has overwhelmed you. Fear not, you do not have to answer now. My heart beats in rhythm with yours and I understand your every feeling, your every emotion, as though mine. I will take my leave and let you regain your composure. But my pet, I will return in one week for your answer.'

He bowed deeply, straightened, and then made a great show of carefully folding the envelope and placing it in his breast pocket. He patted his jacket as though making sure the envelope was safely secured next to his heart, and took his leave.

Georgina collapsed into her chair. What gall. Had that despicable man just proposed to her? Or threatened her? Or both? Yes, both! That was what the loathsome reptile had done. Think, she instructed herself. You are still and always will be the guardian of Charles's reputation. Remember your oath made all those years ago – to protect Charles's standing for as long as you live. The scoundrel must be stopped. But how? By marrying him to keep him quiet? Impossible!

I need help. Frank Beard... yes, Frank will know what to do.

Chapter Thirty: Purple Passages

Before leaving for London yesterday to see Clatterbuck, Dunston had dispatched Nick to Windsor Lodge, Ellen Ternan's house in Peckham, armed with a formal request for any letters from Charles Dickens that could provide background for the novelist's 'officially authorised' biography being written by Dunston Burnett. Dunston wasn't sure the effort would bear fruit, but Nick had a way with women and, given the demise of the mistress of the house, his good looks and glib tongue might do the trick with her likely stand-in – her parlour maid.

The idea had come to him at breakfast on Monday as he wondered what additional avenues might be explored in search of his uncle's son, William. Prompted by the note he'd found in the desk drawer, it occurred to him that there might be other letters, not *to* his uncle, but *from* his uncle, and there was one person he must surely have written to about the illegitimate birth. Hence, Nick's assignment.

Dunston was up early Tuesday morning. He was anxious to read the small stack of letters that Nick had brought back from Peckham, before going to Gad's Hill Place to report to Georgina what he'd learned from Clatterbuck. He was hurrying to the library after a gobbled breakfast, letters in hand, when he spotted his manservant biting a ring to test the quality of the gold. What was Nick doing with a gold ring? Dunston knew Nick had grown up in his mother's opium den and suspected his manservant had done his share of thieving in his youth. Had he fallen back into old habits? Dunston was keen to read the letters but the moral wellbeing of his manservant might be at stake and he took his responsibilities as master seriously.

'Nick, I... er...' Not a particularly arresting opening but enough to make the makeshift assayer, caught unawares, jump out of his skin, lending weight to Dunston's suspicions.

'Oh! It's you, sir. Thought you were still breakfasting.' Nick stood, the ring magically vanishing from sight.

'I was,' Dunston acknowledged, 'but now I'm here... and saw a ring.'

'Ring, sir? What ring was that, then?'

'The one in your breeches pocket,' Dunston replied evenly. He might lack the wherewithal to ever be a proper gent, but Dunston did have an enormous reservoir of perseverance, and side-tracking him was more difficult than prising a knuckle bone from a bulldog's maw.

'Oh, you mean this ring?' Nick reluctantly drew the offending article from its not very effective hiding place. 'Ma gave it to me,' he said. 'Asked me to pawn it for her.'

To Dunston this sounded like the first story that had popped into Nick's mind as he sought some way of fobbing off his master. Nick hadn't visited his mother for over a month.

'I see.' Dunston actually saw all too clearly. Innocent Dunston was learning about life in the real world and had little doubt that his manservant had just lied to him. But what should he do? The letters were burning the flesh of his hand, demanding attention.

'Perhaps it would be best for me to look after this... item until we have time for a longer conversation regarding its origins.' He held out his hand.

Nick hesitated, obviously reluctant to give up the gold band, but the relationship between master and man being what it was, he had little option.

'Right you are, sir,' he replied.

Dunston took the ring, slipped it in his waistcoat pocket and, with a curt nod to his manservant, continued on his way to the library, the incident already forgotten.

Dunston settled in his chair and laid the letters on the library desk. Not many, he noted, disappointed. Fearing another hopeless enterprise, he beseeched Jude, patron saint of lost causes, for a beatific helping hand or, better yet, a tiny miracle. He whispered a quick Amen and started to examine what remained of the twenty-one-year, author-actress liaison – Charles Dickens's love letters to Ellen Ternan.

Dunston did his utmost to remain focused on his task but on at least four occasions he exploded out of his chair like an overweight Guy Fawkes blown up by his own gunpowder, exclaiming 'Oh, my goodness!' and looking all around to make sure no eye other than his had seen what he'd just read. After each outburst, he mopped his brow, re-seated himself, took a deep breath and resumed his reading.

Such behaviour, odd though it was, must have some rational explanation, and indeed it did. As he perused his uncle's letters to Ellen, he discovered writing of such enchanting lyricism and infectious rhythm he knew he was reading some of the finest prose ever penned in the English language. Each word was perfectly chosen for its own special purpose, no other could convey the nuance of meaning, no other could maintain the harmony of sound, no other could flow so effortlessly from its predecessor and yet meld so seamlessly with its successor, as the one chosen by the master. The reader was swept along, captivated, and then, without the slightest warning, BOOM! the writing erupted with a power and passion that took the breath away.

It was these purple passages that caused Dunston to leap to his feet, stirred to the core by their feverish fervour and searing sexuality. He could not conceive how any normal human being could have such an animal-like obsession for another. Nothing in his experience, certainly not his recently awakened interest in Miss Georgina, came anywhere close to what his uncle had felt for Ellen.

The last letter read, he sat in his chair perspiring, exhausted, lost in wonder. He had no idea what would become of these letters, but he could imagine Miss Georgina's reaction. Left to her, these gems of English literature would be destroyed as surely as fire consumed the priceless manuscripts of the Ancient Library of Alexandria. She must never see them.

He cleared his mind and reread the letters, this time looking past the miracle of the prose to their content, and gradually but undeniably, his worst fears were realised. No mention of offspring. No word of arrangements for an infant. No hint of monthly payments for the growing boy's care. Nothing. Not a word. He stared sightlessly at the stack. He'd so hoped Ellen's letters would yield the information he sought, but... nothing. There *must* be something in them, somewhere. Not ready to admit defeat, he decided on one last effort.

This time he saw the pattern. Ellen had kept only a dozen letters but each contained descriptions of torrid love-making or arrangements for their next rendezvous. Very clever of her. This damningly explicit evidence of his uncle's obsession with her provided the ideal ammunition to extort financial support from the novelist should the need arise.

She'd obviously had no interest in keeping the usual pieces of news that a man might share with his partner. Nothing about his latest novel. Nothing about the people he'd met. Nothing about his various ailments. Nothing... except for one odd incident. Dunston had skipped over it on previous readings precisely because it was an account of an everyday event, but now that he understood her purpose in choosing which letters to save, it was clear that this passage held some special significance. He read it again, this time more carefully.

> *I must tell you about my visit to Saffron Hill's Field Lane School. After my speech in the assembly hall, a schoolboy — scruffy, skinny, spotty, no more than ten years of age — timorously approached me, eyes downcast, arms hanging loosely at his sides. I naturally assumed he wanted to pose some question or other, but, to my utter astonishment, he squared his shoulders, looked me in the eye and in front of the entire school announced that I was the subject of a blackmail plot and that he, this CHILD, was there to save me!!!!!!!!*

Not much, Dunston conceded. Could be just an unusual occurrence, something worth relating in a couple of sentences and then forgotten. But Dunston thought otherwise. He had no idea what the reference to a blackmail plot meant, but the capitalisation of *child* and the multiple exclamation marks struck him suspiciously like a signal to Ellen. Could Uncle Charles be telling her he'd had an unplanned and rather awkward meeting with their illegitimate son? He checked the date on the letter. September 13, 1860. Yes, William would have been about ten at that time.

Not much perhaps, but worth pursuing. Should he inform Miss Georgina? Or press ahead by himself? Dunston, mindful of the lady's likely reaction to the purple passages, for once threw caution aside and settled firmly on the latter course of action. Tomorrow he'd set off for London again, and see what he could learn at Field Lane School.

Chapter Thirty-One: Field Lane School

The globule of snot sliding down the urchin's upper lip left a yellow-green trail from nose to mouth. Dunston stared at it with some alarm. Would it continue in slug-like fashion into the creature's mouth? Or would the grimy sleeve of the child's grubby shirt be put to good use? Neither as it turned out. One mighty sniff and the offending discharge disappeared into the mucus-encrusted ragamuffin's right nostril.

It was mid-morning Wednesday, and Dunston had returned to London to follow up the one possible reference in his uncle's letters to his illegitimate offspring. The owner of the runny nose, a scruffy eight-year old, had apparently been instructed to meet him on his arrival at Field Lane School.

Lady Moffet had funded the charity school quite liberally and the gold-lettered sign above the doorway was impressive enough:

DR MAXIMUS FULLERTON, MA, LL.D
HEADMASTER
Field Lane School

Apart from that, he saw no evidence of her generosity. The building, with its broken windows, loose tiles, crumbling brickwork and gaping crack running diagonally across the frontage, was in marginally better condition than its immediate neighbours, but that was simply a measure of their near collapse.

His attention was drawn back to the lad, who, momentarily snot-free, was eyeing the new arrival with interest while running his hand over his shaved head. Lice! The word screamed it's presence in Dunston's mind and he promptly increased the distance between him and the diseased wretch.

'Good morning... er... young man. I'm here to see the headmaster,' Dunston said.

'Office is thru' there.' The boy pointed to the main entrance. 'An' up the stairs.'

'Yes. Thank you,' Dunston replied, but his impish attendant had already disappeared, leaving Dunston to climb the stairs and face the much-lettered Dr Maximus Fullerton.

'Come in!' a deep, authoritative voice commanded in response to Dunston's timid knock.

Dunston opened the door and entered what proved to be a well appointed study with a splendid oak desk in the centre, an oblong conference table with four chairs to the right, and to the left, a pair of comfortable-looking armchairs and a side table bearing a selection of ports and sherries. Lady Moffet's donation had obviously been put to great educational effect.

The headmaster was seated at his desk, head bent over a report, the pale moon of his bald pate, not unlike the rascal's shaven crown, on full display. He finally looked up and rose to greet his guest, his welcome conveying all the importance of his position but none of the cordiality a visitor might expect. 'Ah, Mr Burnett. I'm pleased to receive you in what I call my cathedral of educational enlightenment.' He gestured to the wooden chair on Dunston's side of the desk and then reclaimed the well upholstered swivel chair on his side.

A well-fleshed man of some forty years, he wore an academic gown over a dark brown jacket and scrupulously starched cotton shirt. His ample jowls were liberally endowed with reddish whiskers, their profusion complemented by tufts of similarly coloured hair sprouting from his ears. He may have gleaming white teeth but the world would never know because when he smiled, his lips, two narrow, colourless strips, elongated without ever revealing a speck of enamel.

'You've timed your visit to perfection, sir, if I may say so,' he continued. 'An opportunity to observe pedagogical history in the making.'

'I beg your—'

'I'm referring to my forthcoming treatise entitled *Dr Maximus Fullerton's Modern Methods of Schooling for the Lower Orders*,' the headmaster announced. 'Thanks to my primer, the entire world, yes sir, the entire world will soon be learning the Three R's.'

Dunston was less than impressed. 'Forgive me, but I was taught Reading, Riting and Rithmetic at Dullsbury's Evangelical Academy more than twenty years ago. The Three R's are hardly revolutionary.'

'Ah, *those* Three R's,' Maximus Fullerton exclaimed disdainfully. 'It's so unfortunate, my dear sir, that my fellow educators are incapable of spelling the three activities they claim are fundamental to their professional beliefs. *Arithmetic*, let me remind you, begins with an *A*, not an *R*. How can these imbeciles profess to be the intellectual guides of unopened minds when they can't even spell the third tenet of their pedantic philosophy? Absolutely disgraceful.'

'Yes, but—'

'I assure you that Arithmetic, and certainly not *Rithmetic*, finds no place in my Three R's. The third R in Maximus Fullerton's Modern Methods stands for *Religion*. Much more important. I ask you, of what value is adding and subtracting for the under classes? None whatsoever. Arithmetic may have some merit for lowly tradesmen and common bookkeepers but it's of no use whatsoever to the wretches I have the doubtful privilege of teaching.'

Dunston, a bookkeeper to the core, felt rather belittled by the headmaster's sally. The rejoinder taking shape in his mind would, he was sure, put this supercilious teacher in his place. He smiled in anticipation of the headmaster's comeuppance.

'But, unless I'm much mistaken,' he said, 'the second R which I assume stands for writing even in your Three R's, doesn't begin with R.'

'Well, I don't know where you learned your letters, sir, but the middle component of *my* three R's is spelt R-I-G-H-T-I-N-G.'

'Oh, *that* righting,' a crestfallen Dunston said.

'Exactly. How else can you teach Religion unless you Right the beasts when they sin? And let me tell you, the little sinners sin with a perseverance that never fails to amaze.'

'I see,' Dunston said, not really seeing at all. 'D'you mean to say you don't actually teach writing, that is writing with a W?'

'Waste of time. Best we can hope for is that they learn how to spell their names.'

Dunston was about to contest the Great Educator's contention when he realised that arguing with this buffoon was not likely to further his quest for information about his uncle's offspring. He'd best get to the purpose of his visit.

'Of course. I'm sure you're right,' Dunston said conciliatorily. 'With your permission, perhaps I should come to the reason for my calling on you today.'

'Ah, yes,' Fullerton replied eagerly. 'I believe you mentioned a biography of the great Mr Dickens in your telegram. A wonderful endeavour, if I may say so.'

'Thank you,' Dunston responded. 'The biography I intend to write, with a W that is, will treat both Uncle Charles's novels *and* his interest in social issues, especially education for the poor.'

'Excellent, Mr Burnett. Most commendable.'

'Indeed, headmaster. You see, Uncle believed that drunkenness, debauchery and crime have become a way of life among the lower classes because they have no escape from their self-destroying hopelessness. I'm sure you recall how Uncle captured the bleak future of the boy named Ignorance in the *Christmas Carol* in that single word emblazoned on his forehead – DOOM. That child, and many others like him, are damned as soon as they are born. But education, your chosen profession, provides an opportunity for them to better their lives.'

'Wonderful. Quite wonderful. Your words fill my heart to the brim. Your uncle made the very point when he visited our humble establishment, a famous moment in my school's history,' Fullerton preened.

'Ah, then perhaps you remember a young lad confronting Uncle.'

'Lad? What lad?' the headmaster spluttered, face reddening, ear hairs agitating, nose suddenly requiring vigorous wiping.

'The one who warned Uncle about a blackmail plot,' Dunston replied.

'Oh, that one. I'd totally forgotten,' Fullerton lied. 'Yes, quite deplorable. Claimed he was Dickens's son. Can you believe that? Not the school's fault,' he hastened to add. 'Child was *not* a pupil of this school.'

'Oh, no,' Dunston cried despairingly. 'If he wasn't a pupil then... you have no record of him?'

'None whatsoever,' the headmaster declared firmly.

'Dear me,' Dunston said forlornly. 'What happened to him?'

'Thrashed, of course.' The educational innovator raised his eyebrows, the look on his face making clear his doubts about his visitor's grasp of even the most basic principles of pedagogy.

'Ah... yes.'

'I have a talent for it, you know.'

'Teaching?'

'No, no. *Righting*. I can deliver a magnificent flogging when in the mood. All in the motion. Extraordinarily supple in wrist, elbow and shoulder, you know.' Indeed, there was a looseness about his movements, both sinuous and sinister. 'But the real power comes from the calves, thighs and buttocks. I think of it as a special gift from God to—'

'Yes, quite.' Dunston struggled to put his indignation aside and stay focused on the purpose of his visit. This was his last chance of tracing the child. He must find out all he can. 'And the young boy... did he ever come back to the school?'

'Come back?' The headmaster was much surprised. 'I should think not after the thrashing I gave him. Certainly not to this school and, I'm confident, not to any other school in the land. Probably went straight to the best place for good-for-nothings like him, straight to Heaven—'

'What? He died?'

'No, no. I mean that place in Bleeding Heart Yard, just minutes from here, Heaven's Haven. Home for orphans and foundlings.'

'Heaven's Haven, you say.' Dunston sensed a new possibility. 'Why do you think he went there?'

'Because, sir, besides being the first step on the path to redemption, a good flogging is also the most direct route to extracting any information that may contribute to the fulfilment of our divine mission. And while the child was being delivered, as I like to think of it, he was pleased to reveal the name, nature and location of his residence most promptly.'

'I see,' Dunston murmured, more to himself than to Dr Maximus Fullerton, MA, LL.D. He frowned in concentration, ignoring the headmaster who began to idly practice his swing. But then, the puckered brow cleared. Exhibiting more decisiveness as his investigation proceeded, Dunston quickly thanked the headmaster and took his leave, his next step already determined.

Chapter Thirty-Two: THE Wednesday

Dulcet's spirits waned throughout the day. At their zenith when the sun ushered in Wednesday – THE Wednesday – they were at their nadir by late evening. And for the same reason. It was Wednesday. THE Wednesday. And it was almost over.

'His sister wrote he'd be back today,' the maid wailed.

'Well Dulcie, that's as may be, but if he's gone, he's gone.'

Cook's counsel was greeted with a fresh outbreak of sobbing, prompting her to switch to the tried and trusted method of piling drudgery on top of toil as the best means of mending a broken heart. 'Right, young lady. That's enough. Up to the servants' hall with you and bring down the dirty dinner dishes,' Cook commanded.

Dulcet moved as though in a fog, forlornly climbing the stairs from the kitchen while Cook busied herself with a cauldron of leftover lamb stew.

'AAAARGH!'

The high-pitched shriek struck Cook like a physical blow – 'spooked me outta me bloomers', as she put it later – causing mutton and mixed veg to splatter vomit-like on the flagstones. 'Dulcet!' she cried out. Cook skirted the mess on the floor and pounded up the stairs to the servants' hall.

'Dulcie! What is it?'

Dulcet, her back to Cook, was kneeling over a still form slumped in the doorway like a sack of potatoes.

'H-heard this scratching at the d-door,' the maid sobbed. 'When I opened it, he just fell in and I saw it was… him. That's when I screamed.' She turned and looked up at Cook who could now see that the sack of potatoes was a young man, and, what's more, the young man was Isaac. It was Wednesday. THE Wednesday. And he'd returned.

Cook took a step closer and peered at the body… the DEAD body. For that's what it was. Dead as the rabbit hanging from the meat hook in the pantry. The ugly red gash across his forehead told its story – Isaac had been struck by a vicious blow with a heavy club, enough to finish anyone off – but he'd also been well and truly pummelled, his left eye shut tight and purpled like a ripe plum, his lips bloodied and split, his right cheek a bulge of bruised flesh.

Dulcet buried her head in Isaac's chest, murmuring his name over and over again like a never-ending prayer. Cook reached down and gently began pulling her to her feet.

'Come on, lovey. Nothin' you can do for him now. The lad's gone to his Maker. Leastways them what done this to him can't hurt him no more. Come on, Dulcie.'

Dulcet gripped Isaac's corpse more tightly. Strong though she might be in her moment of grief, she was no match for Cook, and with one mighty yank, Dulcet was hoisted off the body.

'Cook! Dulcet! Whatever's going on?' Georgina swept into the room, took in the scene with one glance, and, ignoring the embracing women, marched directly to the body.

'It's Isaac, miss,' Cook offered.

'I can see that, you silly thing.' Georgina bent down to examine the corpse.

'He's dead, miss,' Cook added.

Georgina said nothing, her sharp eye travelling speedily over the visible injuries. She felt for his heart inside his loose jacket. Nothing. No sign of a beat. Cook was right. He was dead. She moved her hand to the young man's face and tenderly drew back the lid of the undamaged eye. He groaned. She checked his heart again. Just the faintest of flutters, but a flutter nonetheless.

'He's alive.'

Dulcet was back at Isaac's side before Georgina's words were fully out of her mouth.

'Isaac, you're alive,' she breathed into his ear.

His good eye turned to her and for a moment the dimness was replaced by a flash of recognition and a flicker of the purest, sweetest, truest love ever borne by man for woman.

'Dulcet… I came back… for you,' he gasped through swollen lips and loosened teeth.

Dulcet's emotions seesawed – thrilled he was alive, devastated at the severity of his injuries; on top of the world at the words he'd just whispered, worried sick he'd die. About to speak, Georgina hushed her with a stern look.

'Dulcet, I know his face looks badly damaged but I'm not too worried about that,' she said, as confidently as she could given the real possibility of more serious injury to the lad's body. 'Properly tended, the cuts and bruises will mend. D'you understand me?' she asked the girl.

'Y-yes, miss.'

'Good. Now, get hot water and my medicine chest and take them straight to the front bedroom, Mr Dickens's room. Cover the bed with a sheet and wait for us to bring Isaac. He needs rest. That's the best cure for him, but first the blood has to be cleaned off and his wounds bandaged. Can you manage that?'

'Yes, miss,' Dulcet said and rushed off to carry out her mistress's instructions.

It was mid-morning, the day after THE Wednesday, when Isaac finally came to and muttered his first words: 'Y-you… saw me… naked? W-without me clothes on?' His face might be badly bruised and his ribs so battered breathing was a torture, yet what apparently concerned him most was the possibility that Dulcet – DULCET! – had seen him naked.

'Aye, naked as the day you was born.' She was enjoying herself immensely.

Isaac was cautiously feeling under the bedclothes to discover which bits of him were properly clothed and which bits embarrassingly exposed. All he could feel was a bandage around his ribs. Nothing else!

'Oh, don't worry Isaac. I was much too busy cleaning up all the blood and dressing your wounds to look at anything else. Well, 'cept for one tiny peek,' she added mischievously. 'Anyways, weren't much to see. You ain't got nothin' on Dad's young bull, and he's only six months old.' She laughed a happy laugh, but one that was also full of caring for her discomforted patient.

Despite his embarrassment, the exhausted young man soon drifted back to sleep. When next he woke, he repeated the under-the-bedclothes inspection, groaning as his fingers passed over his bruised ribs, but relieved to find he was clothed, his own night shirt, no less. He peeked at Dulcet. She beamed at him. He managed a small, puffy-lipped smile in return, and Dulcet mentally patted herself on the back, pleased she'd decided to dress him while he slept.

'Dulcet, I came back for you,' he said.

'I know,' she murmured tenderly. 'You must rest. Don't speak.'

'No, I must tell you. Have to be honest with you. When I left Gad's Hill Place, I was set on taking ship to Australia, like I told you when you was asleep.'

She nodded, unintentionally revealing the sleeping beauty had been sufficiently awake to follow his every word with avid interest.

'I couldn't take you with me,' he continued, her little slip going unnoticed. 'Wouldn't be right, young girl like you in that wild place. I had to go... but by myself. D'you understand, Dulcet?'

She squeezed his hand but said nothing, her heart bursting with love... and fear. What was he going to say next?

'But I wanted to see you... so bad,' he resumed after a pause, 'and now I know... I could *never* leave without you.'

'Oh, Isaac. I'd go to the ends of the earth as long as I was with you,' the maid whispered adoringly. 'First, though, we must get you well. You rest, my love. I'll be back.'

'No, wait. I want to tell you what happened. There was two of 'em,' he began, 'waiting for me at Dillywood Lane. I was thinking of you, Dulcet, not paying no mind to nothing. Then, afore I knew it, this giant ramper was blocking me path. Knew him right off, but that didn't do me no good 'cos this other pikey grabbed me from behind. Didn't have a prayer.'

Two men, at Dillywood Lane, one in front as decoy, one behind to do the business. Dulcet also knew the attackers – the two tramps who ambushed her. She was horror-stricken as she listened to his account of the brutal beating they'd dished out, her whole attention focused on Isaac... except for one tiny grey cell quietly repeating *the RING... the RING.*

One grey cell wasn't much, but its persistence and a major change in circumstances – Isaac dozing off again – conspired in its favour, and Dulcet's mind gradually seized on the fact that the two footpads, the pair who stole the master's ring, were still in the area. And if they were still around, perhaps the ring was as well. She must tell miss at once.

Chapter Thirty-Three: Heaven's Haven

Dunston exited the Adelphi Hotel where he'd lodged overnight, hailed a cab and set off along the Strand, arriving half an hour later at Bleeding Heart Yard. A pulsating heart might lie somewhere in the rubbish scattered everywhere by its inhabitants, a motley mix of Irish laborers, Jewish tailors and laundry-women from Lancashire and Yorkshire, but if so, Dunston was at a loss as to its whereabouts. Well, he shouldn't be surprised. After all, the Yard was in the same filthy, crime-ridden district in which his uncle had located the den of that loathsome child-corrupter, Fagin.

The only person in sight was a ragged urchin. He was about the same age as Dunston's guide at Field Lane School, but there all similarity ended. Yesterday's child still possessed a spark of life. Today's child was dying. His sunken eyes showed not a flicker of understanding; his twig-like arms and legs were no better than a scarecrow's; and he stank. How could this paltry piece of skin and bone give off such an overpowering stench?

In response to Dunston's query, the emaciated child pointed to a weathered sign bearing the name *Heaven's Haven*.

'You wants Burt an' Gert Mawgsby. They runs the 'ome,' he mumbled. 'I should know. Lived there all me life.'

A racking cough bent the withered stick-figure double. When he straightened, a trickle of blood was leaking from his mouth. So, Bleeding Heart Yard still boasted some blood. Dunston handed him a gold sovereign, a fortune to this hopeless consequence of society's neglect, but the empty eyes failed to register the magnitude of the gift.Perhaps later.

He knocked on the indicated door, and a flat voice bade him enter. Dunston's first thought as he stepped inside and saw two outwardly identical figures sitting at the kitchen table was, Tweedledum and Tweedledee in person. Dressed alike in dull grey smocks with woollen berets on their heads, both were pudgy in the body and plump in the arms with nothing to suggest which was male and which female. Which was Burt? And which Gert?

Whiskers. Yes, thought Dunston, whiskers would provide the necessary clue. And indeed the one to the left had some straggling grey strands about the jowls and the hint of a moustache. Must be Burt. Best be certain though. He stole a quick glance at the other who, much to his consternation, sported a similarly haired chin and upper lip.

Eventually, he hit upon a fail-safe strategy. Like Pythagoras bisecting an angle, he directed his gaze halfway between the pair and said: 'Mr Mawgsby, please forgive this intrusion. My name is Dunston Burnett and I would beg your indulgence for a brief interview.' He paused, confident he'd soon learn the identities of his two hosts.

'Aaaaye, we can spare him a little time, can't we, Mother?' came the reply from Tweedledee.

Ha! Got him. He's Mr Mawgsby, he's Burt.

'Right you are, Father,' Tweedledum said, her answer confirming she was Gert. 'Ain't interested in buyin' no childr'n, tho', are we Father?'

'Right you are, Mother. Got 'nuff of the little buggers as is,' Burt clarified

Dunston, aghast at the thought of children being bought and sold, stared at the Mawgsbys in astonishment.

'Um… no… er… no children to sell, I assure you. I'm here… that is… I'm looking for a child.'

'Ahhh, you wants to buy a young'un.'

'No, no… I fear you misunderstand me.'

'Well, if you ain't in the selling or buying business, why you here then? Best you take the weight off your feet, an' tell us what you do want.'

Dunston did as he was bid and sat on the three-legged, noticeably grimy and distinctly wobbly stool, the only option presenting itself. 'Thank you.

You see, I'm trying to trace a child I believe had the... er... good fortune to be under your... excellent care,' he explained.

'Well, that ain't so easy,' Gert said. 'Keeping track of all the little squeakers we got now is hard 'nuff, never mind all them what've passed on.'

'Yes, I... um... quite understand,' Dunston said, 'but you may recall *this* child because Miss Ellen Ternan, the... er... famous London actress, arranged for him to enter your... establishment.'

'Never heard of her, have we, Father?'

'Right you are, Mother.'

Silence. Dunston considered how much he should reveal regarding the child's parentage. This was his last hope. Best do whatever was required.

'Yes, well, it's just possible that Mr Dickens,' he gulped, 'Mr Charles Dickens, the novelist, made the arrangements.'

'Dickens, you say.' Burt's brow puckered in thought. 'Noooo, don't ring no bells with me.'

'I see.'

Stumped, Dunston let his eyes wander around the kitchen. What a pigsty. He saw a dresser crammed with crockery and cooking pots, all of doubtful cleanliness; a sink brim-full with dirty platters and mugs; and an iron cauldron, its contents more like pig's swill than gruel. Yes, pigsty was the right word for this place. His gaze came back to Burt and Gert. They sat so stolidly and comfortably. What a pair.

Wait a minute. What was that on the dresser? There, beneath a stack of greasy plates was a ledger, similar to the ones he'd used for so many years as a bookkeeper. Burt and Gert's heads swivelled towards the dresser, their gazes fastening on what had caught his eye.

'Ha!' Dunston exclaimed. 'Records. For the beadle, I imagine.'

'Nah. Can't read nor write our names, let alone keep records,' Burt retorted indignantly.

'Perhaps not. But someone could, because *that*,' Dunston pointed towards the dresser, 'is a register. And, with your permission, I'll take a look.'

Burt and Gert exchanged glances, but said nothing.

Dunston removed the ledger and opened it. The records, organised by year, listed arrivals (a steady stream), departures (a few), and deaths (a lot). He flicked through to 1850. Eleven entries. He was not sure what he hoped to find. Neither Miss Ternan nor Uncle Charles would leave any written record to link them to the child. So what clue could he hope to discover? He ran his finger down the page. Just as he feared, no sign of a Dickens or a Ternan. He tried again, and suddenly, right there, the fifth entry stopped him dead – *William Tringham, admitted July 28, 1850, parents unknown.*

William! The name mentioned by Clatterbuck. And that wasn't all. No, the clincher was the child's surname – Tringham. That was the name, according to Aunt Catherine, that Uncle used to lease Ellen Ternan's house in Peckham. No one but Uncle could have come up with that combination. Dunston had found the missing child. He looked at the Mawgsbys. They stared back, inscrutable as a pair of Sphinxes uprooted from the Giza Desert and deposited in this English fleapit.

'I've found the child. William Tringham,' he announced, his finger stabbing the entry.

'Ahhh, *him's* the one you mean, is it?' Burt said, apparently much surprised. 'Well, long time ago. Must've slipped me memory. William, you say. We always called him Billy.'

'Billy or William, doesn't matter which, you found out he was Charles Dickens's son, didn't you?' Dunston challenged.

'Not right off,' Gert said guardedly. 'He was brought here from France by a midwife. Just a few days old, he was. Must've been taken from the womb and put straight on the first ship to England. We wouldn't've known the child's mother was Ellen Ternan if that silly bitch of a midwife hadn't let it slip, and even then we didn't know who Ellen Ternan was, did we, Father?'

'Right you are, Mother. Wasn't until some years later. We was in The Laughin' Leprechaun and Paddy – he's the landlord – was talking about this writer bloke, Dickens, and how he was coming to speak at Field Lane School jus' up the road. Turns out, Paddy's wife used to be cook for some actress lady, and this Dickens visited her regular. Stayed overnight, if you get me drift. And who was the fancy woman? None other than our Miss Ellen Ternan. Am I right, Mother?'

'Right you are, Father,' Gert took over. 'Our Billy was their little bastard. Can yer believe it?' For the first time, the sphinxes came to life, two sets of eyebrows shooting up, eyes widening. 'Not a good-for-nothin' nobody,' she continued, 'but an acorn fallen from a very grand oak tree.'

'Did you tell Billy?'

'Aye, when we got back from the pub,' Burt said. 'He was pleased as Punch. Couldn't stop yapping 'bout his big-name father, and how he'd written all them stories he was reading.'

'Billy could read?' a surprised Dunston asked.

'Oh aye,' Gert replied. 'Luke Mallick teached him. Smartest lad we ever had in Heaven's Haven, Luke was. He could read an' write, but, best of all, he could draw. Why, he painted the sign for The Leprechaun, and he done ours. Got his own painting business now, opposite side of the Yard.'

'I see,' Dunston said. He was only half listening, his mind recalling his uncle's letter to Ellen and that odd reference to a 'blackmail plot'. Blackmail! So *that* was their game.

'You wretches,' he exclaimed angrily, 'you were going to blackmail Unc—, I mean, Mr Dickens.'

'Whoa, there,' Burt said. 'Blackmail… now that's a nasty word, not one we likes to hear, and not what we had in mind. We was thinking this Dickens might like to *share* some of his earnings from his writings so we could care better for his little'un.'

'Bah! Doesn't matter how you whitewash it. It's quite clear what you were up to, and Billy found out, didn't he?'

'Aye, little tyke got wind of it,' Burt acknowledged dejectedly. 'Had a real fit. Mad as a ferret in a sack, he was. Then, before we could get to Dickens, Billy went to Field Lane School and warned him 'bout our little… sharing idea. Don't know what Dickens said to him, Billy never told us, an' he never let us see his backside neither, tho' it was plain as day he'd been thrashed good an' proper for his trouble. Lad was changed after that, an' I don't mean just 'cos of the beating, tho that was bad 'nuff.

'Right you are, Father. It was like his spirit was broke. He just moped 'round the place. Still, don't matter now, I s'ppose,' she concluded.

'Why not?'

'Well, he's dead.'

'What? He's dead?' Dunston screeched.

'Aye,' Burt confirmed. 'A few weeks later, it was. He was always sickly. Pale, skinny little feller. Weak constitushun, if you ask me.'

'I can't believe it,' Dunston moaned.

'Well, we wrote to that Miss Ellen Ternan, leastways Luke actually done the writing, but we told her,' Burt said huffily.

'And you can check the ledger if you don't believe us,' Gert added just as huffily.

Dunston quickly leafed through to 1860. If the lad was ten when he visited the school as Uncle Charles had said in his letter, this was the year when the death would be recorded. He prayed the ledger was innocent of any such notation. But there it was: *William Tringham, died, October 3, 1860, cause unknown.*

Chapter Thirty-Four: A Discovery

Georgina's failure to complete the household accounts on Tuesday, her usual end-of-month practice, was a measure of how much that vile Mr Wurmsley had upset her. Where did he get the nerve to make such a preposterous proposal to her? And Dunston. Where was he all week? She saw him last on Sunday, but hadn't heard from him since and here it was Friday afternoon. Georgina was miffed he'd deserted her, and, strange to say, she missed his presence.

Ruby, the scullery maid at Gad's Hill Place and stand-in for Dulcet while she tended to Isaac, burst into the drawing room.

'Oops, sorry miss, forgot to knock again. Beg pardon.'

'Yes, Ruby. What is it?'

'Mr Burnett, miss.' She ushered the gentleman in.

'Dunston, where have you been? I haven't seen you all week,' Georgina gently scolded him. 'Come, sit here on the sofa and tell me what's been keeping you so busy you've been unable to spare any time for me.' Was she flirting?

'Forgive me. I was… I mean… I…'

'Dunston,' she said in her school-teacher voice, 'when my nieces and nephews had something to tell me I always encouraged them to do so in an orderly manner. So, why don't you start with your visit to Mr Clatterbuck on Monday, and then proceed through the week until you arrive at today?'

'Yes, the beginning… let me see.' Dunston told her how he learned the name of his uncle's child – William – from Clatterbuck, skipped over the purple passages in Charles's letters to Ellen, and then recounted events at

165

Field Lane School and Heaven's Haven, ending with the ten-year old's death.

Georgina almost smiled, pleased with Dunston's news, more pleased perhaps than she should have been at the death of a young boy. Silently upbraiding herself, she set aside her sense of relief and gratitude, and returned her attention to Dunston.

'...Miss Ternan has behaved despicably,' he was saying. 'Can you believe she dispatched the baby to England the very day it was born? A death sentence, if you ask me. Exactly what it turned out to be. What's more she continued collecting payments for the boy *after* he died, lived off the son she'd murdered. Uncle Charles didn't even know he was dead.'

'Ellen Ternan has indeed behaved despicably, Dunston, but she's paid in full measure for her sins. And now, you've found out that the issue of Charles's sinful union with that vile woman has also passed into God's care. Charles's reputation is *safe* from both quarters, and that's *all* that matters. Exceedingly well done, Dunston.'

This time she did smile. Things were falling into place rather nicely. The novelist's funeral had proceeded as majestically as she had hoped, and countless tributes had already poured in honouring him exactly as he deserved. She was still nervous about the deadline, set for one month after Charles's passing and now only eight days away, when Frank would inform the police of the real cause of his death. That could well set off a frenzy of lurid accounts in the newspapers about Charles's dalliance with the dead actress. But with Lavelle already behind bars, the authorities simply had to change the charge from burglary to murder and with luck, any 'unpleasantness' in the press would be short-lived.

Dunston, though, did not appear to share her satisfaction with the outcome. Nor, she observed, had he reacted in his usual fashion to her praise – a blushing, sweaty confusion. In fact, to her eye, he looked distinctly glum. What was troubling him? Was he upset about the death of Charles's bastard? A child he didn't even know? Or was it something else? What a strange man. I'll never understand him.

Still, I'm not going to spend time mollycoddling him out of his sour mood. I have my own news to share. 'Now, let me bring you up to date on events here at Gad's Hill Place. I'm sad to say, Dunston, that Isaac, my stable-boy, was beaten almost to death by those two tramps who ambushed Dulcet.'

'What? Another attack? By the same two men?'

'I fear so.'

'Miss Georgina, I'm at your disposal to… to hunt down these villains,' Dunston offered earnestly.

'That won't be necessary,' Georgina said quickly, 'I've informed Inspector Line, such an impressive man, and he's already instructed his men in Kent to keep a look-out for the pair.'

'I see, Inspector Line, yes, such an impressive man,' Dunston said gloomily. But then, more positively, 'Well, I hope the police capture them before they hurt anyone else. And since your stable-boy is out of commission, allow me to have Nick drive for you and help with the horses until your lad is recovered.'

'That's so thoughtful of you. Nick's help would be most welcome.' Georgina was genuinely touched. 'But that's not all that happened.' She proceeded to tell him about Wurmsley's proposal and the evidence he had concerning Charles's child.

'Disgraceful!' Dunston exclaimed. 'I had no idea. Never liked the man but this behaviour is… scandalous. Fellow deserves a good thrashing. We must act at once. I am, of course, at your service and will do everything—'

'Thank you,' she said hastily. 'Most kind of you, but Frank Beard is handling this matter for me. I have great confidence in him and don't want to muddy the waters by involving you… much as I value and appreciate your offer, of course.'

'Frank Beard… yes, excellent choice,' he muttered, looking even more dejected.

'Good, I'm glad you approve because your support is very important to me.' Georgina smiled again, pleased that Dunston had approved of the way she'd dealt with both the tramps and Wurmsley.

'Well, since *my* services are obviously not needed, Miss Georgina, perhaps it's best I take my leave,' he said, a little reproachfully. 'Nick will be here tomorrow morning.'

Dunston rose to his full five feet two and bade her a cool good-day. Georgina was taken aback. What was the matter with the silly man?

A crestfallen Dunston returned to Woods View House. Georgina had placed her trust in the *impressive* Inspector Line to deal with the tramps and in the *confidence-instilling* Frank Beard to handle Wurmsley. Dunston had been made brutally aware he was a distant third on the totem pole. He was thoroughly upset with her.

But it wasn't only Georgina. In truth, he'd been despondent ever since his return from Heaven's Haven. And very annoyed with himself. He'd jumped too easily to the conclusion that the illegitimate child, grown to manhood, was the second burglar, Uncle's poisoner and Ellen's murderer. Everything had seemed to fit. The lad, new to reading, was enthralled by Uriah Heep, Mr Pickwick, the Artful Dodger, and a host of other fascinating characters. So imagine his delight, when he learned that their creator was his *father*. And imagine his dismay when he was cruelly rebuffed by his idol at Field Lane School.

Hero-worship changed to cold hatred, and hatred was the fertile soil from which sprang the thorns and prickles of revenge. The lad bided his time, eventually making his way to Gad's Hill Place. There, fortune favoured him. He saw Lavelle break into the house with the help of one of Dryker's gang, and then re-emerge and disappear into the night.

The young man seized his chance, slipped into the study through the still open window and poisoned Uncle's tonic. That was when he saw the drawer, found the letters, learned that Ellen Ternan was his mother, and resolved to see her. Whether his intention was reconciliation or blackmail, the end-result was the fatal bludgeoning of Ellen.

Yes, it had all seemed so clear… until he saw that entry in the Mawgsby's ledger and learned the lad never reached manhood and never committed any of the deeds attributed to him by Dunston. He'd been so stupid. How could he, a retired bookkeeper, have possibly imagined himself a real-life Detective Datchery? He should have known better.

Dunston moped the rest of Friday and all day Saturday, but on Sunday, when he was dressing for the day, buttoning his waistcoat to be exact, he was suddenly transformed. He hurried through breakfast and rushed out of the dining room. At least, he displayed all the bustle of rushing but not the speed, his gait, a peculiar combination of scuttling crab and waddling duck, allowed at best an awkward trot.

'Nick!' he yelled as soon as he'd made his way to the backyard.

'Ain't here, mister,' a young boy said.

'What? Where is he?'

'Gad's Hill Place.'

'Ah, yes, helping out Miss Georgina, now I remember. Never mind. Harness the phaeton carriage at once, boy!'

'Ain't here neither.'

'Why not?'

'Gad's Hill Place... with Nick.'

'Ah, quite so.' Dunston paused and regarded the boy for the first time. 'Who are you?'

'Walter, boot-boy,' the lad said solemnly.

Yes, Dunston vaguely remembered Nick telling him he'd taken on a young lad from the workhouse. This must be he. Boy couldn't be more than seven or eight. Seemed willing enough, though. Much more alert than the poor soul he'd encountered at Heaven's Haven. This lad was bright-eyed, with a firmness to his flesh that suggested Cook had been generous with his meals, and Nick ditto with his chores. Probably been using the boy in the stables. Indeed, there was a ripe, dung-smell about the child, pungent but not unpleasant.

'Yes, Walter... quite. Now listen. It's most urgent that I go at once to Gad's Hill Place. D'you understand?'

'Moccles!'

'Mockels? What're mockels?'

'Moccles, the carter, mister. He'll have a carriage for yer, or my name ain't Walter Walterson.'

'Walter Walterson?'

169

'That's me.'

'Well, Walter Walterson, off you go. Half a sovereign if you're back with the carr—' Dunston didn't manage to finish his sentence, Walter Walterson was already on his way.

True to his word, the lad was soon back, proudly sitting alongside the driver of one of Mr Moccles somewhat battered, but still serviceable, vehicles, and true to his word, Dunston provided the promised reward to the grinning child. Well worth it, he thought, given the discovery he'd made.

And what a discovery it was. He felt in the waistcoat pocket of his dark grey three-piece. Yes, it was still there, safe and sound. Why ever didn't he examine it when he first saw it? Had he done so, he could have told Miss Georgina during Friday's depressing visit. Still, better late than never, and maybe his find would nudge him a little higher up the totem pole. Yes, he must talk to Miss Georgina. But first, Nick.

Chapter Thirty-Five: Georgina's Deduction

Ten minutes later, Ruby opened the door at Gad's Hill Place in response to Dunston's knocking, and showed him into the drawing room. 'I'll tell miss you're here, sir.'

'Yes, well actually, I...' Ruby looked at him expectantly. 'I'd like to see Nick first.'

'Very well, sir. I'll fetch him for you.'

She set off to find Nick, but not before popping out to the back garden where her mistress was taking advantage of the sunshine to pick a few geraniums, Charles's favourite, for her bedroom. The young girl had caught on to the interest Roly-poly, as she called Dunston, had in her mistress – and perhaps, hers in him – and was not for a minute going to leave her in ignorance of his arrival.

Still dressed from head to foot in black, Georgina smiled as her stand-in maid imparted her news. 'Thank you, Ruby. You did right. Except Nick's not here. He's in Shropshire.'

'Oh, yes. Sorry, miss. Forgot.'

'Never mind. Tell Mr Burnett I shall be along presently.'

'Presently' arrived sooner than she'd intended, and in no time at all she found herself in the drawing room, wondering whether Dunston really had business with Nick or was using that as an excuse to visit her.

'Miss Georgina, I've been remiss,' Dunston began before she was hardly in the room, his tone plaintive, his look that of a puppy tossed outside in the pouring rain. '*Very* remiss.'

'So I gather. Perhaps you'd better tell me in what way,' she said in a calming manner.

'I should have brought it before. Could have told you last Friday if only I'd examined it.' As he spoke, he drew something from his waistcoat pocket and handed it to Georgina.

She inspected the object with mild interest, head bent, then, with a sharp intake of breath, she looked up, eyes disbelieving, and exploded into a loud HURRAH! She pirouetted with the stiff grace of an arthritic prima ballerina and bestowed a kiss, just a peck really, on the cheek of her much surprised visitor.

'Oh, Dunston, I'm so happy. How can I ever thank you?' She looked again at the gold band and the eleven letters engraved on the inside: C M K W F A S H A E W.

'It's Uncle's, isn't it?' Dunston cried triumphantly.

'It is indeed.'

'I knew it. Soon as I saw the letters. Aunt Catherine said Uncle Charles sent the ring to the jeweller every time a new child came along. The letters are the children's first initials, aren't they? C for Charles, his first-born, all the way to E for Edward, his tenth.'

'Yes, you're right, one letter for each of the ten children he had with my sister.'

'The eleventh letter, that last W, threw me for a moment, but then I realised it stood for… *William*, Uncle's child with Miss Ternan,' Dunston declared.

'Yes, yes. William, I expect,' Georgina muttered. She grimaced as she found herself suddenly thrust back into the unpleasantness of Charles's infidelity.

'Adding that W was Uncle's first step in acknowledging his illegitimate child,' Dunston continued apace. 'That W on his Progeny Ring as he called it, was there for his eyes only, but once he'd started down the path of admitting paternity, he couldn't stop. He planned to go further in the final chapter of the Drood mystery by hinting that he'd abandoned William as a baby, admittedly through the words of Detective Datchery, but once published, the confession would be in the public domain, there for anyone to decipher.'

'Enough of such upsetting thoughts,' Georgina said. 'Please don't spoil this wonderful moment. This ring was supposed to be on Charles's finger when he was buried but those horrid tramps stole it and I thought I'd never see it again. I was sure it was lost forever. Now it's here. Tell me how you managed this extraordinary feat. Where did you find it? Let's sit, and then you can tell me everything.'

Georgina gestured Dunston toward one of the cane-bottomed easy chairs and seated herself on the sofa. Dunston took the proffered seat and related how he'd found Nick with the ring, apologising again and again for not examining it there and then, until Georgina raised her hand to stem the torrent of sorrys.

'And how did Nick come by it?' she asked.

'He said his mother gave it to him to pawn for her, but I didn't believe him. That's why I came today to talk to him and get to the bottom of this.'

'I'm afraid that's not possible,' she told him. 'Nick's taking my stallion to Mr Mason's stables in Shropshire to breed with one of his young mares. Won't be back until Saturday afternoon. Now, back to the ring, why didn't you believe Nick? You couldn't have known it was your uncle's ring at the time, so what made you question his explanation?'

'He hadn't been to see his mother for a month,' Dunston replied, 'so the ring turning up when it did seemed very odd. Apart from accompanying me to London for the funeral, the only place he'd been was Peckham.'

'Peckham? Whatever for?'

'I sent him to Windsor Lodge last Monday to—' He stopped in mid flow, evidently remembering just in time that Georgina didn't know about Charles's love letters with their purple passages. 'To collect some... er... items from the maid.'

'What maid?'

'Miss Ternan's. Madge or Midge or something like that, the one who found the body. Apparently, she came back from her day off to find her mistress dead in the parlour.'

'And how, may I ask, are you so knowledgeable about events at Windsor Lodge?'

'Nick told me on his return from Peckham.'

'And when did you find him with the ring?'

'The very next day.'

'I see,' she said thoughtfully. 'Let me make sure I have this right. Miss Ternan is murdered in Windsor Lodge. Nick is sent there on an errand. And when he comes back, you find him with a gold band that turns out to be Charles's signet ring.'

Her pensive expression slowly disappeared, replaced by a below-the-surface tenseness, a building excitement. She knew who killed the actress! Truth be told, she wasn't much interested in avenging the actress's murder, but she was nonetheless rather proud that she'd just had her own Dunston-like flash of inspiration. He'd come up with the twice-robbed drawer and the Charles-William, father-son link. Well, now it was her turn to surprise him.

'Dunston, listen. The ring was taken by the tramps when they attacked Dulcet. It next turns up in Nick's possession at your house *immediately after his visit to Windsor Lodge.* D'you see?' She looked at him and, although he nodded, it was clear he had no idea what she was driving at.

'For goodness' sake, Dunston. *Those two ruffians killed Ellen,*' an exasperated Georgina exclaimed. 'She interrupted them during an attempted burglary, one of them killed her, and dropped the ring in the process. The maid must have picked it up when she discovered the body, otherwise the police would have found it. Then I expect she gave it to Nick... probably to pawn for her. Yes, that's it. He was pawning it for the maid, not his mother.'

He regarded her doubtfully. 'Yes, possibly. Suppose the maid could have stumbled across it and passed it to Nick as you say. That is, if those two fellows really did commit the murder.'

'Of course they did,' she asserted confidently.

Dunston looked unconvinced. 'The ring does appear to link the tramps to the two crimes, but... A possibility, I grant you,' he said in a tone that conveyed the exact opposite, 'but it raises several questions in my mind.'

'Such as?' Georgina demanded sharply. She was annoyed her deduction wasn't being greeted with the enthusiasm it deserved.

'Well, for one thing, why should the two footpads who attacked Dulcet here in Kent suddenly show up in Surrey and burgle Windsor Lodge?' he asked reasonably.

'I don't know,' she snapped. 'Perhaps, they found out Ellen was Charles's… concubine and reckoned she'd have jewels ripe for the picking.'

'Yes, but—'

'But what?' The man could be so infuriating sometimes, she fumed.

'Well, they didn't actually take anything,' he pointed out, obviously determined to keep everything bookkeepingly straight.

'Of course not. Because Ellen interrupted them. That's why they had to *murder her,*' she grated. Then, in a softer but still accusing tone, she added, 'Dunston, you're being obtuse.'

'Beg your pardon,' he said, 'I was simply trying to eliminate any weaknesses or flaws in your argument.'

'Weaknesses? Flaws? What *do* you mean?'

'Forgive me. Yes, the tramps, very possible… I suppose,' he replied and lapsed into silence.

And just as well. Georgina's patience had run out. She was more annoyed with him than she cared to admit. What a maddening man. At the same time, she couldn't forget his extraordinary service in returning the ring. And, he had a right to probe for shortcomings in her theory, she grudgingly conceded. But there were none. She was certain, as unyielding in her conviction as any Elder of the Kirk in his. The tramps were the guilty party.

Keen to prove her point, ever practical Georgina quickly arrived at a sure way of bringing Dunston on board. 'Dunston, thank you *so* much for your very perceptive questions,' she began, 'so helpful and so like the questions that would spring to Inspector Line's mind.'

Dunston perked up at this. She knew he had tremendous respect for the inspector and was, as she'd expected, pleased by the comparison.

'And speaking of the inspector, I feel we should let him know of your miraculous recovery of the ring. We can then leave it to *him* to decide what it means and how best to proceed. What do you think of this course of action?' she asked politely.

Dunston was neatly trapped. He could hardly refuse to involve the detective. He signalled his agreement, and in short order yet another telegram was dispatched to the man Georgina now considered her personal policeman.

The reply was faster than even she had expected. Line's assessment of the ring's return aligned more closely with hers than Dunston's, and he informed her he would be in Higham on the morrow. His men in Kent had been on the lookout for the two vagabonds ever since he'd received her telegram informing him about the attack on Isaac. Now that there was a link to Miss Ternan's murder, he'd decided to come down and take charge of the search himself.

Chapter Thirty-Six: Dinner at The Athenaeum

The Earl of Toxington waved his arm at the head waiter who glided to his side like a moth drawn to a candle's flame. It was dinner hour on Sunday at the Athenaeum and the earl and his companion were seated at a discretely positioned corner table in The Picture Room, so called because of the many portraits of members hung around the walls. From there, the dusty faces stared down glumly on the best the club's kitchen had to offer, although, truth be told, the Athenaeum was not noted for its culinary achievements.

Lord Toxington glanced at his fob watch. Almost five o'clock. 'Show my guest in as soon as he arrives,' he instructed the waiter.

'As you please, your lordship.'

The two men did not have long to wait. On the hour, Mr Wurmsley was escorted to their table. There was no mistaking his delight as he entered. To be invited to the Athenaeum for dinner by one of its wealthiest members was an honour of the first order. The smile squirming across his face was only slightly diminished when he realised he and the earl would not be dining alone. What was Frank Beard doing here? Still, dinner at the Athenaeum was dinner at the Athenaeum, and he took his seat at the table with a brief nod to Beard and a transparently fawning bow to the earl.

'Ah! Here you are, Wurmsley. Right on time. Excellent,' the earl said in good humour. 'Expect you know Beard.'

'Dr Beard, a great pleasure to see you.' Wurmsley, outwardly polite, was wondering why on earth Beard had been invited.

'Evening,' Frank replied in a neutral tone.

'And an even greater pleasure, Lord Toxington, to receive your gracious invitation.'

'Not at all,' the earl said expansively. 'As chair of the membership committee, I'm aware that your nomination for the club was turned down again, so thought a spot of dinner might cheer you up. Of course, the food is decidedly average. Take tonight.' He studied the hand-written menu. 'Now, the mock turtle soup is usually edible and the Beef Wellington's palatable if not as good as in the Iron Duke's day. And what do you say to a bottle or two of burgundy? Club has a wine cellar, I'll concede that. Only reason I keep up my membership. Ha! Ha!'

Their orders, as prescribed by the earl, were duly conveyed to the waiter.

The Athenaeum was often described as the nerve centre of the empire, more important than the monarchy or parliament in driving Britain's imperial ambitions. Military targets were routinely decided during dinner; boundaries of distant colonies were redrawn over port; a whispered exchange in the lobby and huge sums were withdrawn from one of the world's great banks causing its immediate collapse. Yes, the Athenaeum was the place where far-reaching plans were launched as if by accident. And it was the place where the hopes of mere mortals could be shattered by a single word in the right ear.

The three diners were supping their soup when Frank, as though prompted by the earl, dropped the first conversational bombshell.

'By the by, your lordship, did I tell you about the letters that were stolen from Dickens's desk?' he asked casually. 'About a week before he passed.'

'No, you didn't,' the earl replied. 'Nothing important, I hope.'

'Dickens couldn't remember what was in most of them, but one, he said, dealt with such a sensitive matter he could recall every word. Even remembered the date – third of May, 1850.'

Wurmsley's heart skipped a beat, his spoon stopped midway between bowl and mouth, and mock turtle soup spilled messily on to the tablecloth. May third, 1850, the date on the envelope in his breast pocket.

'And what did it say?' the earl inquired.

Wurmsley was all ears. He was about to learn the contents of the missing letter. Something about Ellen Ternan and the arrangements for the child, for sure.

'From Clatterbuck that prattling lawyer of his,' Frank replied.

Knew it! exulted Wurmsley, inwardly bubbling with anticipation like Scotch broth simmering beneath the stockpot's lid.

'All about that big bust-up with his publishers, Chapman and Hall.'

'What? Can't be!' Wurmsley exclaimed, too flabbergasted to keep his silence.

'Why d'you say that?' Frank leaned across the table. 'What do you know about this? Do you have the letter?'

'No... just the envelope,' Wurmsley blurted out, the words escaping before he could stop them.

Two pairs of eyes fixed on Wurmsley with such intensity he could feel them burning holes through his skull. A full minute passed before the earl broke the silence.

'What a remarkable coincidence,' he observed dryly. 'Here we are casually talking about a letter stolen from Dickens's study and here you are in possession of that very letter's envelope. Perhaps, you'd care to explain this odd circumstance.'

Wurmsley, a pale, shaken semblance of the man who'd strode into The Picture Room relishing the prospect of an intimate dinner with the all-powerful Earl of Toxington, struggled to gather his wits. Deciding the only option was to tell the truth, he related how he came by the envelope at Windsor Lodge and how the maid swore it was empty when she found it beside her murdered mistress.

His two interlocutors exchanged glances. The earl nodded to Frank, as if to say follow my lead. 'My, my. At Ellen Ternan's you say. Well, Sir Edmund will be most interested.'

On cue, Frank chimed in, 'Sir Edmund, your lordship?'

'Yes, Sir Edmund Henderson, my good friend the Police Commissioner,' Toxington clarified. 'Be most upset if he learns evidence was removed from the scene of a crime. Fine man, Sir Edmund, but has some odd ideas. Thinks the law should apply to the upper classes just like it applies to any common fellow. Quite extraordinary. But there you are, that's modern thinking for you. Still, doesn't bode well for you, Wurmsley.'

'Oh, dear, I had no idea. I just thought—'

'Well, what you thought is of little consequence, old chap,' the earl said with a touch of sympathy in his voice. He tapped Wurmsley on his arm and beckoned him closer. 'Here's what I'd do. Best say you intended to hand the envelope over to the police but then forgot all about it. If you like, you can give it to me and I'll make sure it gets to Sir Edmund. There, what do you think of that?'

Frank murmured his agreement, and Wurmsley, pathetically grateful, jumped at the proffered solution.

'Yes, thank you so much.' He handed over the envelope with its unpleasant stains, an envelope now destined not for Sir Edmund's hand but the nearest fire, the surest way of squashing any threat of blackmail.

'Well, that's settled then,' the earl said jovially. 'You can of course rely on us not to mention this conversation. Mum's the word.'

His lordship winked broadly at Wurmsley, who had little idea that he'd just experienced the standard Athenaeum scheme-scuttling ploy at its efficient best. A little conversation, a passable soup, a fine bottle of wine, and a significant part of Wurmsley's plan had been scotched, crushed to dust beneath the aristocrat's gouty foot.

A second bottle of Beaune Greves Premier Cru, the earl's favourite, was presented, tasted and served, and the diners moved on to the Beef Wellington. Halfway through the main course, Frank dropped his second bombshell.

'I fear poor Georgina Hogarth is not too well,' he informed the earl. 'Seems she received a marriage proposal from a most undesirable quarter.'

Wurmsley froze, a soggy mouthful of beef and pastry sliding from his fork and depositing itself in a mound of over-cooked cabbage.

'I say, you alright?' Frank asked solicitously.

Wurmsley stared at him blankly before recovering enough to reply, 'Ye-es, quite alright. Um… touch of indigestion.'

'Told you the food wasn't up to much,' the earl said with a sad smile. 'Now, where were we? Ah, yes, Miss Hogarth. Bit old for a marriage proposal, if you ask me,' he commented, more matter-of-factly than unkindly. 'Woman was born to be a spinster.'

'Had the same thought myself,' Frank said, 'so I probed a little deeper. Seems she isn't sure herself if it really was a proposal. May just have been a misunderstanding. And it's this uncertainty that's really upsetting her.'

'Humph! Have to sort this out,' the earl declared belligerently. 'Who is this shameful fellow?'

'Afraid she didn't, or rather wouldn't, say.' Frank looked hard at Wurmsley.

'Well, whoever he is, the blackguard should clear this up immediately,' Toxington said, and took his turn to glare at the unfortunate Wurmsley.

'Quite right, your lordship,' Frank concurred. 'We must do everything possible to help Miss Hogarth. What d'you say, Wurmsley? Can we count on you to do your bit?'

His bit may not have been defined, but the target of the two intense perusals was under no illusion whatsoever that his marriage proposal must be withdrawn, or he'd be the mortal enemy of his dinner companions for the rest of his days.

'Coming back to your nomination,' his lordship remarked a little later over desert – Norfolk treacle tart, also a favourite of the earl. 'As I said, that's why we invited you to dinner tonight. Not just to cheer you up,' he informed the decidedly uncheerful Wurmsley, 'but to see if we can move the process forward.' Wurmsley perked up at this turn in the conversation. 'Of course, I have to sort out the little problem of the envelope and devote some time to making sure Miss Hogarth's unfortunate situation is satisfactorily resolved, so I won't be able to attend to your membership just yet, but I will take it up in due course… assuming, that is, the other matters are proceeding satisfactorily.'

And that was all it took. The blackmailer cum suitor had been turned into a puppet on the Earl of Toxington's string. Will his lordship incinerate the envelope? Most certainly. Will Wurmsley withdraw his marriage proposal? Absolutely. Will he become a member of the Athenaeum Club? Not in this lifetime.

.

Chapter Thirty-Seven: Inspector Line in Action

Inspector Line crouched behind an outcrop of rock high on the west-facing side of Bluebell Hill, half a mile south of Rochester. He swatted at a cloud of bothersome summer gnats as he cast a critical eye over the terrain around a shack nestled at the foot of the hill. Sheltered on three sides by old oak trees, the shack – more like a lean-to, its slanting roof propped up against a tree – was the hideout chosen by the pair of footpads who'd attacked Dulcet and then ambushed Isaac. At least, that was what Ackworth, the local constable, had informed him on his arrival at the city's railway station early Monday afternoon.

Ackworth, in dark blue uniform, black varnished belt holding truncheon, lamp and whistle, squatted beside his superior officer, his eyes locked on the lean-to. A tall man with the fair skin and blue eyes of his Norse ancestors, Ackworth's intelligence and strength, sadly missing in so many of Line's London subordinates, had already caught the inspector's eye.

'How did you find them?' Line asked.

'Lavelle, sir,' the young constable replied. 'A few days in jail and he finally remembered that it was Stingo Pete, the scrawny fellow who scouts houses for the Dryker gang, who helped him break into Gad's Hill Place. When we picked Pete up, he told us that the two pikeys who attacked the maid are fellow gang members, sir.'

'And?'

'Gave us a description. One's a big lump of a fellow. They call him Nobbler.

183

The other's young, slender, name of Snatcher. Been teamed up ever since they were together in an orphanage in Bleeding Heart Yard. Seems Pete had some business with them, but, whatever that was, he had no trouble blowing the whistle on them.'

'That's honour among thieves for you. Works to our advantage every time.'

'Yes, sir. Then, we had a bit of luck. Dawkins spotted a man who looked like Snatcher heading for the shack late last night. He figured the big one, Nobbler, was inside. He kept watch all night, then Braxton,' Ackworth gestured to his colleague, 'took over this morning, but to be honest, they could have slipped away under cover of darkness. Haven't seen hide nor hair of them today so it's hard to say if they're still there or not.'

'You did well,' Line commended.

Their position was well chosen, allowing them a clear view all the way down the slope to the shack. But by the same token, it made approaching the lean-to without being detected almost impossible. Need more than the three policemen on hand, Line concluded.

'Where's Dawkins now?' he asked.

'Sent him home to catch up on his sleep but Braxton can pick him up from his cottage, it's just outside Strood, if he's needed.'

'Fine. And what about a couple of hounds?'

'Moccles, sir.'

'What?'

'Local carter, sir. Got two of the best trackers in the county.'

'Good. That'll give us four men, two dogs and the handler. Should be enough. It's four o'clock now. We'll move in at six, well before it gets dark. I doubt they'll make a move in broad daylight, assuming they're still inside. Get cracking.'

'Yes, sir.'

The inspector, still plagued by the pesky gnats, watched the shack from the cover of the rocky outcrop. No sign of movement. An hour dragged by and Braxton returned with Dawkins but no dogs.

'On their way, sir. Moccles says he'll get 'em here soon as he can,' Braxton informed Line.

The minute hand on Line's fob watch completed another rotation. Six o'clock and still no dogs. It was early July so he could count on another three hours of reasonable daylight, but he was reluctant to delay much longer. They'd have to make do without the hounds. With the River Medway a quarter of a mile or so away serving as a natural barrier behind the shack, he sent Braxton to the left and Dawkins to the right with instructions to stay out of sight. He and Ackworth would approach from the front.

He watched as Braxton and Dawkins took up their positions on the edge of the woods either side of the shack. The trees provided some cover but at the same time limited their view. Line waited until both men signalled they were ready, and then nodded to Ackworth. Together they stepped out from behind the rocks and began the descent towards the hide-out. Now clearly exposed to anyone inside, speed was their best policy, and the two men moved down the hillside at a fast trot.

They quickly covered the distance to within a few yards of the shack, and as far as Line could tell, they'd not been spotted. He motioned Ackworth to wait while he took a closer look. He cautiously approached the lean-to and placed his ear to a crack in the wooden board that served as a door. He heard breathing. Someone was there. It was laboured, interspersed with a low moaning sound. Was one of them injured? Were they both there? Or just one?

The inspector returned to Ackworth and filled him in on what he'd heard. He was signalling to the other two constables that he and Ackworth were going in, when CRACK! the summer silence was shattered by the sound of splitting wood coming from the back of the shack, followed by the crashing of feet through the undergrowth. Line had been seen; the villains were making a run for it.

'Let's go! NOW!' the inspector yelled, and he and Ackworth dashed towards the lean-to.

Line shoved the makeshift door aside and charged in, the young constable at his heels. The inside was cramped, the air rank, worse than a shit-stinking latrine. A large plank had been ripped from the back of the hut, obviously the point of escape. As the two policemen rushed forward, the younger bumped into the older in the narrow space, knocking him off balance. Line fell, landing hard on the body of a man. A big man. *Nobbler.*

Line scrambled to his feet and saw the blood-soaked front of Nobbler's shirt and the black, encrusted socket that once held his left eye, now a blind emptiness. Someone's knife had found its mark and no mistake. He stared at the vitreous fluid oozing down the man's face and, there, stuck on his cheek, the gelatinous globule that was once his eyeball.

He skirted the prostrate form and made his way to the opening at the back of the shack. About to poke his head out, a loud yell sliced through the early evening quiet from the left.Braxton! He moved aside and signalled Ackworth with a jerk of his head. The young officer squeezed through the gap between the planks and set off to his colleague's assistance.

Hearing Nobbler groan, Line returned to the man. He was struggling to speak but could manage no more that a slurred mumble. Line bent his head close to Nobbler's face, straining to make out what the man was trying to say. He heard, 'Billy done me…' followed by, 'Snatcher,' missed the next word, then, 'Billy.'

A guttural noise came from the man's gullet. He was going fast. His mouth opened once more, but all that came out was a trickle of pink saliva, the fetid odour of death sour on his breath. The throat gurgled again, then cleared enough for him to speak. The policeman, his ear at Nobbler's mouth, could only catch a word here and there: 'I', something impossible to make out, then 'my chance' followed by more muttering lost in a gush of blood, sputum and spittle, after that 'fix 'im', another pause, and finally, 'in Heaven…'No, that was not all, there was one last word but what it was Line had no idea.

The man was still fighting to speak, but it was not to be. His undamaged eye closed, his head fell back on the straw, he was dead. The words made no sense to Line. A dying man's ravings. Probably been delirious for days. It was Snatcher they had to focus on now. He rushed out. Dawkins had come in from his post to lend a hand, and with him was the carter and two Newfoundlands, black, muscular, straining at their leashes. Snatcher's days of freedom were numbered.

Chapter Thirty-Eight: Filling in the Blanks

Inspector Line was sitting in the drawing room at Gad's Hill Place, sipping a well-earned glass of sherry. He'd come straight from Bluebell Hill to report to Georgina and Dunston on the death of Nobbler and the still-in-progress pursuit of Snatcher.

'Oh dear! I hope the poor man is alright.' Georgina was inquiring about Constable Braxton.

'He'll be fine, Miss Hogarth. A sore head, that's all,' he replied. 'Snatcher took him by surprise and walloped him over the head with a branch. The lad must've seen us approaching and decided to make a run for it, but the dogs soon picked up his scent and I'll wager by time I get back, the boys will have him bound tight as the whip-knotted end of a seaman's rope.'

'Well, that's a relief. I've had enough of those two victimising my staff. Shameful, if you ask me. That big lout got exactly what he deserved in my opinion. I suppose the other one is responsible for his death?' Georgina arched an eyebrow in the inspector's direction.

'Looks that way,' the policeman agreed. 'The pair, members of Dinky Dryker's gang by the way, have known each other since their days in an orphanage in Bleeding Heart Yard but that didn't stop the one from killing the other as far as I can tell. Odd thing is though, right before he died, Nobbler said "*Billy* done me," not "*Snatcher* done me". No idea who Billy is. Just the senseless gabble of a dying man, I expect, because his next words, the last he ever spoke, were complete gibberish.'

187

'What were they?' Dunston asked.

'Let me see.' Line consulted his notes. 'I couldn't catch everything he said, but I'll read out what I did hear. I'll say *blank* whenever I missed a word. This is what Nobbler said, "Billy done me," as I told you, then "Snatcher *blank* Billy." And finally, "I *blank blank* my chance *blank* fix him in Heaven *blank*". That's it. Makes no sense to me. Nobbler's not going to fix anyone in Heaven. He's headed in the other direction or my name's not Archibald Line.'

Georgina saw Dunston, open mouthed like the village idiot, gaping at the policeman. So rude. What was wrong with the man?

'It's really most considerate of you to keep me informed, inspector,' she said. 'It's a great comfort to know that we are protected by such a wonderful body of men'.

'You're too kind, miss. With luck, we'll have this whole business wrapped up soon. We've got Lavelle and Stingo Pete, the fellow who helped him break into Mr Dickens's study, in jail, and as for the vagabonds who attacked your maid and then your stable-boy, one is dead and the other as good as in police custody. I'm staying at The Bull in Rochester tonight and will stop by tomorrow morning to bring you up to date.' The inspector stood. 'I bid you good night.'

'And I you, Inspector.'

The policeman gone, Georgina turned to Dunston. 'Really. What *is* the matter with you? The way you stared at the inspector. Most common.'

'I know what he meant.'

'Who? Who meant what?'

'Nobbler. *I know what Nobbler meant.*'

'What? That gibberish?'

'Not gibberish. Quite the opposite. Thanks to Nobbler, I now understand the events leading up to Miss Ternan's death.' Dunston was steaming with barely contained excitement like a geyser readying to blow. 'And you were right.'

'Right? About what?'

'The tramps.'

'I knew it,' Georgina exclaimed. 'I'm glad you've finally seen the light. But what persuaded you when I obviously failed?' she asked with a hint of spinster-to-bachelor banter in her tone.

'This: I believe *Snatcher* was the second burglar,' he explained.

'The twice-robbed drawer,' she murmured.

'Ah! You remember.' He beamed like a tutor whose pupil has just recited yesterday's Latin declensions word-perfect. 'After our fake lord, the first robber, had taken the notes to the Drood mystery from Uncle's desk drawer, Snatcher, the second robber, removed the letters. Something in one of them led him to Miss Ellen Ternan and Windsor Lodge where he killed her. *He's* the tramp responsible for her murder. Exactly as you surmised.' He paused to gauge her reaction to his explanation.

'It's possible… *if*, that is, Snatcher broke into Charles's study,' she said, doubt sculpting a question mark on her face.

'He did… and for a very specific purpose – *to kill Uncle.*'

'Nonsense! Have you lost all reason? Why should some no-good vagabond want to harm dear Charles? Really, you're being ridiculous.' Georgina stamped her foot, a clear signal Dunston had gone too far.

'Forgive me, but Nobbler revealed something else with his dying words,' he persisted.

'Not that gibberish again.'

'No, not gibberish at all. Listen. Nobbler's final words were, "*I* something something *my chance* something *fix him in Heaven* something". The inspector thought Nobbler was trying to say, "I will have my chance to fix him in Heaven above". But, as he said, that makes no sense. Saint Peter will turn Nobbler away at the Pearly Gates as surely as the debit balance matches the credit balance,' Dunston said with the conviction of a practiced, double-entry bookkeeper. '*This*,' he continued with a gleam in his eye, 'is what I think Nobbler said: "I should've taken my chance to fix him in *Heaven's Haven.*"'

'Heaven's Haven? You mean that orphanage you visited?'

'Precisely, the orphanage in *Bleeding Heart Yard*, where Line said the pair first met up.'

189

'What an extraordinary coincidence.'

'Not a coincidence. Nobbler told us a lot more. His first words to the inspector were, "Billy done me," meaning Billy murdered him. Then, "Snatcher blank Billy." An odd conjunction of names, you might think, unless the actual words were, "Snatcher *is* Billy." Even at death's door, Nobbler must have seen that the inspector had no idea who Billy was. So what did he do? He made sure Line knew that Snatcher's real name is *Billy.*'

'Billy? But that's what those horrid people at the orphanage called Charles's son.'

'Exactly. I believe we've found Uncle's offspring in the shape of Snatcher.'

'But that can't be. The Billy in the orphanage died. You saw the proof in the Mawgsbys's ledger.'

'I saw an *entry* in the register,' he corrected her. 'I have no way of knowing if that was a record of a true event or a complete fabrication.'

Georgina's head was whirling like a spinning top, faster and faster with each detail Dunston revealed. This was really too astonishing for words. Dunston might have been open-mouthed when the inspector was talking, but his neural network, or at least its supernatural, dot-connecting one-percent must have been working furiously.

'Quite a history, Miss Georgina,' he continued. 'Somehow Nobbler and Snatcher link up with Dinky Dryker. This is perfect for Snatcher because the gang is operating in Kent, exactly where his intended victim resides. He sees Uncle's study window left open after Lavelle's break-in, slips inside, poisons his father's laudanum, and learns from the letters in the drawer that Ellen is his mother. Whatever transpired between them when he confronted her at Windsor Lodge, he ends up smashing her skull.'

'Are you saying that this young rogue, this Snatcher, or Billy as you say, murdered his father *and* his mother?' Georgina asked.

'Indeed... *and* Nobbler,' Dunston pointed out.

'Yes, of course. "Billy done me." That's what Nobbler said.'

'Yes, Nobbler's death-bed identification of his murderer,' Dunston said. 'I suspect the pair fell out over something, perhaps one blaming the other for losing Uncle's ring at Windsor Lodge, but whatever it was, Snatcher ended his companion's life with one vicious stab to the eye.'

'How horrid.' Georgina was aghast.

Dunston crossed the room to her side and placed a comforting arm around her shoulders. There they sat on the sofa, each in closer proximity to a member of the opposite sex than either had ever previously experienced. No more than a minute or two passed, though, before the pair somehow contrived a return to the safety of their customary, at-a-distance positions. Georgina, discovering an urgent need for tea, summoned Dulcet and in short order the maid returned with the propriety-restoring beverage.

Still distressed by the loss of life resulting from Charles's indiscretions, Georgina stirred her tea deep in thought. She stirred a little faster as sorrow turned into anger. How could some worthless excretion from an orphanage cause so much devastation in the lives of innocent people? The spoon spun even faster as her Scottish genes came to the fore and anger transformed into the urge for vengeance.

Charles's bastard must suffer the ultimate punishment, he must hang for what he's done. Yet her mind was still consumed with her vow to preserve the novelist's literary and personal reputation at all costs. She pondered the situation, the spoon assuming a more reflective rate of rotation. How could she reconcile these goals?

The spoon's motion shifted gear once more, criss-crossing the teacup as though in search of inspiration. Slowly, an idea took shape in her mind. Yes, perhaps there was a way of seeing the villain jailed, sentenced and hanged for murder *without* ruining Charles's reputation.

The spoon, coming to an abrupt halt, was removed purposefully from the still eddying tea. She eyed Dunston. He was key to making this work. She must get him to agree to his part.

Chapter Thirty-Nine: An Eventful Morning

The next morning, Georgina was sitting by herself in the drawing room at Gad's Hill Place, enjoying a more routinely stirred cup of tea.

'Post, miss.' Dulcet entered with a letter and a telegram on a silver platter.

Georgina took both. 'Thank you, Dulcet. And how is that young man of yours today?' she asked.

'Oh, Isaac's *wonderful*,' the young girl said with a blush.

'Yes, I'm sure.' Georgina smiled. 'My inquiry, however, was actually with regard to his health.'

'Beg pardon.' The maid half-curtsied in apology. 'On the mend. Should be back to his chores in a few days.'

'Excellent. I'm glad he's progressing so well.'

'Thank you, miss.' Dulcet bobbed her head shyly in Georgina's direction, and Georgina, setting aside the usual mistress-to-maid nod, responded with a warm woman-to-woman smile, cementing the bond that had been building steadily over the last few weeks.

Rat-a-tat, rat-a-tat.

'Ah, that will be Inspector Line or Mr Burnett. I'm expecting both gentlemen,' Georgina said. 'Please show whomever it is in while I take a quick look at the post.'

A minute later, Dunston entered the drawing room to find an ecstatic

Georgina flapping her arms like an out-of-control semaphore signaller. She rushed over to a startled Dunston and thrust the just-arrived letter into his hand. He took it, backed up two or three steps, and began to read.

My Esteemed Miss Hogarth:

I pray this letter finds you well and that Gad's Hill Place continues to prosper under your splendid stewardship.

I write with a heavy heart, my dear lady. It pains me greatly but I fear I may have misled you, entirely unintentionally, in certain respects when I visited you last Tuesday. If, through some misplaced action or stray word, I have left you with the impression that I entertain certain ambitions in your direction, let me assure you that such is not the case. I beg you to accept my sincerest apology for any confusion I may have unwittingly caused, and beseech you to extend to me your gracious forgiveness if I have given offense in any way whatsoever.

I remain your most humble servant,
Snodrick Wurmsley

'Wurmsley!' Dunston exclaimed. 'He's withdrawn his proposal.' He returned the letter.

'Indeed, he has,' an overjoyed Georgina replied. 'In fact, according to him, he never actually proposed. Can you believe the man? Anyway, I don't care how he rewrites history as long as he never darkens my doorstep again. I have no idea how Frank accomplished this, and so quickly.'

'Remarkable. Dr Beard has more than justified your confidence in him,' Dunston said enthusiastically, even though his expression clearly conveyed his dismay at Frank's proficiency. But then he bucked up, plainly pleased for her. 'What marvellous news. And Wurmsley's envelope? What of that?'

'Destroyed.' She held up the telegram. 'From Frank. He says Wurmsley claimed Ellen's maid found the envelope beside her mistress's corpse but there was no sign of any letter.'

'Ha! It all fits.' Dunston rubbed his hands in obvious delight. 'Snatcher *did* rob Uncle's drawer. Then, at Windsor Lodge, he dropped the envelope, probably while taking the letter out to show Ellen. Or while administering the fatal beating. Either way, it ended up on the carpet as did the ring he'd stolen from Dulcet. Snatcher is the *only* person who could have left both envelope *and* ring at the murder scene.'

'Yes, I expect you're—

Rat-a-tat, rat-a-tat.

'Ah, that must be the inspector. Dunston, don't forget what we discussed last night,' she whispered fiercely as Dulcet showed the policeman into the drawing room.

'Inspector, how good of you to come,' Georgina said in welcome. 'You had a busy night, I daresay. Come, sit and have some tea.'

Line settled in one of the cane-bottomed easy chairs while Georgina took one end of the sofa and Dunston the other. The tea served, Georgina, in her usual no-nonsense manner, came straight to the point. 'So, do tell us. Did you capture the villain?'

'Indeed, we did, miss. A resourceful lad, I'll give him that,' Line acknowledged. 'Led us a merry old chase, but there's no escaping those Newfoundlands. They trapped him in a coppice about four miles from Bluebell Hill. Lad was going to have another go at getting away, but the dogs were too much for him. Constables cuffed him and he spent the night in Rochester jail. He wasn't fit for anything when they brought him in, exhausted, wet from where he'd tried to cross the Medway, and hungry. The men cleaned him up and fed him, and then this morning I spent the best part of an hour questioning him.'

'And what did the wretch have to say for himself?'

'Not much,' the policeman replied. 'Hard nut to crack, I'm afraid. Lad's no fool and he's figured out that his best defence is to deny everything. We have enough witnesses to convict him of the attack on your maid, but the rest, murdering Miss Ternan, ambushing your stable-boy, stabbing Nobbler, even stealing the ring, he denies them all, and frankly we don't have any hard evidence to prove otherwise.'

Just as Georgina had feared. Time for Dunston to act. She nodded to him to get on with it. He coughed and shifted uneasily in his chair.

'Inspector... I...' Dunston cleared his throat nervously.

Georgina groaned silently. She could see that he was still feeling uncomfortable with the course of action they, well, mainly she, had decided upon yesterday evening, obviously still worried about withholding vital information regarding both envelope and ring from the inspector, not to mention Billy's parentage and his Uncle's poisoning. She urged him on with another nod.

'I was... um... wondering how this Snatcher explained Nobbler's death?'

'Claimed Nobbler went out for food a few nights ago and came back with blood streaming down his face, took a knife in the eye while stealing a loaf of bread from a baker's in Strood. Snatcher did what he could for him, but he knew Nobbler was dying, so when he spotted us he made a run for it in hopes of saving his own skin. A plausible story, and since no one can prove otherwise, I see little chance of convicting Snatcher for Nobbler's murder,' Line concluded gloomily.

Georgina nodded to Dunston yet again, this time cluck-clucking her tongue like a cabby prompting his horse to walk on.

'Ye-es, I see...' he began much to Georgina's consternation, but then he hit his stride. 'Inspector, I may have a shred of information... that is to say more of an interpretation that may be of some assistance.' He paused. The policeman waited politely. Georgina rolled her eyes impatiently. 'You see I believe Nobbler's dying words prove Snatcher killed him.'

Line listened with great interest as Dunston explained that the Billy, proper name William Tringham, mentioned by Nobbler grew up in Heaven's Haven, the orphanage in Bleeding Heart Yard where Nobbler teamed up with Snatcher. Hence, when Nobbler, on the point of death, gabbled about his chance to fix 'him' in 'Heaven something', he was not referring to the future and Heaven *above*, but to the time he and Billy were together in Heaven's *Haven*.

Line nodded his understanding, clearly persuaded by Dunston's analysis. But when Dunston continued with his conviction that Nobbler was trying to say Snatcher *is* Billy and that therefore his first words – *Billy done me* – were tantamount to a death-bed indictment of Snatcher as his killer, the inspector shook his head.

'Very clever, sir, and may well be true, but Nobbler never actually said Snatcher is Billy,' Line pointed out. 'All I heard was Snatcher *blank* Billy. He could have been trying to say Snatcher *saw* Billy… *knew* Billy… even *killed* Billy. Your interpretation that Snatcher *is* Billy won't stand up. Too many other possibilities. And without proof that Snatcher and Billy are one and the same, I'm not sure this takes us very far.'

Georgina couldn't believe her ears. She was beside herself, her plan in tatters, tossed aside as easily as the scullery maid dumps left-overs in the pig trough. She'd been sure Dunston's explanation would be sufficient to convict Snatcher of Nobbler's murder without any mention of the villain's parentage or the novelist's poisoning. And then, when Charles's bastard son was strung up for killing a no-account ruffian, she'd have the comfort of knowing that the ultimate punishment had been meted out, not just for Nobbler's death, but for all Snatcher's evil doings without Charles's name being dragged through the mud. But it was not to be. It was nothing but wishful thinking.

'I see,' Dunston said. 'May I ask what evidence would be required to make this identification between Snatcher and Billy?' Georgina glanced at him. Did he have a new plan?

'Well, we'd need someone who could vouch that Snatcher's real name was Billy,' replied the policeman. 'That would do it.'

'Inspector, what are your plans now?' inquired Dunston.

'I'll take Snatcher up to Scotland Yard and he can cool his heels in our cells until the court's ready to try him for attacking Miss Hogarth's maid. He can't squeeze his way out of that one,' Line said firmly.

'Inspector, I know someone who can *confirm* that Snatcher is Billy,' Dunston announced to the astonishment of Georgina and the delight of the policeman. 'I'll be at Scotland Yard this afternoon with my witness.' So saying, he set down his teacup, stood up and marched out of the drawing room, much like Napoleon at the start of the Moscow campaign, short of stature but brimming with confidence, leaving Georgina and the inspector staring wordlessly at each other.

Chapter Forty: Billy's Friend

An hour later, the Napoleonic confidence exuded when Dunston had boldly announced he'd have his witness at Scotland Yard that afternoon was rapidly dissipating as Russian-winter reality set in. Seated in a first-class compartment on his way to London, Dunston fretted that his intended witness – Burt or Gert Mawgsby, either would do – wouldn't return with him to identify Snatcher as Billy. Still, he had to try. He disembarked at Charing Cross and hurried to the cab rank.

'Bleeding Heart Yard, if you please.'

The cabby, a scruffy man in woollen cardigan and cloth cap, with a pox-scarred face and a huge, purple-veined nose, an ever-present beacon signalling his whereabouts to would-be passengers, nodded and with a 'Giddy up!' and a flick of his whip they were off.

Every clip-clop of the horse's hooves increased Dunston's foreboding that he'd promised more than he could deliver. The Mawgsbys had made that entry in the ledger, or someone had made it for them, because Billy really was dead, or because that's what they wanted the world to believe. Either way, they'd produce the entry as evidence and that would be that.

'Eh! Guv! We're 'ere. Bleedin' Heart Yard,' the cabby shouted for the second time to his worry-deafened passenger.

'Er… yes. Thank you, driver. I'll be back shortly. Please wait.'

'Alright, guv. Take yer time. Got all day.'

Dunston entered the Yard and let his eye wander over the mishmash of ramshackle sheds, grimy workshops, dilapidated hovels, bright yellow sign… BRIGHT YELLOW SIGN! So out of place in the greyness of the Yard, the bold black letters on a brilliant yellow background held his gaze like an ocular magnet:

Luke Mallick
Artist —Painter — Printer

Ah, yes, Luke Mallick, the lad who'd opened a painting business when he left the Mawgsbys's orphanage. Hmmm, who would be better able to identify Billy than the youngster who taught him to read? Worth paying Mr Mallick a visit before approaching the Mawgsbys, Dunston decided, and duly turned his step towards the yellow sign.

'In here,' a husky voice growled in response to Dunston's timid knock.

Dunston peered in and was astonished at the scene greeting his eyes. The workshop was cheerful, sunny almost, the yellow of the sign brought inside, coating all four walls and making the room brighter and airier than one would have thought possible for an establishment in Bleeding Heart Yard. And so clean and ship-shape: a small printing press, old but shiny, occupied one corner; samples of lettering and graphics covered an entire wall; paint brushes hung from a row of hooks; and pots of paint, from white through a rainbow of colours to black, lined a long shelf. But it was the almost-completed painting of partially clad, lissom nymphs at play in a field that caught and held Dunston's eye.

He dragged his gaze away and turned to the young man standing behind what was part-desk, part-workbench. He looked like a lumberjack from the vast forests of North America. He had on a heavy shirt and cord breeches, and had a logger's barrel chest and bushy, brown beard. He also had unusually large, spade-like hands. How such hands could have brought to life the delicate nymphs captured so gracefully on the canvas was beyond Dunston.

'Ain't got all day. You gonna tell me what you want?' he asked gruffly.

'Yes... quite. Mr Mallick, I take it.'

'Aye, that's me.'

'Ah... well, I'm here to... um... inquire about... an acquaintance of yours,'

Dunston explained.

'Not sure I have any *acquaintances*. Social life in the Yard's a bit limited,' Luke replied in his surly manner.

'Quite… I take your point. Actually, I had in mind a young boy you befriended at Heaven's Haven—'

'Oh, aye. Lots of young lads at Heaven's Haven, that being the purpose of the place,' Luke cut in unhelpfully.

'Yes, indeed, but this was a boy you taught to read, a boy by the name of Billy, and—'

'Billy? What d'yer know 'bout him, then?' Anger flashed from his eyes and the very big hands clenched into very big fists.

Taken aback by Luke's strong reaction to Billy's name, Dunston replied cautiously. 'Well, only what the Mawgsbys told me.'

'The Mawgsbys? Ha! What a pair. What'd they tell yer?'

'More what they showed me – the entry in the ledger recording the poor boy's death – and I wanted—'

'Ha! Knew that would come back to bite 'em,' Luke said with a serve-them-right smirk. 'Same with that letter to Miss Turner or whatever her name was.'

'You mean, Miss Ternan?'

'Aye. Never liked being part of their little scheme.'

'*Little scheme?* Was there something inappropriate in what you wrote, then?' Dunston asked.

'Inappropriate? Depends what you mean by inappropriate. If you mean saying the lad's dead when he was live as you an' me, then yes, it was inappropriate.'

'WHAT?' Dunston couldn't believe his ears. Was he right in thinking the boy didn't die? 'Billy's alive?'

'Didn't say that, did I?' Luke scowled. 'You gotta listen. Said he was alive *then*. How should I know if he's alive now? Best you tell me why you're asking all these questions 'bout Billy.'

Sinking deeper into the sordid world of untruths, Dunston searched for a version of events sufficiently concrete to satisfy Luke Mallick yet free of any hint of Uncle's murder. Just stick to the tramps, he decided. He explained that Snatcher, a vagabond, was suspected of killing his mate, a lump of a fellow named Nobbler, but Nobbler, moments before he died, claimed his murderer was called Billy.

'Nobbler and Snatcher teamed up in Heaven's Haven, so I'm here to see if anyone can attest that the grown-up Snatcher used to be known as Billy,' Dunston concluded.

'Hmmm. Maybe we can help each other. If I see this feller called Snatcher and he turns out to be Billy, then that'll help the scufters nail him for murder, right?' Dunston nodded. 'Good,' Luke said coldly. 'Then, here's what I know.'

Luke confirmed much of what Dunston had already learned from the Mawgsbys about Billy's encounter with his father at Field Lane School but then moved well beyond their account. According to Luke, Billy swore he'd track down his father and avenge the novelist's cruel rejection of him at the school. Luke reasoned with him, and for a while Billy settled back into the daily routine at Heaven's Haven. But that wasn't the end of it.

'One day, he came into the shop, all wild-eyed and twitchy,' Luke continued. 'Said he was running away and needed my help. Still thought of the bugger as a friend so I was willing to do what I could. Asked me to tell the Mawgsbys he'd gone to Gravesend to take boat to France, and was never coming back. That way, he said, they'd never be able to blackmail the writer bloke, his father, 'cos the evidence, by which he meant himself, would be gone.'

'What a generous act given the way his father treated him,' Dunston said.

'Bollocks!' Luke snapped. 'Knew right away he was pitching me the gammon. Still bent on getting even with his dad, he was. Tried to talk him out of it, but it weren't no use.'

'What did you tell the Mawgsbys?' Dunston asked.

'Told 'em the story he'd made up, but it really didn't matter 'cos the Mawgsbys was just glad to see the back of him, worried he'd blow the gab 'bout their blackmailing scheme. That's why they got me to write in their ledger that he'd died 'cos then nobody would give his disappearance another thought and they'd be safe. Wrote the same to that lady. And that was that. Haven't seen the bastard since. Just as well. Strangle the sod if I ever set eyes on him again,' Luke growled, fists clenching again.

It all fitted with what the Mawgsbys had told Dunston except for the all-important fact that Billy didn't die. But what he'd heard so far didn't explain Luke's fist-clenching hatred of Billy. Something else happened between them.

'I take it… you and Billy had a… a falling out?' Dunston prompted.

'Falling out?' Luke snarled. 'More than a falling out to my mind. Filching shuffler stole my pa's silver pocket watch, the only thing I had of my father's.Kept it safe all those years I was in Heaven's Haven, but then, after Billy'd been to see me at the shop that last time, the watch was gone. Little thief took it. So if he hangs thanks to me, we'll be even, him an' me. And if the Mawgsbys get nabbed as well for saying Billy's dead, so much the better. Done everything I can to repay what they lent me to start my business but it's never enough.Worse than the bleeding money-lenders, they are.'

What a sad story, thought Dunston. Luke was doing his best to make something of himself but he was being hindered at every step by the grasping Mawgsbys. Still, the Mawgsbys's greed and Billy's thieving worked to Dunston's benefit, because Luke, when asked, readily agreed to accompany him to Scotland Yard.

Luke went into the back room, took a tin canister from the window sill and removed a piece of paper. He put his jacket on and placed the paper in the coat's inside pocket. When he returned, he found Dunston furtively eyeing the half-naked nymphs.

'Painting ain't finished,' he said brusquely, but not as sourly as before. 'Come on.' The pair left the shop and headed towards the waiting cabby.

Chapter Forty-One: The Naked Truth

Inspector Line cast a doubtful eye over the witness Mr Burnett had brought to Scotland Yard. The man was dressed in a coarse woollen jacket over a faded plaid shirt open at the neck. One over-sized hand held a cloth cap, while the other scratched at a reddened spot on his cheek until it was rubbed raw. The hand, its job done, dropped to his side and hoisted the leather belt supporting rough, working-man trousers, bringing into full view a pair of heavy, hobnailed boots.

'And who might you be?' he inquired as his visitors sat themselves in the two chairs in front of his desk.

'Luke Mallick,' came the surly reply.

'Ah, yes, Mr Mallick.' Line was already sensing he'd have to handle this fellow carefully if he was to get anywhere. 'Understand you may be able to assist us in our inquiries regarding a young man you were acquainted with at Heaven's Haven. Name's William Tringham but going by Billy when you knew him.'

'Depends.'

'On what?'

'On what you wants me to do, don't it?'

'Quite simple, really. All you have to do is take a look at the prisoner in his cell, you don't even have to go in, and tell us if he's Billy,' Line explained.

'And if he is, what happens then?' Luke demanded, his tone angry, his stance aggressive.

'We thank you and you'll be on your way,' Line replied.

'Not to me, you fool. To him, the prisoner.'

The policeman struggled to control his annoyance at Mallick's impertinence, but did so without any change in countenance. His granite mask fell into place and there it remained for the rest of the interview.

'Yes, of course, the prisoner. Well, it's not for me to say, but, if you do identify the man, twenty years on the force tells me he'll hang for murder.'

'Then, I'll help you. And I don't care if the bugger sees me.'

'Excellent. Please come this way.' Line guided his guests out of his office and towards the jail.

'What d'you lot want, then?' Snatcher demanded from the wooden bench in his cell where he sat, elbows on knees, chin in hands. He glared at the three faces peering at him through the bars of the prison door.

'Alright, that's enough lip from you. Stand up and let's have a look at you,' Line commanded.

Snatcher scowled at him, but nevertheless got to his feet. Luke stared at the inmate, taking a good look. He rubbed one of his big hands over his face, his fingers probing the blemish just as his eyes probed Snatcher, searching in the prisoner's hardened features for traces of the young boy. At last, he nodded to the policeman, turned on his heel and set off towards the inspector's office. Success, Line thought, pleased his doubts about Mr Burnett's witness had proved groundless.

The threesome re-sat themselves in Line's office, exactly as before.

'Well?' the inspector asked.

'Not him,' Luke said curtly.

'What?' Line exclaimed.

'Never seen him before. He's got Billy's scrawny build and holds himself a bit like Billy, but he ain't Billy,' Luke insisted.

'Are you sure?' the policeman pressed.

'I am. And I can prove it if you don't believe me.'

'You can prove it? How?' a perplexed Line asked.

Luke fished in his inside pocket and pulled out the piece of paper he'd taken from the tin canister. He unfolded it and handed it to Line. The inspector saw an odd design in faded red ink on a white background. He handed it to Dunston who inspected the drawing, turning it this way and that, equally puzzled.

'That's Billy's mark,' Luke explained. 'Right here.' He patted the left side of his chest just below the collar bone.

'You mean a birthmark?'

'Aye. Deep purple, it is. Real ashamed 'bout it, Billy was. Never showed it to no one. Only ever saw it that once when he came to me after the thrashing he took at Field Lane School. Made him take his shirt off so I could clean up the criss-cross of welts, all raw an' bleedin', on his back. Even then he did his best to hide it with his hand. Felt real sorry for him, I did, and then he steals my pa's watch. That's thanks for you.'

'Is that when you made the sketch? After he took the watch?' Line asked.

'Aye. Wanted to be sure I'd recognise the light-fingered little sod if ever our paths crossed again. Maybe his looks would change as he grew older, but that mark, can't change something like that, can you? Silly bugger was branded for life, and that's how I'd know him.'

Line was on his feet. He snatched the drawing from Dunston and marched out of the office. In a matter of minutes, he was back.

'It's not him,' he said tersely. 'Stripped him naked. Not a blemish anywhere on that lad's body.'

Chapter Forty-Two: The Signet Ring

The next morning, Ruby opened the front door at Gad's Hill Place and found Dunston Burnett standing on the doorstep. Before he could say a word, the maid blurted out, 'They're going to get married.'

'Married? Who? Miss Georgina and that swine Wurmsley?'

'God bless you, no, sir.' Ruby laughed in astonishment that Roly-poly could think such a thing. 'Miss'll have no truck with him. No, Dulcie an' her young man, Isaac. They're in the drawing room now with miss.'

'Oh, Dulcet and Isaac,' a visibly relieved Dunston said.

'Miss said I was to show you straight in if you was to call, so if you please, sir.' Ruby turned and led the way into the drawing room.

'Ah, Dunston. Excellent timing,' Georgina exclaimed in greeting.

Her glance took in his slightly askew cravat, unevenly buttoned jacket and noticeably crumpled shirt, clear signs something was amiss. In contrast, Georgina was as prim and proper as ever in her black mourning dress. Her dark hair, scrupulously parted at the centre, framed her pale face, the style's severity only slightly softened by ringlets at either side. The warm glow, though, in those too-often frosty eyes revealed her genuine affection for the young couple standing in front of her, and her eagerness to ensure their nuptials proceeded according to plan... her plan, of course.

'Now, you two,' she said to Dulcet and Isaac, 'don't forget. Mr Clatterbuck will be here on Saturday morning. I'll need about an hour with him to clear up some matters in Mr Dickens's will, so you should be on hand to meet with him at ten o'clock. Understood?' Dulcet curtsied and bobbed her head.

206

Isaac touched his forelock. 'Good. That will be all.'

The pair took their leave and Georgina turned to Dunston. The sad-clown look on his face told her immediately the news was not good. He gets so involved, she mentally scolded. Best try to cheer him up.

'It's *so* exciting,' she enthused. 'Dulcet and Isaac to be married. It's perfect. I interviewed both of them myself before employing them, and thought then they'd make exemplary servants but I had no idea they'd marry. Isn't it exciting?'

'Yes, indeed.'

The dejection in his voice told her she really had her work cut out. Must be another one of his mishaps, something to do with his silly claim about a witness, she imagined. She'd have to find out what it was, and then see what could be done to remedy matters.

'Come, sit here, on the sofa,' she said, 'and tell me what happened in London.'

Without looking at Georgina, Dunston recounted yesterday's events in a muted monotone.

'Billy didn't die,' he began.

Georgina nodded cautiously. She would have preferred Billy to have remained dead, especially with the one-month deadline fast approaching, but if he was alive then perhaps Dunston's theory that he was Snatcher was back in consideration.

Dunston's next words disabused her of that hope. He continued with an account of his meeting with Luke Mallick and their visit to Scotland Yard, and with his head sinking lower and lower, ended with Luke's opinion, confirmed by his sketch of the birthmark, that Snatcher was not Billy.

She could see that he was crushed, trampled under the booted feet of this latest failure. Georgina shifted slightly from her end of the sofa and placed her hand on his arm, a simple yet tender expression of sympathy, albeit short-lived. Suddenly realising its improper location, the hand was hastily withdrawn, and there they sat, pilloried in the frigid formality of upper-class sensibility, he reliving every minute of his most recent reverse, she, always the practical one, desperately searching her mind for some way to relieve his misery.

'Dunston,' she finally said, 'all Luke's evidence proves is that Snatcher is not Billy. You only thought they were one and the same because that was the way you interpreted Nobbler's dying words. Rather tenuous, you must admit.'

Dunston groaned.

Georgina promptly switched tactics. 'Dunston, take heart,' she encouraged him. 'Listen, Snatcher stole the ring and it subsequently turned up next to Ellen Ternan's body after the tramps' attempted burglary, so *Snatcher* remains the leading suspect in *her* murder. But he is not Charles's out-of-wedlock child, so he had no motive to murder your uncle. Billy though, *is* Charles's illegitimate son, and had *every* reason to kill his father. *Billy* was the one who broke into Charles's study and remains the leading suspect in *his* murder. You see? You were on the right track, only instead of one murderer, there were *two*.' There, that should buck him up.

Dunston's second groan, this one even more anguished, made clear her approach was seriously misguided. Perhaps she shouldn't have pointed to the obvious weaknesses in his investigation with quite so much enthusiasm. Probably not the best way to reassure and rebuild the confidence of a male member of the species, especially this one. Like an infantryman executing a smart about-turn, she swiftly switched tactics again, unintended criticism giving way to sincere praise.

'Dunston, you've done more than anyone, more than even Inspector Line could have done, to sort through this business.'

Dunston's head rose an inch or so. Ha! Now she was on the right track.

'Think of all you've accomplished. You solved the Drood mystery, engineered Lavelle's arrest, and on top of all that you tracked the child from Field Lane School to Heaven's Haven and finally to Luke Mallick. An amazing performance. Nobody could have done more.' His head notched up another degree or two. 'But, *you*, you *did* do more. You recovered the most treasured of treasures, the ring I feared was lost forever.'

The head came upright, just in time for Dunston to see Georgina take his uncle's signet ring from her skirt pocket and hold it out to him.

'I never thought I would again let this out of my sight. But I want you to have it as a small measure of my deepest gratitude for all your efforts on my behalf and a token of my heartfelt affection.'

She pressed the ring into his hand and, as she did so, he looked at her and their eyes meet. Several seconds passed. His usual reaction to praise from the splendid Miss Georgina – a cheek-reddening, perspiration-drenched dither – was absent on this occasion. Instead, his look returned in multiples the tender feelings she'd revealed to him.

Georgina rose. 'Dunston,' she said softly, 'let me give you a moment by yourself.'

The next day after lunch, Dunston entered the drawing room at Woods View House, sat in his favourite armchair, and examined the ring. What a gift. His uncle's signet ring, his Progeny Ring. He treasured the inkwell, that fount of flowing ink-blue inspiration, bequeathed to him by his uncle, but the ring was ten times, no, a thousand times more precious.

He tried it on his middle finger. Too tight. Then his little finger. Still too tight. Made originally for his small-boned, spare-of-flesh uncle, it was never going to fit the chubby digit of an overweight, retired bookkeeper. What could be done? A solution was not long in presenting itself. He slipped the gold band on to his watch chain and let it rest against his abdomen where he could fondle it whenever he wanted, like a chair-bound old lady stroking her lap dog. Exactly the right place for the ring.

Strange, he mused, sitting back in his chair, how a ring featured so prominently in his investigation into his uncle's death *and* in his continuation of *The Mystery of Edwin Drood*. He smiled, remembering how Jasper was fooled into believing Rosa Bud's diamond and ruby engagement ring was in the tomb. Hmmm… could he have been similarly fooled? Misled into believing his Uncle's signet ring was beside Miss Ternan's body? What if it was *never* beside the actress's corpse, just as Rosa's ring was *never* in the Sapsea family sepulchre?

He sat up straight. Facts have to be facts, the first principle of detection as expounded by Inspector Line. And he had blithely ignored it. Was the signet ring's presence on the carpet at Windsor Lodge a fact? Not really. It was Georgina's inference based on two propositions: that one of the tramps dropped the ring in Ellen Ternan's parlour; and that the maid found it and gave it to Nick. Neither was fact.

Miss Georgina had become such a huge presence in Dunston's tiny universe, he unhesitatingly accepted her word as gospel. But this time even he had to acknowledge that her conclusion, far from being a biblical truth, was nothing but guesswork. The only *fact* in the entire concoction was that the ring was in Nick's possession at Woods View House the day after he'd collected Uncle's letters from Windsor Lodge. How he acquired it was an open question.

Dunston's mind jumped to the envelope, the other piece of 'evidence' allegedly found in Miss Ternan's parlour. That was what Mr Wurmsley told Frank Beard and Lord Toxington. But how reliable was Wurmsley? All that was known for certain was that Wurmsley had the envelope when he made his preposterous marriage proposal to Georgina. But did he get it at Windsor Lodge?

Dunston's head sank into his hands. He should have verified the facts before jumping to conclusions. Lesson learned. Perhaps it would be best to resume interviewing his list of 'suspects' under the guise of writing his uncle's biography, he mused. *No*, not until he was *sure* of the facts. Before doing anything else, he had to check every detail of Georgina's conjecture and Wurmsley's claim. But how? Ah! There was one person who could do both. Tomorrow, he'd get to the bottom of what really was beside Ellen's body once and for all.

Chapter Forty-Three: The Two Maids

'Good morning,' Dunston said. 'Midge, I believe.'

'Oh, no, sir. She's the pretty one.'

Not one to take much notice of appearance, Dunston was nonetheless struck by the beefy arms, wart-spotted face, bulging brown eyes and lank hair of the eyesore confronting him. Midge, no matter what her looks, had to be the pretty one if this potato-bodied fright was the point of comparison.

'I see. And you are?'

'Molly, scullery maid, sir.'

It was Friday morning and Dunston was carrying out his plan to interview the one person – Ellen Ternan's maid, Midge – who could confirm whether envelope and ring, the two pieces of evidence at the heart of his investigation, were found beside her mistress's body and subsequently delivered to Wurmsley and Nick respectively.

As arranged the previous evening, Moccles himself had arrived at Woods View House at 8 o'clock. He was suitably dressed for the journey in travelling coat, woollen muffler and scruffy top hat, but otherwise managed to present a decidedly glum appearance – stooped at the shoulder, turned down at the mouth, gloomy in the face and drooping in the moustache. He was driving a run-down, faded-yellow post-chaise – old, but fast, he assured Dunston – and in three hours they'd arrived at Windsor Lodge in Peckham.

'Very well, Molly. Now where is Midge?'

'Shopping. Does a lot of shopping ever since miss got walloped. Like to wait for her, sir?'

'Yes, I would.'

'Best come to the parlour then.'

Dunston entered the parlour and glanced around nervously, his gaze drawn involuntarily to the candlestick on the piano.

'Him's the one used to bash her head in,' Molly volunteered helpfully. 'Cleaned the blood an' brains off, and it don't look so bad now.'

Dunston hurriedly backed away, not stopping until his legs bumped against the sofa and he sat down with a thump, his breath whooshing out of him as he landed.

'You alright, sir? Shall I bring some tea?' she inquired.

'Th-thank you, Molly.' Dunston took a deep breath and sat up, striving for a more business-like manner.'Yes, tea would be most welcome, but first, since Midge isn't here, let me ask you one or two questions. Now, think back to the day Miss Ternan died—'

'Oooh!'

'It's alright,' he soothed. 'Just tell me what you remember about finding the body.'

'Well, Midge found her.'

'You didn't go into the parlour?'

'Wild horses wouldn't've got me into that devil's den. Most I done was peep from the door while Midge went in.'

'And what did you see?'

'Well, Midge was looking at this body and I jus' knew it was miss.' The maid's mud-brown eyes deadened in terror at the memory. 'I screamed and threw my apron over my head like this.' She demonstrated the pinafore's defensive properties with practiced ease.

'You didn't see anything else?' he asked once the apron was lowered to half-mast. 'Nothing on the carpet?'

'Funny you should say that, 'cos when I peeked over my pinny, I did see Midge pick up an envelope, take a quick look inside, and then tuck it in her apron pocket.'

'An envelope. Very good. Anything else?'

'No, sir.'

'She didn't pick up a ring, then.'

'Ring? No, didn't see no ring. Jus' the envelope.'

'Excellent. You've been most helpful.' He smiled reassuringly. 'Perhaps, now I will have some tea.'

After Molly had served the tea, Dunston sat, cup in hand, still kicking himself for not establishing the authenticity of alleged facts earlier, but pleased that he was now making up for lost time. He'd confirmed the envelope was on the carpet just as Wurmsley claimed, an important point in that it established a direct link between the burglary of Uncle's study and the murder of Ellen Ternan. But Molly didn't see the ring, an equally important point because it was the only 'evidence' tying Snatcher to Ellen's murder. The envelope was a fact; the ring, a red herring.

Miss Georgina's two-murderer theory was rapidly falling apart. The absence of the ring *eliminated* Snatcher as Ellen Ternan's murderer. Miss Georgina was wrong on that point. And the presence of the envelope *implicated* Billy. Miss Georgina had rightly noted that of the two, Billy, Uncle's illegitimate son, was the only one with motive to poison the novelist. But she'd missed the obvious possibility that Billy stole the letters when doctoring Uncle's laudanum, and later dropped the envelope on the carpet after murdering Ellen.

He'd been right all along. Taken together, Molly's two pieces of evidence resurrected his one-murderer theory – the illegitimate son killed both father and mother. That Snatcher is not Billy, only meant that the *real* Billy was yet to be identified.

Dunston sipped his tea, pleased with his progress on the murders, but increasingly puzzled about how the ring ended up in Nick's hands if it wasn't on the carpet at Windsor Lodge and wasn't given to him by Midge. What happened between Dulcet losing it at Dillywood Lane and its appearance at Woods View House in his manservant's possession?

Dunston cast his mind back to the day the ring was lost. He recalled the search after the tramps had scarpered and distinctly remembered Nick picking something up from the ground and staring at it closely. Whatever it was glinted in the sunlight. Feeling Dulcet's anxious eyes on him, Nick signalled with a shake of his head that, sadly, it was not the hoped-for object. But could it have been the ring? Did Nick find the ring?

Well, if he did, it would explain how it ended up at Woods View House, and the guilty, pilfering-the-offertory look when Dunston caught him checking the gold content of the ring with his teeth. Someone with his history would know exactly how to turn a stolen ring into ready cash. The scoundrel. The tramps didn't take off with the ring. Nick did. Dunston's eyes had been opened and he was furious. His manservant had some explaining to do.

A knock on the door interrupted his thoughts and in stepped an eye-catching bundle of perky innocence and carnal promise, appealing to saint and satyr in equal measure.

'I'm Midge. Molly says you're looking for me, sir.'

Nothing about Midge could be described as fashionable or even tidy, but the overall effect, from the dishevelled hair and saucy cap to the high bosom and tiny waist, was devastatingly attractive.

'Was you one of her men friends, then?' she asked with an engaging tilt of her eyebrows.

'N-not exac—'

'Didn't think so,' she said with conviction. 'What can I do for you, then?'

'I… I'm assisting Inspector Line of Scotland Yard,' he fibbed.

Midge's pretty eyes narrowed. 'Oh! You are, are you? Well, what d'yer want with me?'

'Please, don't alarm yourself,' he reassured her. 'I simply need to clear up a few points regarding Miss Ternan's murder.'

'Like what?'

'Well, I understand you found an envelope next to your mistress's body.'

'Envelope? Didn't find no envelope, and that's the God's truth,' exclaimed the maid, unease registering on the adorable face.

'But Molly saw you pick—'

'Bah! That Molly. Got donkey droppings for brains, that one. Pair short of a brace, she is. Anyways, when I was in the parlour she had her face in her pinny.'

Dunston stared at Midge in astonishment. Why was it so difficult to discover the truth? Lies spewed forth whenever anyone opened their mouth. But who was lying this time? He saw craftiness and cunning in the sparkle of Midge's pale blue eyes, whereas Molly's lacklustre brown ones had displayed none of the imagination or creativity necessary for deception. Molly and I are fellow spirits, he thought. She was telling the truth, Midge is lying.

'Let me repeat that I'm working with the police, and already know about the envelope.' He strove to project an image of authority. 'There's little use in lying. My only concern is to confirm you found it next to Miss Ternan's body and handed it to my... colleague, Mr. Wurmsley.'

'That weasel of a man who was here the day she died? Why didn't you say so,' a relieved Midge said. 'Told me I wasn't to say nothin' 'bout it or it would be worse for me, but if you works with him, then s'pose it's alright.'

'Quite alright.'

'Then, yes, I did find an envelope and I give it to old ferret-face. There, satisfied? Is that it, then?'

He put a mental tick against 'envelope'. Now to confirm 'no ring'. 'Just one other small matter...'

'Yes?'

'I was wondering if you found anything else beside Miss Ternan's body.' The blue eyes narrowed again. 'Like what?'

'A ring for instance.'

'A RING!' Blue eyes spit shards of icy indignation. 'I'd never take none of miss's jewellery, on my life. You ain't got no right blackening my name like that.'

'No, no,' Dunston said hastily. 'You misunderstand me. I mean this ring.' He stood and showed her the gold band on his watch chain.

'Never seen—' She stopped, peering hard at the signet ring. 'No wait! Let me see!'

She grabbed the ring, almost yanking the chain out of his waistcoat, and checked the inscription.

'That Nicky!' she screeched. 'Wait 'til I get my hands on him, the slimy piece of shit! I'll squeeze his dobblers to mush!'

Dunston shifted uneasily. 'Please, calm yourself,' he implored her. 'Are you saying you recognise the ring?'

'Course I do,' Midge snarled. 'It's the one I give Nicky to sell for me. Wish I'd never seen his face. Too handsome by half, he is.'

'But where did you find it? Molly said you only found the envelope on the carpet, nothing else.'

Suddenly sullen and subdued, the maid muttered, 'For once in her stupid life, Molly's right. The ring wasn't on the carpet. It was inside the envelope.'

'INSIDE THE ENVELOPE?'

'That's what I said. Inside the sodding envelope. Why else would I take a buggery envelope, you old fool. A piece of paper's no good to me 'cept for wiping my arse. But a ring. A ring's different. A ring means money. Least it should've.'

Chapter Forty-Four: The Crooked Finger

After leaving Windsor Lodge and making his way to The Crooked Finger, Peckham's only inn, a brooding Dunston sat motionless, wooden as the tavern's rough-hewed dining table on which his lunch languished untouched, everything blotted out by Midge's baffling testimony. The maid's words echoed in his head like a relentless drumbeat – *inside the envelope... inside the envelope... inside the envelope.*

Since Nick had the ring following the scuffle with the tramps at Dillywood Lane, was he the one to drop it on the carpet at Windsor Lodge beside Ellen Ternan's corpse? And if the ring was inside the envelope, did he also have the envelope? That seemed unlikely. Nick chanced upon the ring, whereas the envelope was acquired as part of a premeditated murder by Uncle's illegitimate son. Whoever broke into Gad's Hill place and took the envelope was there to poison Uncle, and Nick had no reason to want the novelist dead. Unless... unless *Nick was Billy.*

Could Dunston's boon of a manservant be a double-murderer? A disbelieving Dunston wanted to discard this troubling thought, but he soon found himself tracing a possible sequence of events implicating Nick. He pictured him finagling a job at Woods View House where he'd be within striking distance of Gad's Hill Place and his despised father. One night, he spies Lavelle entering and then exiting Uncle's study through the window. Seeing his opportunity, he steals inside and poisons the laudanum. He spots the rifled drawer and finds the letter that tells him Ellen Ternan is his mother.

Then, after routing the tramps at Dillywood Lane, he stumbles across the missing ring, his father's signet ring with his initial – W – engraved on the inside. He now has two pieces of evidence – the ring and the letter – confirming his parentage. He puts the ring in the envelope along with the letter for safekeeping and waits for his chance to confront Ellen Ternan. It comes on his next day off. He goes to Windsor Lodge, shows the letter to Ellen and when she disowns him, kills her.

Later, when he checks his jacket pocket, he finds the letter but realises he must have dropped the envelope with the ring still inside it on her parlour carpet. No one saw him remove the envelope from Uncle's study, but several witnesses saw him at Dillywood Lane where the ring was lost, so its subsequent appearance at the murder scene *is* a real threat to him. Whoever found the body – probably the parlour maid – must have picked it up, hoping to make a few bob off it. He has to find her and get the ring, and Dunston unwittingly obliges by sending him to Windsor Lodge to collect Uncle's letters to Ellen. There, he sweet-talks Midge into handing over the proof of his guilt.

Dunston was horrified at this imagined unfolding of events and tried desperately to bury it, but fresh suspicions kept springing up. Luke Mallick described Billy as 'scrawny'. Well, Nick, small boned and wiry, could easily have been a scrawny child. And he was the right age, about twenty, exactly the same as Billy. Then there was Billy's birthmark. Despite all Nick's outdoor work in the past month, Dunston hadn't once seen him bare-chested. Was he hiding something? Nick also had opportunity – he was on hand to poison Uncle's laudanum, and Ellen Ternan was killed on a Sunday, Nick's day off. Nor could Dunston forget that Nick grew up in crime-ridden Spitalfields and was doubtless well schooled in the mechanics of poisoning and bludgeoning.

Should he inform Inspector Line? Heart and head were far apart on this question, the first pleading Nick's innocence, the second insisting on his guilt. The evidence, Dunston sadly concluded, was just too compelling. The unpleasant truth had to be faced. Still, best not be too hasty. He'd been wrong before. Has he got the right man this time?

No! Of course he hasn't. What a fool he's been. *Poppy juice!* Ma's 'medicine business' as Nick called it. He could see her, a humpbacked crone, silently stirring her narcotic concoction, an image owing more to the opening scene in *The Mystery of Edwin Drood* than anything he'd actually experienced, but, no matter what she looked like, the real-life proprietress of the opium den, was *Nick's mother*.

Nick, then, could *not* be Ellen Ternan's son, Billy, and once that was ruled out, the notion of him exacting revenge on her, and on Uncle for that matter, broke down. Since they were not Nick's parents, he had no reason to want either dead, and without motive, ring and envelope, damning though they appeared, must have some innocent explanation. He'd go straight to Ma's opium den, speak to the woman, and confirm that Nick was her son. Then, he could put this unsettling line of inquiry behind him, and get on with the business of identifying the real killer.

Chapter Forty-Five: The Saracen's Head

W hat's yer fancy then, luv? Here for a puff... or something else... something more like... me? I knows how to give a gent a good time.' Hand on hip, the timeworn slattern who'd been idling in the doorway leaned forward and caressed Dunston's cheek.

Moccles's post-chaise had conveyed Dunston from Peckham to Spitalfields and The Saracen's Head, the inn in Thrawl Street, where Nick's mother had her 'medicine business'. The tavern was easily spotted even though its colourful sign of a turbaned Turk had long ago been severed from its wooden joist by drunken patrons, much as the crusaders sliced off the heads of infidels in the Holy Land.

The ramshackle, three-storey hostelry had a well-earned reputation, not for its ale or its meat 'n' taters, but for its capacity to indulge every sin known to man. The top storey, strewn with straw mattresses, served the many young, and not so young, ladies touting for customers in and around the inn. The middle floor was reserved for dice, cards, and betting, and the inevitable fist-fights and knifings that followed. The ground floor, though, was the real hive of activity. Here, a man could arrange to be serviced by a child, negotiate a murder over a pint of ale, fix a horse race with the exchange of a few pounds, plan a burglary free of interruption, in short, if a price could be set on an article, person, or service, that article, person or service could be acquired at The Saracen's Head or supplied in short order.

It was here, in a cheerless, windowless shed behind the main building, that Ma had her 'medicine business'. And it was here that Nick had spent, or more likely misspent, his youth, thought Dunston grimly.

The tawdrily dressed strumpet who'd accosted Dunston on his arrival at the inn adjusted her sales pitch.

'What's up, darlin'? Cat got your tongue? Don't have to be shy with me,' she prompted, ever ready to give a first-timer a little push. 'Ain't going to bite... unless you wants me to.'

'N... no, you don't understand.' He took a step back.

'Aye, that's what they all say. But you can tell me, dearie.'

'Yes, well, you see, it's about my manservant, miss.'

'Miss? Ha, that's a good un'. Ain't nobody calls me miss. You can call me Maggie.'

'Yes... Maggie... thank you. Er... about my manservant, name of Nick—'

'Nick? Young feller what used to help out 'round here?'

'Just so, my manservant. If you'd be so kind, please inform his mother I'd like a word with her.'

'Well, that ain't so simple,' she replied with a frown. 'You see, he never had a mother.'

'WHAT?' Dunston squawked. 'What are you saying?'

'Sorry, sweetheart,' Maggie said quickly, obviously startled by the pudgy gent's violent reaction, and with good reason. She'd had more than her fair share of backhanders across the face and boots to the belly from the sots and roisterers she serviced, but it was the respectable-looking ones like this gent who were the most vicious.

'Course he had a mother, same as all of us, otherwise he wouldn't be on God's earth, would he?' she explained carefully. 'But, that lady dumped him soon as he took breath.'

'Nonsense. Nick's forever talking about Ma and her... um... business establishment.'

'Ah!' The woman visibly relaxed. 'You want to speak to Ma.'

'Exactly. Ma, Nick's mother.'

'Oh, now I see why we've been at cross purposes. Ma's alive. But she ain't Nick's mother.'

'But he calls her Ma. That means mother, doesn't it?'

'True enough, but it's like my Auntie Mabel.'

'Your Auntie Mabel?'

'That's right. Calls her auntie, but she ain't really my aunt, just my mother's friend. Same with Ma. Everyone calls her Ma, including Nick. But she ain't his mother. Definitely not.'

'Not his mother?'

'No, sir. Fact is, Nick never knew is mother. Ma took him in off the street after he ran away from a home for foundlings and orphans.'

'Oh, no,' Dunston groaned. 'W-was it in Bleeding Heart Yard?'

'Funny you should say that. No one knows for sure. Some of the girls say it was in Limehouse, down by the docks. Others say it was up Hackney way. But most of 'em think it was Bleeding Heart Yard, like you said. And they're probably right. Stands to reason, don't it, it's closer than them other two.'

Dunston groaned again, reeling as Maggie's explanations pounded his brain one after the other like toppling dominoes except unlike their unvarying clack-clack-clack, each of Maggie's revelations was more devastating than its predecessor with the final one leaving no room for doubt – *Nick was Billy.*

'You alright, luv?' Maggie asked. And then, giving it one last try, 'Reckon you could use a good quiffing.'

But Dunston had already turned, staggered to the post-chaise and stumbled in, collapsing on the back seat like an over-the-hill rake after a night of loose women and hard liquor. With a click of his tongue Moccles set the horses off at a walking pace.

'Where to now, sir?'

'Scotland Yard.'

Chapter Forty-Six: Scotland Yard

Moccles moved the two horses along at a steady pace and before Dunston was ready, they were at Scotland Yard. Dunston felt more despicable than a twofaced snitch peaching on his mate, but he knew he had to share his troubling findings about Nick with Inspector Line. He intended to confine his report to the signet ring, something Line already knew about, and how, sadly, it tied Nick to Ellen Ternan's murder. But once in the inspector's office, other bits and pieces, including the envelope, spilled out as a still-shaken Dunston garbled his way through recent events.

Nick's Ma, or rather non-Ma, was the most damaging unintended disclosure. The policeman, obviously not following, probed the inept fibber as he might a gallows-bound Newgate lag, and under pressure, Dunston let slip that his manservant was Billy, the illegitimate offspring, cast aside at birth, of his uncle and Ellen Ternan. Dunston was aghast that he'd revealed one of the two skeletons in Uncle's cupboard that Miss Georgina was most anxious to keep hidden. Thank goodness he'd not divulged anything about his uncle's murder, although the inspector cast some questioning looks at him as the story poured forth.

Line fell silent, head on chest, evidently deep in thought as he digested Dunston's startling news. When he at last looked up, his worried expression was enough to unnerve Dunston, but his words shook the poor man even more.

'Mr Burnett, I fear Miss Hogarth's in grave danger.'

'Miss Hogarth? In grave danger? H-how?'

'Revenge, that's what's driving Nick, or Billy as he really is... and he's not finished. He could've taken off after killing Miss Ternan and been in the clear, but he came back to Woods View House. Why? Because he's intent on settling the score with *everyone* involved in his abandonment as a baby.'

Everyone? Nick had already killed his mother and father. Who else was there? Dunston wondered. And what did this have to do with Miss Georgina? Dunston had no idea, but the inspector did.

'Nick must've spied on Gad's Hill Place and seen enough of Miss Hogarth's comings and goings to realise she managed all of Mr Dickens's household and personal matters, and naturally concluded that she'd handled the arrangements for his birth, that she was the one who'd despatched him to an orphanage. *That's* why he's after her.'

Miss Georgina! Nick's next target! And where was the villain now? At Gad's Hill Place on loan to his unsuspecting victim... *thanks to Dunston*. Any lingering doubts about the man's guilt vanished, swept away like a puff of cigar smoke snatched by a stiff sea-breeze.

'Inspector, Nick is on loan to Miss Hogarth!' he squawked.

'Damnation! Perfect opportunity for the man. Quick! We must leave for Gad's Hill Place at once.' The inspector started to rise.

'No, hold on. Miss Hogarth sent Nick on an errand. He's taking her stallion to Shropshire.'

'Thank God. Miss Hogarth is safe for the moment. When is Nick due back?'

'Late tomorrow afternoon.'

'Alright, we have time.' Line resettled himself in his chair. 'Let me think.'

Dunston was on tenterhooks for what seemed like an age but was in fact no more than a few minutes before Line spoke.

'Mr Burnett, there's not enough evidence to arrest Nick for Miss Ternan's murder, but maybe what we tried with Snatcher will work with Nick. If Luke Mallick identifies your manservant as Billy, then Nobbler's death-bed indictment that "Billy done me" would be enough for me to arrest him for the tramp's murder.'

Dunston eagerly nodded his understanding, and approval.

'Here's what we'll do,' the inspector continued. 'First thing tomorrow I'll collect Luke Mallick from Bleeding Heart Yard and bring him to Gad's Hill Place. Then, when Mr Nick Sharpe shows up in the afternoon, we'll have a nice, little welcoming party for him.'

Chapter Forty-Seven: Back Where It All Started

It was Saturday, July 9, exactly one month after the novelist's death, and at long last the author's study was back in use. Miss Georgina and Mr Clatterbuck had just completed their business meeting, a mind-dulling review of provisions in Charles's will, when the arrival of the young couple at precisely ten o'clock irradiated the room. Who could possibly be immune to Dulcet's blushing smiles as she gazed adoringly at her husband-to-be? As for Isaac, he looked overwhelmed, even embarrassed by all the attention, but there was no mistaking his passion for the maid.

Georgina ushered the pair towards the desk where the lawyer was laying out a rental agreement for the cottage she'd found for them in the village of Little Hermitage, barely a ten-minute walk from Gad's Hill Place.

'Thank you, Mr Clatterbuck, everything seems to be in order. Let me send for Nick to witness our signatures.' She rang a bell on the wall and when Ruby appeared, instructed her to fetch Nick.

Rat-a-tat, rat-a-tat.

'Drat!' Ruby exclaimed. Having delivered Nick to the study, she was half way down the stairs to the kitchen on her way to a nice cup of tea when the sound of the front door knocker obliged her to turn around and hurry back up.

'Lawks a mussy!'

Poor Ruby. Never before had she been confronted by a bunch of men crowding the front steps with what looked like every intent of storming the house. Worse still, three of them were wearing the dark blue uniform of the police, their whistles, billy-clubs and lamps conveying not a sense of security, but the threat of immediate incarceration. She jumped back in sheer panic and started to close the door, only for an authoritative figure in a bowler hat to place one large boot in the jam.

A roly-poly figure emerged from behind Mr Bowler Hat.

'Ruby, Ruby! It's me.'

Ruby stared at him. 'Mr Burnett? Is that you?'

'Yes, it is. And Inspector Line... from Scotland Yard,' Dunston explained.

'Don't care where he's from. Got no right scaring the dumplings out of honest people,' she blustered.

'Miss,' the inspector said firmly, 'this is a matter of life and death. Where's Nick?'

'Nick? What d'you want him for?'

'Is he still in Shropshire?'

'Shropshire? No, got back yesterday, day early. He just went in the study to see miss.'

'Good God!' Dunston cried. 'Is she alone with him?' His eyes swivelled wildly from Ruby to Line and back to Ruby.

'No, sir. Mr Clatterbuck's there, and so's the two love birds, Dulcie an' Isaac.'

'It's alright, Mr Burnett,' Line reassured him. 'She's safe as long as other people are with her. He won't harm her with witnesses present.' He turned to Ruby, pointing to his right. 'That's the study window, correct?'

'Yes, sir.'

'Good. Just the one door into the study? Off the main passageway?'

'Yes, sir.'

'Thank you, Ruby. You've done well. Now, listen, I want you to go to the kitchen and stay there 'til I send for you. D'you understand?' The inspector was speaking softly now but there was no mistaking his expectation that Ruby would do exactly as told.

And she did. With a final 'Yes, sir,' she scurried off.

227

Line quickly positioned his three constables. 'Braxton, stay here. No one in or out unless they're with me. Got it?'

'Aye, sir!'

'Ackworth, take Dawkins and station yourselves outside the study door. Not a sound, mind. And same procedure – no one in or out unless I tell you otherwise.'

'Right, sir!'

'Mr Mallick, I've every reason to believe the person you know as Billy is in the study.' Luke Mallick, the sixth man in the party, nodded, having clearly figured this out for himself. 'I want you to confirm we've identified the right man this time, but don't let him see you,' Line continued. 'Don't want to give him any chance to scarper. D'you understand?'

'Aye, I follow you.'

'Right then, here's what we'll do.' The inspector laid out his plan.

'Mr Burnett, you're first.'

Dunston's anxiety-racked five-foot-two-inches quivered like a just-plucked harp string as he inched his way to the study window and carefully looked in. Everyone was standing around the desk busy with some papers. Nobody was interested in the window. He returned to the front porch.

'It's Nick. He's in there,' he reported breathlessly.

'Your turn, Mr Mallick,' Line said.

The young man edged to the window and peered in. His look lasted longer than Dunston's, but finally he turned and retraced his steps.

Desperate to know what Luke saw, dreading what he might report, Dunston sputtered, 'W-well?'

'It's him alright, it's Billy,' Luke replied.

In the study, Georgina blotted the final signature. 'Thank you so much for helping, Nick,' she said with a warm smile. 'Is that everything, Mr Clatterbuck?'

'Indeed, it is Miss Hogarth.' The lawyer bowed and withdrew a step or two.

'Excellent. Then I think a little toast is called for.'

She turned to a small side table, picked up a silver tray with its already-filled glasses of sherry and, reversing their usual roles, served the maid and stable-boy. Dulcet curtsied, bursting with pleasure. Isaac took his glass not knowing where to look until his sweetheart squeezed his free hand and his lost-at-sea gaze found the blissfully safe harbour of her eyes.

After the lawyer and Nick had taken their drinks, Georgina replaced the tray, lifted her glass and addressed the young couple.

'Isaac and Dulcet, I'm so pleased—'

CRASH! The study door flew open and Line burst in, Ackworth and Dawkins hard on his heels.

'Miss Hogarth, please excuse this intrusion.'

Georgina turned, shocked into silence by the inspector's grim expression and the revolver held close to his side. Dulcet clutched Isaac's arm, spilling his sherry. Clatterbuck flinched, his glass dropping from his hand. Nick, body tensing, gulped a mouthful of sherry and stared, stone-faced, at the intruders.

'William Tringham,' Line barked. 'I hereby arrest you for—'

'NOOO!' The agonised cry checked the inspector mid-sentence. 'That name... ain't mine. You can't prove nothin', you dirty scufter.'

Line, thrown off stride, reacted instinctively. 'Oh yes we can. The birthmark will pr—'

'Ain't possible!' was the screamed response, part fearful, part confused. 'Nobody's seen it. Unless—' The speaker broke off, looking hard at Dulcet.

'Bitch!' he screamed. 'You saw it, didn't you?' He flung what was left of his sherry in her face and before anyone could move lashed out at her with the empty glass. Smashing on contact, it split her cheek, blood spurting from the gash like rainwater spouting from a gargoyle's mouth.

The inspector raised his revolver. 'Stop! Or I'll shoot!'

The maid's assailant didn't even hear the warning. He tossed the broken glass aside and lunged at the bleeding girl, shoving her across the room until her back was pressed hard against the bookshelves. He pinned her with his weight, his madman's hands swiftly finding her throat.

The inspector steadied himself and lined up his target.

Dulcet, her head swung savagely from side to side by her frenzied strangler, caught increasingly out-of-focus glimpses of panicked faces, shock-stilled figures and… the inspector's finger locked on the revolver's trigger. Fast losing consciousness, the half-choked girl twisted to the right, then pivoted sharply to the left with enough force to rotate their interlocked bodies, his back ending up against the bookshelves, hers directly in the path of the bullet already speeding from the policeman's gun.

Line's aim was deadly, the shot finding the soft spot between her shoulder blades.

Dunston couldn't believe his eyes. Dulcet shot? Yes. He could see the blood spreading down the back of her dress. She was slumped like a forgotten carcass hanging from a gibbet, the man's hands, rigid around her neck, keeping her upright until Ackworth and Dawkins rushed forward, yanked him away, and the maid slipped silently to the floor. Dulcet dead? Yes. He saw her body, unmoving, a macabre obscenity defiling the spotless parquet tiles.

Silence. Nobody moved. The two constables, one either side of the young man, held on to him but only loosely. The inspector, the gun dangling slackly from his hand, gaped in horror at what he'd done. The captive, dazed at first, began to quiver from head to foot, as though hatred was coursing through his body, building up until with one sudden lurch, he pulled free of the policemen's grasp.

'That slammock,' he wailed, his outstretched arm pointing at Dulcet's body, 'she done for me. She's the only one what saw it. The only one to see THIS!'

He tore his shirt open and the birthmark, a dull plum-coloured swathe shaped uncannily like the goose-quill favoured by the great author, was revealed to all. Line stared at the purple blemish, signs of understanding slowly spreading across his face. Dunston, not as quick as the inspector, peered from the doorway, unable to make head or tail of the nightmare unfolding before him. But then he gasped as his eyes slid up from the puce-pigmented breast to the dark, smouldering face, and he realised he was looking at Charles's son… his bastard son… not Nick… but Georgina's stable-boy… *Isaac.*

Chapter Forty-Eight: Luke Mallick

Seconds passed, the group in the study snared in a dazed silence until snapped back to life by a new voice.

'Didn't expect to see me again in this lifetime, did yer?' Luke Mallick, brushing Dunston aside, stepped into the study, stabbing his finger at the dumbfounded stable-boy.

'Luke! What're you doing here?'

'Ha, beginning to understand, are you? Aye... little lass didn't blab on you.'

'Shut yer rattletrap! You don't know nowt. Gabbling prattle-box saw it. When she bandaged me.'

'That's as may be, but I'm the one what told 'em 'bout your purple marking, not her. Thought I'd forget all about it, didn't yer? But I got it right here.' He thrust the sketch of the birthmark in Isaac's face.

Isaac staggered back, mouth slack, spittle dribbling down his chin, eyes locked on that damning drawing in his former friend's hand. Dunston could see from the look on his face that the enormity of what he'd done was slowly penetrating his madness. He was clearly realising that his failure to trust the woman who'd loved him more than life itself had caused her death, by Line's hand, true, but Isaac might as well have pulled the trigger himself. Dunston watched as the madman's face contorted, his mind surely splintering into a thousand jigsaw-puzzle pieces. But then, as though seized by a single imperative, his insane gaze veered towards Line... and stopped.

With a fearsome roar, Isaac charged. Line raised his arms to fend him off, but the lad wasn't interested in hurting the policeman. All he wanted was the revolver. He wrested it from the officer's grasp with a maniac's strength, pushing the inspector to the ground with ease. The gun's barrel disappeared in a trice into the stable-boy's mouth, a moment's hesitation, then, finger tightening, knuckle whitening, the study echoed with the sound of the afternoon's second gunshot, this one oddly muted.

Chapter Forty-Nine: The Missing Letter

'Good afternoon, Inspector Line.' Dunston fiddled nervously with the buttons of his ill-fitting, brown jacket and eyed his surprise visitor warily. 'Delighted to see you. Just having a spot of tea. Please join me.'

It was a full week since the inspector and his men had entered Gad's Hill Place to arrest Nick, only to find that Isaac, not Nick, was Charles Dickens's illegitimate son, Billy. So what could possibly have brought him to Woods View House today? Whatever it was, Dunston was not going to let slip anything about his uncle being murdered. That was still known to only three people – Dr Frank Beard, Miss Georgina and Dunston.

Their deadline for informing the police about Charles Dickens's poisoning had fallen on the same day Isaac and Dulcet had met their deaths, and the three conspirators had convened that evening to decide how much they would reveal to the authorities. The answer that eventually emerged was... nothing, a unanimous decision reached by each in his or her own way: Frank, satisfied that Charles's murderer had paid with his life; Georgina, pleased Charles's reputation was safe; and Dunston, pleased Miss Georgina was pleased.

Their mutually agreed silence shaped the historical record. John Forster, Dickens's literary agent and closest friend, would duly record in his 950-page *Life of Charles Dickens*, the first biography to appear, that the author died from a stroke. Every subsequent biographer, children to his Pied Piper, would blindly report exactly the same deceit. No one would ever know that Charles Dickens was poisoned. As long, that is, as the inspector was kept in the dark.

Dunston poured the tea while Line settled in an armchair which, together with its mate and a two-person sofa, formed a horseshoe facing the fireplace in the sitting room, a light, airy room, with windows overlooking the garden.Sparingly decorated, the room was free of the elaborate ornamentation that overwhelmed many another parlour, but all the more refreshing and relaxing in consequence.

'There's no doubt that Isaac killed Nobbler and Miss Ternan,' Line began, 'but I'd like to clear up a few loose ends if you don't mind, sir.' Ever the professional, he'd put together most of the pieces but it always paid to check.

'Of course. Not sure I fully understand everything myself,' Dunston admitted as he seated himself in the other armchair.

'Then, let's begin with Nobbler's death,' Line suggested. 'Nobbler's dying words were "Billy done me" and we now know that Billy was Isaac, but we don't know when or where Isaac inflicted that deadly eye wound on Nobbler.'

'Yes, I wondered about that,' Dunston replied. 'All I could think of was that Isaac stabbed Nobbler in the eye when the two vagabonds waylaid him as he was returning to Gad's Hill Place.'

'Had the same thought myself,' Line said. 'We don't know that for a *fact*, but it's the most likely explanation. As a footnote, I suspect the ambush was when Snatcher realised Isaac was Billy. He and Nobbler overlapped with Billy at Heaven's Haven, don't forget, so my guess is that when I heard Nobbler say "Snatcher blank Billy," the missing word was *pegged*, and not *is* as you suggested.' The inspector arched an eyebrow in Dunston's direction.

Dunston nodded. Yes, he thought, the inspector's interpretation makes more sense. At least it fits the facts, unlike mine.

'Let's move on to the ring, another murky area. When you came to see me at Scotland Yard, you said you saw Nick pick up something shiny when he and Isaac searched for the ring after the attack on Dulcet at Dillywood Lane. But was it the ring? Did you actually see it?'

'Not… exactly. But it had to be. If Nick didn't pick it up, how did it end up in Windsor Lodge beside Miss Ternan's body?'

'Again, I don't know this for a *fact*,' the policeman said, 'but I suspect *Isaac* was the one to find it.'

'Really? Hmmm… it's true he found Dulcet's purse… but when he handed it to her, it was empty.'

'Ha! There you are,' Line said confidently. 'He took the ring out before giving the purse to Dulcet.'

'Yes, that would certainly explain the ring's presence by Miss Ternan's body, and confirm that Isaac murdered her,' Dunston acknowledged, 'but what I still can't understand is *why* he killed her. It couldn't be revenge for abandoning him as a baby because *she* wasn't his mother. Isaac visited his *real* mother several weeks ago. Apparently, the poor woman was dying and wanted to see her son one last time. Miss Georgina has the letter from Isaac's sister requesting permission for him to go home, and another informing her of his return, and letters are facts, aren't they?'

'I didn't know about these letters but, if they arrived as you say, then indeed they are facts,' the inspector responded. 'But let me ask you this. If you received a letter from *my* sister saying *my* mother was desperately ill, what would you think?'

'Well, naturally I'd be very concerned for your mother and of course for you,' the innocent replied.

'I had no doubt,' Line said, 'but the *facts* are that my mother's been dead thirty years and I don't have a sister.'

'Dead? Thirty years? No sister?' Dunston, as though wading through treacle, struggled to grasp the policeman's point. 'You mean, the mother in the letters received by Miss Georgina was made up?'

'That's exactly what I mean. Isaac probably sent those letters himself, the first so he could disappear without arousing suspicion and kill Miss Ternan, his real mother, the second because he couldn't bear being separated from Dulcet. Only a guess, and the timing would have to fit, but—'

'It does. From what I recall, one letter arrived shortly before and the other shortly after Miss Ternan's death. There, that explains away the alleged mother. Most satisfactory, inspector. Very well done.'

'Thank you, sir. Now, coming to the main reason for my visit. Thought you should see *this* letter.' The inspector took a sheet of notepaper from the pocket of his single-breasted, charcoal-grey jacket and handed it to Dunston. Dunston began to read.

Clatterbuck and Jorrin, Solicitors
7 Gray's Inn Square, Holborn
May 3, 1850

My Dear Sir:
I'm delighted to hear that you have accepted my counsel not to acknowledge Miss Ellen Ternan's child as your own. As I have endeavoured to explain, my advice is based entirely on my interest in protecting your reputation as gentleman and author, and ensuring, I hope, a continuation of your highly profitable career as the country's foremost novelist.

Dunston's incredulous eyes darted back to the date – *May 3, 1850*. This... this is the letter stolen from Uncle's drawer... the letter that must have been in the envelope that was later found empty next to Ellen's body. He looked at Line.

'Where did you find this?'

'Isaac's jacket pocket.'

Isaac's jacket pocket! Dunston gasped in horror, understanding crashing down on him. By a cruel twist of fate, Isaac happened on *this* letter when he broke into Uncle's study, and not the *other* letter, the one from Ellen, the one that Dunston chanced upon. Had he found that letter, he'd have known his father had cared for him enough to provide for his upbringing through the monthly payments to Ellen. Instead, his eye fell on the letter *denouncing* him as Charles Dickens's son, hardening his hatred for his father and triggering a downward spiral of death for father, mother and son.

Dunston, rooted in his thoughts, realised Line was talking.

'...very odd, don't you think?'

'I... beg your pardon.'

'The date. I was saying how odd to find a letter to Mr Dickens dated third of May, 1850, when he was reputed to have burned all his correspondence in a bonfire ten years later.'

'Um… yes… very odd,' was all Dunston could manage.

'My guess,' Line said, 'is that Mr Dickens kept a few important letters from the flames, letters like the one you're holding in your hand. Perhaps in the drawer of his desk, the one that was jimmied.'

'Ah! Very good, inspector. More tea?'

Line hid his smile as he regarded Dunston's open-book face, so transparent even a child could read it.

'No thank you, still have half a cup.' Line was not about to be side-tracked. He reclaimed the letter from Dunston and said, 'Now, if this letter was in the desk, then we can reasonably conclude that that's where Isaac found it. He probably entered the study *after* Lavelle had left and saw it in the open drawer.'

Line knows about the twice-robbed drawer, Dunston fretted. What else does he know?

'Frankly, I was always curious about the timing of that robbery and the subsequent death of Mr Dickens,' the policeman continued. 'Did that thought ever strike you, sir?'

'Yes… I mean *no*… I don't think it ever did. No, I'm sure I never thought that. Not even for a second. Didn't cross my mind.' Dunston knew he was babbling on, spouting denials as freely as a toothless, old man sprayed spittle.

'I'm surprised.' The inspector didn't look the least bit surprised. 'A rejected son, finding he's been disowned by his father might harbour thoughts of revenge, might be tempted to bring that man's life to an untimely end, might, in short, be driven to murder. Of course, just a theory.' Such were Line's words but the look on his face said this was much more than fanciful conjecture.

Danger! What would Miss Georgina say if this particular secret was suddenly made public?Dunston must act.

'Interesting, but as you say, just a theory… and not consistent with the facts, if I may say so.'

'And which facts are they, sir?'

'Well, only one really, but an important one. Uncle Charles died of a stroke, as confirmed by Dr Steele.'

'Yes, sir. Quite right. Must have slipped my mind,' he replied.

Dunston doubted that any fact ever escaped the inspector's strongbox of a memory. No, the policeman recalled the doctor's opinion very clearly, and since he'd obviously figured out that Charles was murdered by Isaac, he must also suspect that Dr Steele was somehow manipulated into misreporting the cause of death. Dunston panicked. The inspector knew every dirty detail of the Frank-Georgina-Dunston conspiracy. They'd all be arrested, and Uncle's murder, by his own son no less, would be bold-print, frontpage headlines in every newspaper in the land.

'Anyway, whatever the truth, sir, we'll never get to the bottom of your uncle's death now that Isaac's dead. And nobody will hear from my lips that the lad was Mr Dickens's offspring. So I don't think there's anything to worry about,' he said kindly.

Dunston nodded gratefully, his body sagging with relief, his estimation of the inspector as detective and human being soaring sky-high.

Line finished his tea and rose to take his leave. 'Mr Burnett, it's been a great pleasure to meet you. It was your extraordinary insight that the unknown Billy was Nobbler's murderer that solved this case. Thanks to your remarkable ability to see beyond the physical evidence,' Line said, unwittingly echoing Dickens's words of twenty years earlier about Dunston's golden one percent, 'and your determination to follow your instincts wherever they take you, justice has been served. Would that my fellow detectives were as astute and persevering as you.' He held out his hand.

Dunston was delighted by the policeman's praise. He stood and shook his hand heartily.

'Sad to say,' the inspector continued, 'this will be the last time we meet, at least in my official capacity.'

'I... don't follow. Last time?'

'Yes, sir. I will be submitting my letter of resignation Monday morning.'

'What? You can't resign. What will the police force do without you?'

Line smiled. 'The police force will survive, I'm sure, and my mind is set.'

'But why?' Dunston asked.

'The maid, a mere child, shot in the back by my own hand. That was the *only* time I fired my revolver in twenty-five years on the force, but that doesn't make it right. As man and police officer, I have no choice but to step down.'

'But—'

'Mr Burnett, I bid you good day.'

Chapter Fifty: Clearing the Air

Later that afternoon, Nick entered the sitting room at Woods View House carrying a large, oblong package.

'This come for you, sir,' he said, his words clipped and icy, relations between the two having been strained ever since Isaac's suicide a week ago.

'Er... thank you... Nick.' Dunston, head down, didn't dare look at his manservant. What a muddle, he said to himself for the umpteenth time. How could I have been *so* mistaken about Nick? How could I have *mistrusted* him so? And how much does he know? Has he guessed what terrible atrocities I thought him guilty of?

The manservant watched his master remove the wrapping paper to reveal a framed painting.

'Luke Mallick brought it,' he ventured, slightly more warmly. 'Said it was a thank-you for you paying off his debt to the Mawgsbys.'

Dunston inspected the painting. 'Ah, the nymphs. How delightful.'

'Can put it over the mantle if you like.' Nick stepped forward and took the painting.

'Yes... thank you.'

Was the glacier of stilted civility beginning to thaw? Possibly, thought Dunston, but it wouldn't be fully melted until the cause of their estrangement had been squarely faced. Dunston coughed, nerving himself to speak, but before he could say a word, Nick grabbed the bull by the cods, as he would have put it, and launched in.

'Now, sir, time I spoke up,' he said.

Dunston groaned, fearing what was coming next.

'That day in Mr Dickens's study when Dulcet got shot an' Isaac blew his brains out,' Dunston blanched noticeably, 'could've sworn the inspector had come to nab me. Looked right at me, he did, when he said, "William Tringham, I hereby arrest you." Now why'd he look at me? And then be taken aback when Isaac piped up? Started the cogs grinding in the old noddle, it did.'

'Yes... most unfortunate, but—'

'Beggin' pardon, sir, best let me get on with it. See, seemed like them crushers was there to snaffle *me*, not Isaac. And that's what I couldn't fathom. Why ever would they think I done Nobbler?'

'And Miss Ternan.' The words slipped out before Dunston could stop them.

'What? Nobbler *and* Miss Ternan?'

'In a way,' the master croaked un-masterly. 'Though the inspector didn't have all the proof he needed regarding Miss Ternan,' he added lamely.

Miss Ternan? Nick stared, incomprehension clouding his face at this new wrinkle. But not for long. Nick might lack a formal education but he was versed in the ways of the world and had long known about the comings and goings at Windsor Lodge.

'Miss Ternan was... um... close to Mr Dickens, real close, if you take my meaning.'

'N... no, I don't think so.' Dunston hated himself for lying, but what could he do? He had to protect his uncle's reputation for Miss Georgina's sake.

'Well, that's queer. See, Mr Dickens's goings on with Miss Ternan may have been swept under the rug *upstairs,* but they was everybody's business *downstairs.*'

'What?'

'Aye. Molly, scullery maid at Windsor Lodge, is the cousin of Ruby, under maid at Gad's Hill Place. Whatever goes on at Miss Ternan's house is known by the servants at the other house almost before it happens. And then there's the midwife.'

'Midwife?'

'One what went with Miss Ternan to France and helped birth her little

241

boy, then brought the new-born back to England and dumped him in some orphanage in Bleeding Heart Yard. That midwife happens to be Molly's mother.'

'No!'

'Yes, sir.'

'Oh, dear,' Dunston muttered. 'You mean the servants knew there was... a child?'

'That they did. Knew all 'bout Mr Dickens's fancy woman, and the little *offshoot*.'

A miserable Dunston was praying for Nick to stop before any more ugly revelations spilled forth. But Nick was not finished.

'Now, I ask you. Seems to me this child, grown to manhood, is much more likely to do away with the mother what abandoned him than me, someone who'd never met the lady, don't yer think, sir?'

Dunston sighed. He'd dissembled too long. Nick was too close to the truth. He had to clear this up before it went too far.

'Yes, you're right.'

Dunston was dreading Nick's reaction when he learned about the allegations his master had made. He breathed in, gripped the arms of his chair, released a whoosh of air as though ridding himself of some noxious gas, and began his explanation.

'You see, when I heard you were brought up in an orphanage in Bleeding Heart Yard, I thought... that is, I thought you were Uncle's—'

'Ha! You thought *I* was Mr Dickens's love-child. Well, polish my piston!' Nick exclaimed gleefully.

Dunston watched in disbelief as Nick clapped his hands and did a little jig.

'You mean, you're not... outraged?'

'Outraged? 'Cos you thought I was Mr Dickens's son? Bless me steamin' hot swingers! Me... son of the famous writer? What could be better? Wish it was true, but it ain't. Never been in Bleeding Heart Yard in my life. Orphanage I grew up in was in Hackney. Still, much honoured that you thought I could be his young'un. Thank you very much,' he said with a broad grin.

Dunston let out a long sigh, thanking his lucky stars that Nick had not made any connection to Uncle Charles's death. And *so* relieved the damage to their relationship was not as great as he'd feared. For the first time in the conversation, he looked Nick in the eye.

Even though language is one of mankind's most remarkable accomplishments, verbal communication is sometimes quite superfluous. A look can speak volumes. The one shared between master and manservant said plain as day that their squire-to-knight bond had been restored, even strengthened. The look also carried a message. Each knew exactly what must be done, but as usual in their odd relationship, it was the servant who had to translate thought into action.

'Nice afternoon, sir,' Nick said conversationally.

'Yes... indeed.'

'You ain't seen Miss Georgina for the past week,' he remarked.

'No... I haven't.'

'Perhaps you fancy a little drive?'

'Yes, believe I do, but... it's a little late, don't you think? Perhaps another day.'

'Beggin' pardon, sir, but where the ladies is concerned, it's my experience that you have to strike while the iron's hot, seize the day, take time by the forelock.'

'N-no doubt, but I don't feel today is... um... right. Not quite... ready. Have to... prepare.' Dunston dithered a little longer, but then found his backbone. 'I'll go... tomorrow... Sunday. Sunday afternoon's a good time for a visit. Yes, *that's* what I'll do. Have the carriage ready... three o'clock sharp.'

Nick nodded. His master was a dilly-dallier, but once he settled on a course of action, there was no stopping him. Come what might, Mr Burnett *would* be at Gad's Hill Place to see Miss Georgina tomorrow afternoon.

Chapter Fifty-One: Bereft

The next morning found a restless Georgina drifting forlornly through Gad's Hill Place, lost in a void once filled to overflowing by *him*. Drawing room... empty, just like the conservatory. The study, his sanctuary... empty. The quirky, larger-than-life characters, vanished; the sprawling, wondrous stories, no more; the speeding quill, stilled; Charles Dickens, *her* Charles Dickens, silenced forever.

She'd never imagined she'd feel so... so bereft by his absence, but she'd had no choice, she *had* to do what she did, *had* to sacrifice the man to save him from himself. Getting hold of the strychnine had been easy – a discreet visit to an apothecary, eight pence in payment, an ounce of white powder in return. After that, it was child's play to doctor the bottle of Battley's Sedative Solution, half an ounce mixed with the laudanum, the rest kept in reserve just in case, but in the end not needed.

Once she'd fully understood what he had in mind, she knew this was one mess that couldn't be cleaned up *after* the event. She had to act *before*. And there was only one way to eliminate *all* possibility of him shredding his own reputation, destroying everything he'd worked for, everything that was as much *hers* as his. *Charles had to die.*

It wasn't his actress-mistress that drove her to act. She'd known about the slut for years. Charles thought he was dreadfully clever, but he was *so* transparent – the cross-channel trips, the house in Peckham, the bills for perfume, all unmistakable signs of a romantic entanglement.

Nor was it the illegitimate brat. She'd learned about that sordid detail soon after Charles's visit to Field Lane School. He'd shut himself in the study, pacing to and fro, his doleful tread setting the tempo for her pounding heart as she pressed her ear to the door, wondering what was weighing upon him. A week later, when she received the jeweller's invoice for the single letter engraved on the inside of his disgusting *Progeny Ring*, she knew. Ten letters for the first-name initials of his ten legitimate children, then one more for his mongrel son – a newly-cut W.

That Charles had a mistress and a bastard was repulsive to her, but she could live with the knowledge as long as it stayed out of the public eye. But Charles, seeking to ease the remorse that plagued him and make amends for callously abandoning his infant son, was bent on acknowledging William as his offspring. The stupid man was set on baring his darkest secrets to the world in hope of earning his son's forgiveness.

The first inkling of trouble reared its ugly head on the last day of May when Clatterbuck delivered a revised will for Charles's signature. As Georgina was showing the loose-tongued toady out, he couldn't resist disclosing that the new bequest, the only amendment, was *huge* – ten thousand pounds. He didn't mention the beneficiary but she knew – ten thousand pounds for *The Whore*. Could he still be so smitten? And so foolhardy? She had to find that will and see for herself.

The next day, Georgina slipped into the study while Charles was out for a morning walk. Her spare key, never used before, turned easily in the desk drawer's lock, and the author's private papers were exposed to her prying eyes. She grabbed the large manila envelope resting on top of a handful of letters, and quickly opened it. But it wasn't the will, just his notes for the second half of the Drood story.

She scanned them, and there, in the outline for the last chapter, she saw exactly what he intended, exactly what she feared. The damning admission about his illegitimate son would be in Detective Datchery's words to be sure, but it would really be *Charles's* confession. The words put in the character's mouth by an author as desperate as his chosen spokesman to right the wrong inflicted on an innocent child. But once published, his flesh-fuelled flaws would be laid bare on the whiteness of the printed page, there for anyone to read… and interpret, as had Dunston.

But the notes were just the tip of the iceberg. Her eyes fell next on a legal-looking envelope. She opened it and found the will drafted by Clatterbuck and awaiting Charles's approval. She saw the bequest to his whore on the very first page. That was bad enough, but the scribbled reminder to himself, a single-word notation in the margin, leapt from the page, stealing her breath, sucking her down in ice-cold quicksand – *William*.

The fool was going to put his bastard son in his will. The little monster as well as the wanton hussy? How could he? He was going to expose all his sins, even confirming his paternity in a legal document. He was going to ruin everything. She could see the headlines, big, black, bold, besmirching his name, debasing his reputation. She had to act quickly.

She returned the will to its envelope and replaced it in the drawer exactly as she'd found it. She couldn't take that, at least not yet. But she could take the Drood notes. Nobody must ever see them. She put several blank sheets of paper in the manilla envelope – enough, she hoped, to cover up her theft for the time being – and laid it on top of the letters. She turned the key in the lock and hurried out.

That evening, she went back to the study after Charles had finished his writing for the day, and laced his tonic with the just-purchased strychnine. She'd hoped the poison would do its work before Charles could instruct Clatterbuck to include William in a new will, but as she was replacing the bottle of Battley's Sedative Solution, she spotted the current draft, torn in half, in the wastepaper basket. Was she too late? Had he already notified his lawyer to prepare a new will? To add William?

She hurriedly checked the letters he'd written that day and left on his desk for her to collect, the usual practice. There were two. One, to a fellow novelist; that one would be placed on the hall table ready for posting the next day. The other, addressed to Clatterbuck and containing, Georgina suspected, Charles's instructions for William's inclusion in a new will, would *never* reach the lawyer.

The guardian of his reputation, then, now and forever, had fulfilled her pledge to protect Charles's standing for as long as she should live. Thanks to her steely will, the greatest danger to Charles's literary standing, the man himself, had been removed without arousing any suspicion. And with the death of the bastard stableboy by his own hand and that of his whoring mother by the same hand, the two remaining threats to Charles's position in the literary universe had been eliminated.

Over a week had passed since the shootings of Dulcet and Isaac, and nothing had appeared in the newspapers smearing Charles's name, nothing about illegitimate offspring, nothing about kept women, and, most important of all, *nothing*, not even a whisper, questioning how he died. His rightful place among the titans of English literature was secure, and his cherished memory would stand unblemished for all time.

Willing herself back to the present, she glanced at Charles's eight-day chiming clock – half past seven. Moccles should be here by now with the coach-and-four. She turned on her heel and walked firmly out of the study. She'd given twenty-five years of her life to the novelist, but that was over; it was time for her to go, never to return. She exited the house and stepped into Sunday's early morning sunshine.

She was no sooner settled in the carriage, when she felt the horses take the strain. A moment later they were pulling through the gates at the end of the drive. With a quick glance back and a whispered goodbye, she left Gad's Hill Place to its memories... and its secrets.

Chapter Fifty-Two: Three Months Later

'**N**ewspaper, sir.' Nick handed the day's Times to his master.
'Bit late,' grumbled Dunston. 'Already finished my breakfast.' He took a last sip of his coffee, wiped his mouth and stood up from the table. 'I'll read it in the drawing room.'

He settled himself in his favourite armchair and shook open the newspaper. He was a selective but thorough reader. Once he'd found an article of interest, he'd read it from start to finish. Today, he read in full an account of the latest parliamentary debate on the Irish question; ditto a piece on whether Britain should become a minority shareholder in the Suez Canal.

He turned the page. The first item's heading read:

BRITISH TOURIST DIES IN SWITZERLAND

Not something likely to interest him. He was already moving on when his eyes were drawn back to the barely glimpsed opening words of the article – *Miss Georgina Hogarth...* Georgina!

It was three months since Dunston had taken that last futile drive to Gad's Hill Place to see her. Second thoughts, a common occurrence for Dunston, were swirling in his mind long before the carriage had crested the rise to the house. He'd set off at 3 o'clock that Sunday afternoon as planned, but as the seconds ticked by he felt more and more uncomfortable. Why was he dong this? What would be say to her? Good questions but in the end irrelevant; Georgina was not at home. A much relieved Dunston had sat back in the carriage and let Nick drive him back to the security of Woods View House.

He'd thought of her often since then, not so much with regret, but with curiosity about why she'd left without a word and where she'd gone. Here at last was some news.

He read the lead sentence. *Miss Georgina Hogarth, a British citizen, died while on holiday in Lausanne.* That was unsettling enough but it was nothing compared with the next sentence. *According to Swiss authorities, Miss Hogarth ended her life by ingesting poison.* Suicide? Miss Georgina? His boggling eyes rushed on to the next few words. *The almost empty bottle of Battley's Sedative Solution found beside her body was laced with strychnine.*

Battley's Sedative Solution? Strychnine? Dear God, just like Uncle! The news exploded in his mind, but before he could collect his wits and digest it, the Times correspondent dropped his second bombshell. *Found among her possessions were several Charles Dickens memorabilia and some papers in the late novelist's hand.*

Papers! In Uncle's hand! He skipped over the list of mementos and keepsakes, and fastened his eyes on the description of the written material. Notes! Six numbered pages of notes. Good Lord! The outlines for the second half of the Drood mystery, one for each of the six instalments.

He scanned the reporter's account. Not much on the first two pages, but the jottings on the third spoke of Edwin confronting Jasper in the tomb. Edwin lived! Just as Dunston had envisaged. Pages four and five sketched how Datchery and Grewgious used Rosa's ruby and diamond engagement ring to trick Jasper into re-entering the tomb, again exactly as Dunston had envisioned.

But what of the final page? Did that last note make clear that Edwin was Datchery's abandoned son, as Isaac was Dickens's? The journalist offered no enlightenment on this point, instead confessing himself totally baffled by a sheet that was blank except for one word – *SON!* But Dunston knew exactly what it meant. He'd been right. The Datchery-Edwin relationship was to be Uncle's acknowledgement, veiled yet in public view, of his own father-son relationship.

Quietly pleased with himself, Dunston leaned back in his chair and rested the newspaper on his lap. His pleasure at this unexpected confirmation of his solution to the Drood story, however, was short-lived. The Times, as if of its own accord, began pivoting upward until it was back in front of his eyes insisting he read more. Was there something else? Indeed there was. Georgina had also kept a letter. Never posted, it must have been in her possession ever since she left Gad's Hill Place.

It was an instruction from Dickens to his lawyer, Clatterbuck, to add a new beneficiary to his will. That much was clear. But, as the article explained, the name of the proposed legatee had been blacked out, or almost. Whoever had done the crossing out had missed part of the initial letter and left traces of a W. W! W for William! Uncle had intended to include his and Ellen Ternan's son in his will.

This time the newspaper slipped from Dunston's hands all the way to the carpet. He mopped his brow and stared straight ahead, his face set. He tried to empty his mind, but the ugly thoughts crowding in could not be stopped. He sank lower and lower in his chair as the article's revelations pierced his brain like darts, each perforation forcing him closer to the horrible truth. *Georgina* took the notes for Uncle's novel… *Georgina* kept the letter about Uncle's will… *Georgina* saved for her own use the strychnine-laced tonic that ended Uncle's life. She removed *everything* that could possibly taint the novelist's reputation, including the man himself. None of this was Line-grade proof of guilt, but in his heart of hearts Dunston *knew* Miss Georgina killed his uncle.

Dunston sat motionless for a full hour, absorbing what he'd read in the article's half a dozen paragraphs. Not for even a single second had he suspected Georgina of killing the novelist but in the end, this failure was of no consequence. The murderess had forfeited her own life for her sin, and that gave Dunston the comfort of knowing his uncle's death had been avenged. He was left, if not with a sense of satisfaction, at least with a sense that matters had been brought to a close, and justly so.

It was several days before Dunston finally felt settled, once more at peace with himself. He didn't know what the future held in store for him. Perhaps the tranquillity and solitude of a contented bachelorhood; perhaps another adventure in tandem with the iconic Archibald Line. Whatever it might be,

Dunston was ready.

The End

What's Fact, What's Fiction

For readers who would like to learn more about Charles Dickens, the options are legion. My favourite biographies are those by John Forster (*The Life of Charles Dickens*, Chapman and Hall, 1874), Edgar Johnson (*Charles Dickens, His Tragedy and Triumph*, Simon and Schuster, 1952) and Peter Ackroyd (*Dickens*, HarperCollins, 1990). Other books I found particularly useful for this novel are *Georgina Hogarth and the Dickens Circle* by Arthur Adrian (Oxford University Press, 1957) and *The Invisible Woman: The Story of Charles Dickens and Nelly Ternan* by Claire Tomalin (Vintage Books, 1990).

Virtually all the material in *Immortalised to Death* pertaining to Dickens is historically accurate. This is true of minor incidents such as the burning of his correspondence in 1860 as well as major events including his death on June 9th, 1870 at Gad's Hill Place although not from strychnine poisoning, or so we are told.

The sole instance where fiction departs from fact is the timing of his separation from Catherine, his wife. Many of the events surrounding the rift, including Dickens's first encounter with his mistress-to-be and his pursuit of her to Doncaster, all happened exactly as portrayed in the novel with one difference – everything occurs eight years earlier than in reality to allow the issue of their union to reach the age of twenty by the time of the novelist's death.

Of the main characters, Georgina Hogarth and Ellen Ternan actually lived. Georgina remained a spinster and a resolute defender of Dickens until her death in 1917 at the age of ninety. Ellen married George Wharton Robinson six years after Dickens's death, and together they had two children. Speculation has remained rife that Dickens and Ellen had a child. The evidence is suggestive rather than conclusive, and Billy in my story should definitely be considered a figment of my imagination.

The evidence of a relationship between Ellen and Dickens, however, is incontrovertible. The first bequest in Dickens's will is to none other than... Ellen Ternan. Telling as this is, evidence of the relationship only began to appear in the 1930s, an amazing sixty years after Dickens's death. Dickens's red leather pocket diary, lost by the author in 1867, resurfaced at an auction in New York in 1922. The entries are highly abbreviated – N, for example, stands for Nelly, Dickens's name for Ellen – but when deciphered, they provide a clear record of the Dickens-Ellen romance.

The other main characters – Dunston Burnett and Inspector Line – are made up, as are their efforts to solve the various crimes, also pure fiction, that drive the tale.

Gad's Hill Place, now a school, is depicted as it was in 1870. The house, a short train ride from central London, is well worth visiting. The study, the setting for some of the novel's most important scenes, is much as it was in Dickens's day apart from the computer that now graces, or disgraces depending on your point of view, his desk.

Turning to the *Mystery of Edwin Drood*, all characters and incidents are exactly as described by the master in the completed half of his story. Forster's account of Dickens's intention to expose Jasper by means of the diamond and ruby ring is drawn straight from his biography of the novelist, as is his recollection of the author's 'very curious idea' for the final scene. Of course, the solution offered in *Immortalised to Death* is entirely a result of Dunston's literary sleuthing.

Whether Dickens intended Edwin to live or not has been the subject of heated debate for almost one hundred and fifty years, a time span that has seen countless attempts to find *the* solution. My own view is that this is a fool's errand for one simple reason – Dickens himself had not decided what to do with Edwin.

This is not as strange as it may sound. Think of *The Pickwick Papers,* his first major literary success. The monthly instalments of that story recount a series of humorous incidents and embarrassing adventures linked, not by a continuous storyline laid out in advance, but by the foibles and eccentricities of the Pickwick Club members.

While this tendency to let the characters drive the story remained throughout his career, he did introduce more structure into his later novels and eventually adopted the practice of preparing notes outlining each story, the earliest surviving set being for *Dombey and Son* published in 1848. The relevant point here is that the notes for *The Mystery of Edwin Drood* stop at Instalment Six. The pages covering the second half of the novel have instalment numbers at the top but are otherwise totally blank suggesting that the story's outcome and Edwin's fate were yet to be decided.

I favoured keeping Edwin alive in Dunston's continuation of Dickens's novel because I wanted the Dickens-Isaac relationship in my story to parallel the Datchery-Edwin relationship in the Drood mystery, and this was best accomplished with Edwin's survival. In *Immortalised to Death*, the plot, not the characters, drives the story.

A Note from the Author

Immortalised to Death is set in nineteenth century England. As part of my effort to place the reader in this location and this period, I have used British spelling throughout the novel and drawn on then-current colloquialisms in dialogue. If an odd spelling or unfamiliar word pops up, blame the British.

Acknowledgements

Writing is a labour of love. I absolutely loved writing *Immortalised to Death*. But it was a labour, or, more accurately, a hard slog over several years, and it would never have been finished without a *lot* of help. Many contributed in all sorts of ways, but I particularly wanted to say thank you to the following.

My agent, Jeff Schmidt (President, Creative Management Agency, New York) proved an enthusiastic supporter and advisor. His extensive knowledge of the publishing industry was a valuable resource in guiding me through the final stages of completing the novel. My editor, Emily Williamson (Senior Editor at Chrysalis Editorial, Baltimore/Washington DC) went through the entire manuscript with a keen eye and a sharp pencil. She spotted an overworked quirk in my writing style which once reduced to its proper place, greatly improved the flow. And my publishers, Harriette Sackler and Shawn Simmons at Level Best Books, who piloted me, a debut author, through the otherwise daunting publication process.

On the home front, my wonderful wife, Jennifer, supported and encouraged me every step of the way. She read draft after draft, corrected spelling and grammar, lasered in on inconsistencies and suggested improvements in the plot and in the development of characters, all with a sense of humour (most of the time). Finally, a special thank-you to my son. Hugh is the poet in the family and he composed the chant sung by the gang of robbers on Bluebell Hill.

More Praise for Immortalised to Death

"*Immortalised to Death*'s ingenious solution to fiction's most celebrated unfinished mystery holds the key to the secret life, and murder, of legendary author, Charles Dickens himself. This novel's cleverly wrought combination of fact and fiction will grip fans of historical mysteries from the opening death scene to the last astounding revelation."—Herta Feely, award-winning author of *Saving Phoebe Murrow* and founder of Chrysalis Editorial

"In this cleverly plotted period mystery, Lyn Squire has crafted a fascinating tale involving the great Charles Dickens and his final, half-completed work, *The Mystery of Edwin Drood*."—Charles Salzberg, three-time nominee for the Shamus Award, author of *Swann's Last Song, Devil in the Hole,* and *Second Story Man*

"*Immortalised to Death* is a lively mystery novel that delights in the particulars of Charles Dickens's Victorian England."—*Foreword Review*

"Lyn Squire mixes the novels of Charles Dickens with real events, adds a bit of his own fiction for a kick, and creates a true old-fashioned cocktail of a book that keeps the reader desperately turning the pages to find the resolution only to be met by yet another twist in the story."—Matt Cost, award winning author of twelve histories and mysteries, most recently, *Velma Gone Awry*

About the Author

Lyn Squire was born in Cardiff, South Wales. During a twenty-five-year career at the World Bank, he published over thirty articles and several books within his area of expertise, and was lead author for *World Development Report, 1990,* which introduced the metric – a dollar a day – that is still used to measure poverty worldwide. Lyn was also the founding president of the Global Development Network, an organization dedicated to supporting promising scholars from the developing world. He now devotes his time to writing. His debut novel, *Immortalised to Death*, introduces Dunston Burnett, a non-conventional amateur detective, whose adventures continue in *Fatally Inferior* and *The Séance of Murder*, the second and third books in *The Dunston Burnett Trilogy.*

AUTHOR WEBSITE:
  https://www.lynsquiremysteries.com/

Milton Keynes UK
Ingram Content Group UK Ltd.
UKHW012226181223
434609UK00012B/693